By the same author

ALL SUMMER
TENDERWIRE

ALL NAMES HAVE BEEN CHANGED

All Names Have Been Changed

Claire Kilroy

faber and faber

First published in 2009
by Faber and Faber Limited
Bloomsbury House
74–77 Great Russell Street
London WC1B 3DA

Typeset by Faber and Faber Limited
Printed in England by CPI Mackays, Chatham ME5 8TD

A CIP record for this book is available from the British Library

ISBN 978-0-571-24237-5

2 4 6 8 10 9 7 5 3

For my mother Helen

PART I

Michelmas Term

October

I

Sinne fianna fáil

We are soldiers of destiny

Nobody wrote about September like Glynn. It was his month. You could say it was his season. September intensified the lush sadness pervading his work, made it complete, corporeal, laden; the late summer drawing to a close, the sun forsaking our remote shores, the long hard winter setting in (he compared it once to an animal settling down to die). A spirit of contented melancholy swept through his eight startling novels, swelling their pages like sea air. You could almost taste it. I could almost taste it.

Abandonment; that was Glynn's great subject. Abandonment and longing. He wrote about anguish with a lucidity that was exhilarating. The autumn equinox in particular, the sun crossing the celestial equator, referred to in three of his novels, (*Prussian Blue*, p. 140, *Gorsefire*, p. 98, *Farm Animals*, p. 20), mirrored the condition of his narrators – each one of them was the Hanging Man, suspended on the cusp between love and hate, fear and hope, remorse and defiance. Oh, his incomparable skies. He sketched them almost offhandedly with a few deft words, evoking them as metal: pewter, silver, iron. Our northerly latitude became him. The cast of Irish light penetrated his every sentence; our fitful island weather infiltrated his every noun. During the decade or so that he spent in the States, academics and critics eagerly speculated as to the nature of his first 'American novel', but Glynn's absence from his native country only compounded his vision of it, and it was whilst there, in Brighton, Connecticut, that he produced his masterpiece, *Hibernia*, land of winter, home.

It was an October day when we formally met Glynn. His season had latterly expired. The sky that day was bright, chill, coppery. Listen to me – I am as bad as him. The workshop looked whiter than it ever had. We had been waiting there for four weeks by then, and had grown accustomed to that attic room, familiar with the variations of light on the floor, its many shades of disappointment. Glynn was the best part of a month late and we had all but given up on him, so implausible did it seem that a writer as great as he should join us in a room as modest as that. It was a problem of scale.

When the front door slammed shut on the ground floor, the seven of us – there were seven of us left by then and, although it is hard to imagine, for a time I wasn't the lone male – the seven of us raised our heads, startled deer. The four, my four, had already begun their descent, but they about-turned without consultation and resumed their seats where they waited in silence, hands folded in laps, looking for all the world as innocent as if they hadn't budged in the first place, they of little faith.

We all of us listened intently to Glynn's tread on the wooden staircase, losing impetus with every step, but gaining substance. His approach lasted for ever and sounded so weary that he might well have been dragging his exhausted bones towards us for weeks, slouching across desert sands, icy plains, no different to the way in which we had found ourselves dragged towards him,

4

when you think about it, and I have.

They were unbearable, those last few seconds spent waiting for him to appear. We were trapped up there on the top floor, no escape. What had we summoned? What baleful spirit, what tormented soul? Too late to call a halt now. We were as charged as thunderclouds before we laid eyes on him, our imaginations sparking every which way, a meteor shower. We could have seen anything, anything at all. That is the effect he had on us. Glynn had been absent from the public domain for some time. We hardly knew what to expect.

It was almost a relief when he finally materialised. It had almost been too much. Guinevere said she found herself blinking back tears upon his entrance, Faye felt a rush of blood to the head. Aisling thought she was going to pass out. Her face went whiter still, if such a thing can be imagined. God only knows what raced through the dark alleys of Antonia's fraught mind – over a year had passed since she and Glynn had last come face to face. Not that the rest of us were aware of their connection at the time. Their history, I suppose you might call it.

If Glynn was surprised to see Antonia there, he betrayed not a trace. What a figure he cut. It looked to me that he hadn't slept during his month-long absence. His red eyes surveyed us from the doorway, then he stalked to the chair at the top of the room and collapsed onto it heavily, throwing his person down like a sack of coal, like so many goods and chattels.

How unlike himself he looked, how unlike his publicity photograph, that is. Older, uglier, yet more impressive. Every inch proclaimed his status as tortured heroic artist – drawn, crumpled, glowering, spent. It was a simultaneously appalling and satisfying sight. September had evidently gone hard on him that year. Afterwards, months afterwards, we discussed how surprising it had been to encounter him there, despite it being precisely where he was supposed to be. He had stared at us like he loathed and pitied us in equal measure. Empty desks floated like icebergs in the no man's land between us. This first meeting is an event I shall return to.

Six of Glynn's novels were set – are set – by the coast, specifically the east coast of Ireland. No sublime Atlantic sunsets for him, no horizons charged with promise, no Americas. The man could in a sentence reduce you to the state of a child by invoking that universal response of helplessness when confronted with a vast and indifferent sky, its impact doubled by the vast and indifferent sea heaving beneath it, growing steadily darker. Glynn was uncannily adept at capturing the feeling of being lost. It is a difficult predicament to write.

One of the many singularities about the man is that the older he got, the more piercing his evocations of childhood became. A further singularity is that the more piercing these evocations became, the more familiar they became, to the extent that it could have been your own childhood he was describing. My own childhood, I mean. Though Glynn was over thirty years my senior, it seemed it was my childhood he was writing about. The incident with the stillborn calf in *The Common-place Book,* for example – the very same thing had happened to me. Or at least I thought it had, but thought so on a second reading.

I see now I replaced my childhood with Glynn's depictions – they were so vivid as to eclipse mine. Sometimes I even think I grew up on a Wicklow headland with lighthouses and what have you overlooking the Irish Sea

and not on our low-lying few hectares of Mayo bog dotted about with rushes and reddled sheep, blue for us, red
for the McGuigans. I went so far as to tell Guinevere
about it once, how as a boy I fell asleep at night listening to waves crash against rocks. What waves, what
rocks? And yet I hear them to this day. Storms were my
favourite. 'There is nothing to beat a good storm,' I
informed Guinevere, adopting the iambic cadence
favoured by Glynn, hungry for her attention. I don't
know what possessed me to impart all this. It didn't even
feel like a lie. You could say I was part-Glynn by the
time I made it to House Eight that October, so thoroughly had I absorbed him by then, so thoroughly had I been
absorbed. To a degree we were all part-Glynn, the five of
us, and he thrived on that, for a time.

Clearly it is problematic to conclude that if a great
artist delineates the intimate contours of your mind,
then you and that great artist are of a mind, yet forging
that link is precisely what the poetical imagination does,
it is precisely the locus of its power. Glynn's aesthetic
vision was so expansive that it bled into our own, where
it was welcomed, where it was invited to flourish. The
five of us, strangers then, had found ourselves in the
jaws of an inimical world, and Glynn's response to it
made sense of our own. No longer did we feel alone,
that is the plain truth of it. Our subsequent devotion was
nothing short of pure. Somewhere along the line, art
stopped being important to the rest of the country, failed
in relevance, ceased to be a faith system. Not to us,
though. And certainly not to Glynn. He must have
known what he represented to us. He had been young,
after all, once.

Of course, we were clear that Glynn had not written

about us, but that in writing about himself, he had formed us. And because we believed we were of a mind, it led to this misconception that we knew him, that we understood him, and that we loved him. Events thus gained a momentum they might not have otherwise. We thought he would be pleased, and in the beginning he was. Or not so much pleased as gratified.

You may ask how it was that the five of us came together, but you might not – indeed Glynn might not – accept our answer: We came because he called us. Glynn set down his words knowing they would mean nothing to most, but everything to a few. We, those few, heard his siren song and followed it, having little alternative under the inhospitable circumstances. He wanted his art to be a dangerous force, alive. Well then, you might say he got what he asked for.

2

The pipes, the pipes are calling

When Glynn published *Hibernia* in 1981, a public reading was organised in the Meeting Room of the Royal Irish Academy to mark the occasion of this, his first novel in four years. The attentive response was in no small part due to the success the writer had for many years enjoyed in North America.

Advertisements were placed the week beforehand in the *Irish Times* and *Irish Press*. We all, it turns out, saw them. This fact is remarkable for its improbability, and not just because the advertisements were scrupulously mean (though even in eight-point font, Glynn's name leapt screaming off the page at us, as if it were our own names we saw printed there) but mainly since none of us much troubled ourselves with newspapers. Too ephemeral. Lasting monuments of art were what was wanted.

We did not know each other, or of one another. Our backgrounds were what you might call diverse, by Irish standards. Beyond our love of Glynn, we shared nothing in common, not a blessed thing.

Guinevere and Aisling were the closest in age, hardly out of their teens back in '81, and still living with their parents at opposite ends of Dublin Bay – Bray and Howth respectively. The two headlands regarded each other benignly across the broad curve of sea, desultorily flashing lighthouse beams at one another, batting commuter trains back and forth.

Faye had travelled all the way from Clonmel to attend, although the Feast of the Immaculate Conception, the day she traditionally came up on the train to Dublin to do her Christmas shopping, wasn't for another fortnight. The Christmas window in Switzers had yet to be unveiled, so it wasn't quite the same, she later told us, quickly adding that it didn't matter, it was fine, she didn't really mind. She was asked by the porter to leave her crammed shopping bags behind in the cloakroom, such was the mill caused by Glynn.

Antonia, in the painful throes of marital separation at the time, mentioned that she had entered a period of depression so bleak, so hopeless, so self-defeating, that she no longer, if she could help it, left the house. She made an exception for Glynn that night. Her hair, she realised as she slipped into the last vacant seat, which was right in the middle of the front row where everyone could see her ('just my luck'), hadn't even been brushed that day. I broke into laughter. This, I could not envisage. Antonia's impeccable grooming, her expensive glossiness, was key to the woman she was, or to the woman I thought she was. 'I know,' she agreed, tapping cigarette ash into the brown glass ashtray. She went on to pinpoint that evening in the Royal Irish Academy as the first step in her journey back to what she called 'civilisation', enunciating the term with the caustic irony she so often employed in an attempt to mask her vulnerability.

Four years passed after Glynn's Academy reading before the five of us came together in House Eight. It took us a number of weeks to establish that we had all been in attendance that wet night in '81. The discovery was made during one of those landmark late-night marathon sessions in Bartley Dunne's which consolidated us from five individuals into a bona-fide group. Those conversations often lasted longer than a working man's day and revealed (to our surprise) that here were five people who badly needed to talk. Enormous revisions to our self-conceptions were incurred by this revelation. Each of us had learned to regard ourselves as solitary to the core. A predominant characteristic of our group was that none in it had been part of one before. The experience was disarming. Within a short period, our guards were down, strewn about us like discarded coats on a hot day. Defences were no longer necessary, as interacting with each other was not unlike interacting with aspects of ourselves. Alcohol, naturally, was a catalyst.

Once securely within the fold, we allowed ourselves to acknowledge the true extent to which we'd privately longed to feel part of a group. This was not a desire any of us would have owned up to in the past, describing ourselves variously as 'loners', 'outsiders', 'misfits' and so on, clamouring to outdo each other with such labels as if they were badges of honour, hallmarks of authenticity. Antonia even went so far as to apply the adjective 'cold'.

Significantly, not one of us reached for the term 'lonely'. That would have constituted an admission of defeat. Over the preceding years, as a protective measure, we had come to regard the need for companionship as something to be disdained, as if the natural impulse to share your life with another human being were a weakness, not a strength. It wasn't until we had come in from the cold and thawed ourselves at the fireside of each other's company that we realised how perished, how neglected, we'd been. Guinevere told me in confidence that there were times during the infancy of the group, as it took its first trembling steps, when she could have cried with relief, this new sense of kinship being so unprecedented, and so welcome. She had never dared hope to belong either. It was the last thing you'd expect a beautiful girl to say.

We fell silent and exchanged meaningful glances over our pints at the discovery that the five of us separately and unbeknownst to one another had come to hear Glynn speak that night. That we had all spotted the newspaper ad was of particular note. So small, so unassuming, no bigger than a matchbox. That ad was certainly, we agreed, barely noticeable, and yet . . . In those early days, we thrived on coincidences of such a nature, being engaged in the great project of constructing our collective mythology, like married couples rehearsing the story of how they met, so that everything, in retrospect, seems predestined. That five strangers at different stages in their lives had gravitated toward Glynn like pilgrims toward a star proved that there was such a thing as fate, and that we were firmly in the grip of it. This desperation for justification is common to all who have taken risks that have yet to pay off.

The weather was especially foul the night of Glynn's reading. The Irish winter threw its entire repertoire at us. Thunder, lightning, sudden downpours, blasting gales, fleeting glimpses of stars. We grimly recalled those adverse conditions which tested our commitment, and did not find it wanting. A torrent of rain had started to fall in Ireland in 1980, after the largely sunny decade that was the seventies. Once the rain started, it did not seem to know how to stop. It rained so heavily and so steadily that we started wondering where it was coming from. Then we wondered whether it could keep coming from there. There was so much of it, we were surely leaving another part of the world short. The surface water drains quickly clogged with the fallen leaves and detritus carried by the coursing rainwater along the gullies. Flash floods formed wide pools on the pavements and streets. It was, by any stretch of the imagination, a spectacularly filthy night, even for late November. (We can confirm the date as it was Aisling's birthday.)

Who could have divined that that fine room was there all along, concealed behind a grey Dawson Street façade like a clandestine church, a priest hole? How many times had I walked past without noticing? I possessed little knowledge of civic Dublin, of the institutional fabric of the city, despite having lived there for four years by then. That feeling of strangeness, of unfamiliarity, of having inadvertently stumbled upon a hidden world, detonated a headiness in me, in us.

Certain minor details from the evening stood out in our minds all those years later. We each recollected with undiminished agitation the faulty microphone, for instance. Glynn stepped up to the lectern to applause, nodded his thanks, opened *Hibernia* to the appointed page, but his voice, when he spoke, did not receive the expected amplification, and thus audience members at the back (Faye, Aisling) failed to hear a thing. Antonia and I, sitting at the top, picked up what the others missed. ('Good eve– *Jesus*' is what he said.)

Not being in the least bit technically minded, and certainly not prepared to give it a bash in front of all those people, Glynn simply removed his book and took a step back. A man appeared and tinkered behind the podium until he found the switch that turned the shagging thing on; the microphone which, when it did eventually decide to work, converted all of Glynn's *p*'s into minor explosions, so that every time he pronounced a word beginning with that letter ('profundity' he used at least twice), the backfire caused him to recoil from the grey foam turtle head as if it had electrically shocked him. All five of us, a full four years after the fact, still harboured resentment towards this unsatisfactory piece of equipment and thought – individually, unbeknownst to each other, scattered throughout the soggy audience of approximately two hundred – Could we not, as a nation, have done better for the man? Wasn't this precisely the class of shabby disregard that drove Joyce and Beckett away in the first place?

And the coughers. Why were they there? And in such numbers. Those dirty sickly people teeming with greasy germs – why had they come out that evening if they were so very unwell? Glynn had to raise his voice to be heard, and repeat sentences, or halt them halfway through until a bronchitic fit subsided. '*Stop it!*' Antonia had hissed at the old man beside her, as if the event were a recital. He did stop, confirming her suspicion that much of this coughing was recreational, stemming from habit as opposed to need. Perhaps it was the same crowd shooed like chickens out of St Anne's Church at closing time, there simply to spend a few more hours in a heated building, hunched up in overcoats like perverts. There was so much coughing, and in such rhythmic patterns, that we discussed the possibility that it was an act of sabotage. Glynn had enemies, jealous rivals. I concentrated on his voice, my hands clenched into fists. The

Meeting Room was beginning to smell of wet dog.

The man who always showed up to readings was first to pose a question, that vain white-haired man who was more interested in listening to the sound of his own voice than in hearing Glynn's response. That man, who didn't know the difference between a query and a speech – all of us remembered him distinctly. A question mark, we observed, could not with any degree of conviction be placed at the end of his concluding sentence. It was merely a verbose statement of opinion. Glynn, we concurred, delivered the most felicitous response. 'Good for you, sir,' he replied cheerfully, and then, swiftly pointing at another raised hand, 'Next.'

In his answers, Glynn demonstrated no desire to entertain or amuse, no tendency towards flippancy, instead speaking about the act of writing with generosity and lucidity. 'The writer's role,' I recall him saying, 'is to snow on things, that is, to pick out the surfaces which go unnoticed when it does not snow, to illustrate the world as it really is: a chaos of peaks and troughs.' Yes, I found myself nodding; yes, that's it exactly! This was what I had come to hear. 'Pliancy–' Glynn continued, but the explosion on the *p* put him off his stride, and we lost whatever he was about to tell us.

At the book signing which followed the reading (badly organised, queue as bloated and malformed as a tumour), the pushiest denizens of Dublin were, as ever, attended to first. Antonia would have been up amongst them but for her delicate state of mind. She feigned rapt fascination with the cover of *Hibernia* to avoid meeting the eye of past acquaintances, though this measure was unnecessary and well she knew it. Her old friends no longer acknowledged her. There'd been much unpleasant talk surrounding her separation, she told us. 'Dublin,' she noted, 'is excruciatingly small.'

The Meeting Room fell suddenly quiet when the rabble of boors left, clattering the double doors carelessly in their wake. The rest of us drifted in single file along the aisle, waiting for a brief audience with the man at the top. At a table, with a publicist standing in attendance to his right – a whole publicist, God forgive us our sins – sat Glynn, listening, nodding, inscribing. He was for the most part obscured from view by those ahead in the queue. We caught a glimpse of elbow here, a silvery flash of curl there. The smell of antiquarian books lining the walls was as musky as incense, the gold titles embossed on their spines arcane as alchemy. The brass fittings of the overhead lamps glinted down on us like thuribles. There was an atmosphere of the midnight mass, though it wasn't past nine.

All manner of thoughts flowed through my mind as I progressed, head bowed, toward Glynn; Russia at the turn of the last century, extreme unction, a handful of uncut emeralds. These images fell beyond the pale of my habitual sphere of reference, and I was happy to break loose for once in my life from the usual banal restrictions that held my imagination in check. My mind glided freely as if it had been released into the locked wing of an old castle in the great forest of a country since dissolved, some long-gone kingdom that exists only in the annals of history and the realm of folk memory and is thus more alluring, more compelling, than the modern-day place could hope to be. Bohemia, say, or Dalmatia; *Hibernia* itself.

Nothing that transpired that evening quite took place in the present tense, nor did it feel as if it were unfolding in the city I knew so well but, rather, in some chamber out of time. More than anything, it seemed that I was reading it, in the purest, most liberating sense of the word reading, that state in which the mind is lifted out of its confines and cut free to roam at will behind the veil of a book. My imagination felt airborne, as if it had set down a great weight it had been carrying for miles, for years, until it had all but merged with it.

I – we – still heard the occasional blast of traffic on Dawson Street, but it sounded improbable, artificial, *noises off* on a stage set. That I hadn't previously been aware of that building's existence compounded the impression that the real world had been temporarily suspended. It was extraordinarily peaceful. I don't recall ever having felt so calm. Things made sense. Faith systems, religious rituals, liturgy, made sense that night as we closed in on Glynn – not as they pertained to the divine, but in the true value of ceremony, the recalibration it induced.

We each of us in our own way attempted to explain to Glynn as best we were able how much his work meant to us. We stuttered and blurted before him, blushed and shifted our weight. Antonia was too curt and said it came out patronisingly, as if she were addressing the hired help. 'Wonderful work,' she informed him, followed by a hearty, 'Well done,' hearing in her voice an echo of the belligerent insincerity of Glynn's earlier 'Good for you!' Antonia was cursed with an unfortunate manner, but couldn't seem to help herself. Aisling was too vague: ('I get it. No, really: I *get* it.') Guinevere, by the time she reached the top of the queue, was trembling from head to toe. She didn't utter a syllable, could barely manage eye contact, and instead spilled warm smiles

17

all over the great writer's hands. Faye said she just closed her eyes.

Despite our tongue-tied stage fright, we came away discerning from whatever way Glynn had responded, whatever glance he had thrown in our direction – this communication must not have been forged through words, seeing as none of us could remember him saying any – each of us came away from the signing believing that he loved us. He may not have said as much, but we felt his love as strongly as we hoped he felt ours. It wasn't a trick, it wasn't a delusion, it wasn't a testament to what a professional he was. His love was perceptible in a capacity that is impossible to define, being expressed not through word or sign, but directed at the soul. Our soul. Glynn hated that word.

We spilled out into the filthy city afterwards, the five of us, and slipped back unnoticed into the driving rain, not to meet for another four years. I was aware as I crossed onto South Anne Street of a foolish reluctance to glance back at the Academy lest it already be magicked away. I longed to be back there the moment I left, amongst the warmth, the shuffling bodies, the lowered voices, the comforting fug. Once, as a small boy, I had hidden in the cloakroom when the school bell rang and spent a happy morning amongst duffel coats and the contents of classmates' pockets while the school day went on as normal without me. All my life I have been trying to return there.

'Do you think he really loved us?' Antonia once asked me, apropos of nothing. She wasn't even drunk. We'd been crossing Front Square when she detained me with a gloved hand and made me turn to face her. It was unusual for Antonia and me to be alone together. This was not a permutation into which the group naturally fell.

Night was almost upon us. The air was growing glutinous, mottled as the cobbles underfoot. The darkness exaggerated Antonia's already dramatic features. She was all mouth and eyes staring urgently up at me, as if my answer mattered to her; Antonia, who generally barely registered my presence. I'd either stopped hating her by then, or had not yet started. She'd voiced the question quietly, careful that no one should overhear, choosing me and not one of the others presumably on the reasoning that I was the sole member of the group who would not lie to her out of common decency, possessing, in her opinion, no shred of it. Whatever way she'd inflected the question made me unexpectedly want to hold her, hold the ball of nervy sinews and resentful bones that was her.

'I do,' I affirmed as vigorously as I could, conscious of how difficult it must have been for a woman like Antonia to have used as intimate a term as 'love', in light of its spectacular failure in her life. I wanted her to know that she was in safe company now, that the restrictions she had experienced in her relationships hitherto no longer applied with us. 'I do, Antonia, I firmly believe he loved us. There is not a shadow of doubt in my mind.'

She accepted this information with a nod of agreement – Glynn's love had felt real to her too – and then she threw me an imploring, almost panicked, glance, which exposed the fragility I hadn't discerned in her until then.

'Well, goodbye then, Declan,' she said, knotting the belt on her long black coat, having learned the invaluable lesson that every mother should teach her daughter, apparently: that a decent winter coat is a good all-round defence against whatever life might throw at you. That, and a good haircut. We hovered by Front Arch a second longer, wondering how to part. This delay decided matters. Antonia abruptly set off alone on her patent stilettos, as if we hadn't previously been travelling in the same direction. The incident was never mentioned again, but I was glad of the exchange. I don't think I ever really hated Antonia, when it comes down to it. It was just a way of channelling insurmountable emotions.

3

Tarry Glynn

I met a woman once who claimed she'd known Glynn as a child, and I can find no reason to doubt her account of him. I had been sitting on my own in the lounge area of a public house in Leeds one Sunday afternoon in the December of 1984 reading Glynn's first novel, *Prussian Blue*, a second time (just twenty-four years of age when he published it – what hope was there for the rest of us?) when the woman seated next to me on the wall-to-wall banquette leaned across to my table. She wore a gold T-bar rope chain over her royal-blue polo-neck jumper, and a black mohair cardigan over that again, stray fibres of which she picked off her lip from time to time like strands of loose tobacco. She had been observing me for some minutes.

'I was in national school with your man,' she finally remarked, nodding at my paperback. Her accent was rural Irish, right enough. 'A holy terror,' she added with satisfaction, pursing her lips in a manner that said, *Go on, ask me more.* She folded her arms and gave herself a brisk squeeze of pleasure at the prospect of throwing in her tuppence worth. We are a nation that likes nothing better than a good story, preferably featuring one of our own, ideally the parish black sheep, and few could hold a candle to Glynn in that field. I frowned at his author photograph on the back of *Prussian Blue* to confirm we were discussing the same individual. 'That's the boyo,' said the woman, 'the very man,' and indeed she looked the correct vintage to have been in Glynn's class: mid-fifties, thereabouts.

'In Wicklow, was this?' I asked her.

'Arklow,' she asserted.

'I see.' So she knew what she was talking about. I was all ears after that.

Glynn's childhood remains what you might call a grey area. It is difficult to even conceive of him as a boy, if the truth be told. Just one short story in his body of work is told from the point of view of a child. The powerful evocations of childhood which characterise the novels are refracted through the narrative agency of a grown man casting his mind back (for yes, they are all male, Glynn's protagonists – all male, all to blame, all contrite to the point of belligerence). Little is recorded of Glynn's early years save for a few bald facts such as which schools he attended, and when. Dr M. J. Hanratty's otherwise exhaustively researched biography, *Glynn: An Irish Paradox* (Oxford University Press, 1982), glosses over the topic in a matter of paragraphs. Glynn himself joked in an interview with the London *Times* that he sprang forth fully grown on the 18th of April 1952, at the age of twenty-one. This was the date his first piece of writing was published, a short story in the *Irish Press*. '*Homo poeticus* was born,' he was quoted as saying, borrowing the phrase from Nabokov without accrediting him. 'Life before writing was hardly a life for me at all,' he elaborated when queried by the interviewer why he so casually discounted his childhood.

Here follows a little cited fact: for a period of eighteen

months commencing in 1948, Glynn was a seminarian. After completing his secondary-school education he entered St Patrick's College, Maynooth, to study to be a priest. Has enough been made of this biographical detail, I wonder? Glynn doesn't exactly conceal this information so much as not exactly publicise it either. Should photographs of him in his cassock exist I have so far failed to come across them, notwithstanding my great curiosity and renowned attention to detail.

Mention is always made in the Note on the Author printed on Glynn's dust jackets of the four years he spent reading Classics in Trinity – something of a novelty for Catholics at the time – but never a whisper of his spell in Maynooth. He was asked about it on the night of his public reading in the Royal Irish Academy, which was the first I'd heard of him harbouring religious inclinations. It made sense, though, when you thought about it. He had an uncommon capacity for awe. 'It's no secret,' Glynn responded, as if the questioner had suggested it was. He did not elucidate on the subject beyond this statement.

Brigid – for that was her name, the Arklow woman in the shedding mohair cardigan that Sunday afternoon in the pub in Leeds – Brigid wasn't in the least bit surprised when her mother told her that young Glynn was studying to enter the priesthood. And she wasn't in the least bit surprised either, she was quick to add, when her mother told her the following year that young Glynn was only after spoiling his vocation. 'I'd put nothing past Patsy!' said Brigid with glee, 'and look it, wasn't I right?' I laughed. Glynn with a Christian name? Ludicrous. Brigid laughed too, for different reasons, I assume. She flicked through the pages of my paperback edition of *Prussian Blue* and snorted in begrudging admiration before passing the book back. 'A gas man for the sermons still, I see.'

As a young fella of no more than seven or eight years, Patsy refused, Brigid informed me, to play Mammies and Daddies or Doctors and Nurses with all the other little boys and girls on his road, instead devising his own game, which he called Mass. Mass was conducted in Patsy's back garden. He was always the priest, and the other children were always his flock. 'Father,' they had to call him. 'Yes my child,' he would reply. None of them ever questioned this arrangement, no one dared to bags the top job from him. Glynn organised his congregation into rows and made them sit, and sometimes kneel, to listen to his sermons in dutiful silence. Brigid corrected herself: there was nothing dutiful about their silence; the children were spellbound. *Gobsmacked* was the word she used. 'The things he came out with!' she cried. 'And the little size of him!' Everything she uttered had an exclamation mark attached, now that she'd hit her stride. I bought her another sherry.

Glynn scared the living bejaysus out of his playmates, issuing arcane threats of damnation that he surely could not spell; Brigid shuddered in lurid recollection, visibly enjoying her day out. Other times, the children were seduced by his lyrical descriptions of Paradise, or regaled with knuckle-whitening stories about bible characters which were entirely fabricated. The stories were fabricated, that is, not the characters. Glynn appropriated names from the Bible – Moses, John the Baptist, Mary Magdalene, Saul – and threw in some period detail to lend the thing an air of authenticity; sandals, locusts, olive trees and whatnot.

The children grew confused as to what was actually in the Bible and what most certainly wasn't, Glynn's stories being so much more memorable than the real thing, and that, I have come to believe, is the measure of a good novel. 'They stayed with you,' Brigid observed, 'do you know what I mean? The trouble he got us into with Sister Mercedes!' Sister Mercedes had to set the kids straight with a cane.

Once a week, young Glynn heard confession. This was a grave, terror-inducing business conducted in the pitch darkness of the coal shed. The children kneeled beside the nettle patch, Brigid related, and prayed to the garden wall until the shed door creaked open an inch or two and Glynn's finger beckoned through the chink. The little ones used to cry. Why they actually waited there like frightened lambs and didn't run off to play normal games with normal children, Brigid would never know. All this, Glynn would argue, is merely hearsay.

This desire to sermonise was misinterpreted by the religious orders as evidence of a vocation, and a seventeen-year-old Glynn found himself packed off to Maynooth with another hundred or so boys similar to him, and probably worse than him, knowing the state of the country then, forties Ireland, mother of God, was there no end to it? The forties dragged on until the seventies. This was hardly the plan, not by a long shot, not to get banged up with them yokes, up there chewing the altar rails. Where were the women, for a start? After an interlude of spiritual reflection, Glynn, now nineteen, discovered that his calling wasn't in fact to serve the Lord after all, but rather to find a flock. And there were easier ways of coming by an audience, what with his talent. I am, it should be said, surmising.

Brigid did not grasp the significance of her anecdote: that Glynn had managed by the tender age of eight to captivate his first audience. His mesmerising faculty with language was evident from the outset, his strange power with words was apparent even then. The audacity of coupling biblical names with historical props to fashion a narrative so authentic that the local kids accepted it as, well, Gospel – you had to hand it to the little chancer, you had to take off your hat. The man was born to hold a pen in his hand.

Brigid stubbornly refused to see the matter in those terms. She had formulated strong opinions of her own regarding Patsy Glynn's coal-shed evangelising and seemed crestfallen, even a little bitter, when I didn't endorse them, when I declined to add my voice to her round condemnation, on the contrary finding it increasingly difficult to contain my mounting excitement. It marked the end of our association.

The timing of my chat with Brigid turned out to be auspicious. Just one of those things. A sign, if you like. A mere matter of weeks later, and a full three years after the five of us had individually, unbeknownst to each other, scattered throughout the soggy audience of approximately two hundred, attended Glynn's Royal Irish Academy reading, I found myself entirely by chance face to face with the man himself. I had never seen him in daylight before. What a pallor he had on him.

It was the Christmas of 1984, and I was home in Ireland for the holidays. I'd just that morning come up on the bus from Mayo to visit friends in Dublin when he joined me at the pedestrian lights on the Ha'penny Bridge, also waiting to cross. There we suddenly were, standing side by side on the banks of the Liffey one brisk breezy afternoon in late December, regarding each other none too warmly. Seagulls with wingspans as broad as eagles wheeled and screamed above the great writer's head, part of the aura he carried everywhere, the raucous extension of his mind into the sky. Glynn protested a lifelong interest in the avian world, coastal species in particular: gulls of all types, terns, gannets, cormorants, guillemots – they feature prominently in his work.

Though I knew the contours of his face almost as well as I knew my own, I still did a double take to make sure it was really Glynn. He looked somehow contrived; not Glynn, but a man dressed up as him. Surely the real Glynn should not have to try so hard to resemble himself, and still not fully succeed? He was shivering despite it being an unseasonably pleasant afternoon, sunny enough to force us both to squint, or, in his case, scowl. In retrospect, it seems likely he was enduring one of his health scares at the time. Mortality; another of Glynn's great topics.

His navy coat was fastened to the throat, the collar turned up around his ears. It looked as naked as a shirt buttoned to the neck without a tie. No one had ever accused Glynn of possessing style. He hadn't shaved in days, and his cheeks, when he coughed wetly without covering his mouth, puffed out the mauve grey of the homeless. About his person, the various appurtenances with which we were to become so familiar: the umbrella, the high grade hat and, in case there was any doubt as to his occupation, the old chestnut-brown leather satchel from his student days. Glynn had been a Foundation Scholar at Trinity in the early 1950s, an honour he shared with Wilde and Beckett.

A fair to middling crowd of bargain hunters had

gathered at the lights, not one of whom had spotted the prodigy walking amongst us. *Hibernia* had been published three years previously to international acclaim. Glynn must have read the jumble of confusion and zeal on my face, because he regarded me with a harried eye, but it was also a speculative one. This was typical of the man, I would come to learn. Jaded by the attention, but nonetheless courting it. He seemed perpetually on the brink of issuing an observation of literary import, of producing poetic utterance. That's how it felt to be standing next to him – braced for epiphanic articulation to burst into the world, your hands cupped in readiness to catch it.

Glynn sighed impatiently and tapped his umbrella against his leg, urging it to giddy up and get him the hell out of there. He had a point: the lights were taking for ever to change. The country should have shown him more respect. The circumstances, it occurred to me then, were unrepeatable. I could not, even on paper, have devised a scenario more accommodating to our first conversation. It was the casual nature of the encounter that was most striking. Two men of the world briefly detained by a set of pedestrian lights. One man, the younger, leans in to extol the work of the elder, and the elder is pleased to hear that his work remains relevant to the next generation. These are his people, after all. This is his country, is it not? Glynn put himself on the line with *The Ashtray Chronicle,* exposed the darkest thoughts, the most pitiful weaknesses, the apparently boundlessly abject nature of man. It wasn't much to ask of me to issue a sentence or two of gratitude in return for such uncompromising honesty. There was another fierce outbreak of shrieking amongst the gulls, their hysteria louder than the thundering traffic. Glynn swivelled his bloodshot eyes upward, swaying on his feet, and I winced at the stale reek of last night's stout.

A lorry hurtled up the quays at a reckless speed, and the crowd back-stepped in alarm, jostling the two of us together. I turned to Glynn and cleared my throat to speak. His speculative appraisal of me hardened into an admonitory glare. How was I supposed to know that the anonymous poison-pen letters had recently put in their first appearance? Sometimes they were delivered through the postal system, but more often than not by hand, dropping through his letterbox at all hours of the day and night. One had even materialised in his coat pocket after a particularly punishing night out on the tiles.

Despite putting his back into it, deploying the formidable powers of observation at his disposal, Glynn never managed to catch the perpetrator in the act. Whoever penned the things was unnervingly conversant with his movements, appearing to know before even Glynn knew where he would be found. It was with great assiduity that they had studied their subject, displaying an eye for detail and a flair for dramatic timing rivalling that of the master himself. How intimate the two must have become, in a perverse way, brooding over each other like lovers all those long hours. Glynn had come to regard every dog and divil as their potential author, a man under siege from an assailant he couldn't see. His tormentor could have been standing right next to him in the crowd at that very moment, for all he knew. Perhaps that explains why he shuddered.

A backdrop of swollen clouds was steadily rising behind him, an assassin creeping up to slit his throat.

Clouds all but had minds in the fictions of Glynn. They were all but sentient. 'The highwaymen of the sky,' he had called them in *The Devil's Party*, flattened in hiding on the horizon, ready to loom up and ambush you the second you came into range, as this one had done just now, all eighty foot of it. The chests of the gliding gulls looked so chalky white against its sodden greyness, and Glynn, he looked so small.

The pedestrian lights turned green and the crowd surged forward. Glynn headed back to the doghouse. He was living in a dank bedsit in a condemned building on Bachelors Walk by then, his wife having thrown him out the week before Christmas. Yet another fact I could never have inferred at the time. 'Wait,' I heard myself calling after him, but Glynn was already out of earshot, taking his retinue of screeching gulls with him. 'Rain!' they shrieked, 'Rain!' Fat drops burst on the pavement as the sky blackened. They fell tentatively at first, and then in a deluge, but still Glynn did not open his large umbrella, using it instead to strike a dustbin, then another, and so on up the quays, *bang bang, bang bang*, confirming an opinion I'd heard muttered in licensed premises the length and breadth of the country: that here was a fellow who did not know what was good for him, and who was unwilling to learn.

On the last bus home that night, I jotted down notes obliquely based on this thwarted encounter, my handwriting juddering across the page like a seismogram. I'd filled a copybook by the time I disembarked, and over the next four nights, before returning to the factory in Leeds, I fashioned a short prose piece. It was my first Chapter One, the first of my many Chapter Ones.

I termed it an excerpt from a novel in my application

to Glynn for a place on his course, though there never was any novel. The piece was about, well, defeat, I suppose. Perhaps that's what Glynn responded to when he read my few pages and added my name to the list alongside the names of the four girls – neither the imagery nor the characterisation, not the plot nor the language, but the all-pervasive tincture of failure. It must have struck a chord.

4

The Rocky Road to Dublin

Ten months later, I was back on the boat, this time going against the tide of panicked young Irish who were bailing off the island like rats off a sinking ship. Not me. I wanted to be there when that ship sank. I wanted to see it happen. It was the final week of September 1985.

The country I returned to was comprehensively and publicly on its knees. My teenage years had been dominated by news bulletins detailing which factories had closed and where, incurring how many job losses, how many new additions to the live register. Having in '82 completed an engineering degree out of a sense of duty to my poor mother, a widow then of some seventeen years, God have mercy on my father's soul, I left Ireland to work in a manufacturing plant in Leeds. We produced components for various domestic appliances. Vacuum cleaners, washing machines, irons, sandwich makers.

Through living an existence entirely temporary in nature, barely an existence at all by Glynn's red-blooded, hot-headed criteria, I had saved enough money to keep myself – were I to continue living frugally – for a full academic year in Trinity. Like many witless young idealists, I was of the conviction that money was of no inherent value in itself. I was twenty-five years old. By that age, Glynn had already published a debut collection of short stories, one novel (the aforementioned *Prussian Blue*) and what he described during the Royal Irish Academy public interview as 'a few aul poems', finding two syllables in the word 'poem', as, very soon, did we.

I spent altogether twelve days trawling the streets for a suitable bedsit, a search that proved more sobering than anticipated. Michelmas term had already commenced, so only the dregs were left by then, the dives every other student had rejected. The full extent of the neglect Dublin had suffered was revealed to me in a series of tableaux presented by bored landlords. They swung doors open onto scenes of dilapidation so grim that they didn't even attempt to defend them. Those rooms told a story not just of a recession, but of a city – once the second of the British Empire, it is hard to credit – that had been in decline for the guts of two centuries.

The rooms were situated mainly in the grand Georgian terraces and squares built in the late eighteenth century. The sad deterioration of those gracious family residences was not a reflection on Ireland's distaste for its colonial past but, rather, on the lack of resources available to bestow on those fine old buildings the specialist care they required. Whole rows, entire streets, had been broken down into the maximum amount of rental units for the minimum possible investment. I encountered rooms with broken windows, rooms with no windows, rooms that were sited partially underground, or in poorly converted attic spaces, shards of daylight piercing the rafters. Rooms that were split into smaller rooms by panels of sheet rock, floor areas not much larger than coffins. Rooms that stank of mildew or grew mushrooms in the corner. Rooms with ivy poking through cracks in the walls, floors squelching underfoot.

Most disquieting of all were the faded traces of genteel living, lingering ghostlike in the details: the incomplete ceiling roses, the crumbling stuccowork, the chipped marble mantelpieces and shattered fanlights. Everywhere, ruined proportions; windows bricked up or knocked through, kitchenettes shoved in hall corners, toilets plumbed into reception rooms. Those unloved rooms pleaded with me to do something, do something, to speak on their behalf, or at least not to close the door again. I picked my way around, observing their condition without comment, mindful to touch nothing, as if they were plague victims or war casualties in a field hospital and my role was solely to count them, to compile an inventory of the condemned and the dead. The relief I experienced upon coming back out to fresh air fell far short of adequate.

The flat on Mountjoy Square, in the heart of Gardiner's Dublin, became available late in the day for reasons that were never specified. It was Aisling, with her great fondness for the macabre, who planted the idea in my head that the previous tenant had dropped dead in it. Suicide, most likely, she reckoned. I followed the haunches of an Offaly man with a beer gut straining the buttons of his tea-coloured shirt as he laboured up the stairs. Up three flights to the top floor he led me, jangling his ring of keys as offhandedly as a jailer, pausing on each landing to catch his breath, all the time profaning softly. 'Mother of God,' he sighed. 'Merciful hour. All the angels and saints.'

The room was clean, bright, plain. A single bed, desk and chair, two-bar electrical heater. The landlord placed his hands on his kidneys and surveyed the room as if seeing it for the first time. 'Snug,' he noted with approval. 'Central location, own sink.'

'Take your time,' he added before retiring to lean out the landing window for a smoke.

In gradient, it recalled that rickety bedroom in Arles that Van Gogh had painted a hundred years earlier, except that his floor sloped upward, not down. It was the shipshape bareness that most appealed to me, as if everything was nailed to the ground. The simple, practical sturdiness of its contents, the sense of things being orderly and under control, was as satisfactory to me as a tightened belt. I could picture myself bent over the stout desk scribbling past midnight, ripping pages from notebooks and firing crumpled balls into the corner. Such were my notions of the writing life. God knows where I got them. Not from Glynn. Can't blame him for that. Out I went to the landing.

'I'll take it,' I told the landlord, pulling out my roll of money. He flicked his cigarette out the window and tossed his head in a manner intended to convey approbation, but which somehow seemed more like a scoff.

I transported my belongings from the temporary student dormitory accommodation to Mountjoy Square that same afternoon. It took just two crossings. All I had were the few changes of clothes and, of course, my books. Local children overtook me on the street hauling tyres and furniture. A convoy of five carried an upended three-piece suite on their heads, ants raiding a picnic. Smaller kids, six-year-olds, lagged behind dragging the matching cushions. They were dismantling the city at a ferocious rate. Unlit bonfires loomed up from every patch of open ground, squat and totemic, some of them already fifteen feet high though Halloween wasn't for weeks.

I moved the desk in my new room from the corner to the window. Van Gogh's window glowed with Provençal sunlight. Mine gave onto a concrete yard jammed with decades' worth of household detritus: paint cans, ironing boards, a rusting cooker, half a bike. Nothing the local children could burn. A buddleia sprouted from the boundary wall, its flowers brown and curling. To the rear of the yard, a back lane ran the length of the terrace, joining up with Fitzgibbon Street and the flats. The rhythmic ticking sound which had promised during the viewing to be a grandfather clock turned out to be a dripping tap. The toilet and shower stall were located downstairs.

I unpacked my reference texts, my foolscap pads, my pens, and laid them out on the windowsill like a set of surgical instruments. The *Irish Times* had printed a large black and white photograph of Glynn in his study when he won the Prix Médicis étranger, the first Irishman to have done so and, to date, the last. I was no more than nine or ten when I saw that image, but it stayed with me all those years. Glynn was seated at a leather-topped desk by a bay window, illuminated by a soft shaft of sunlight. Behind him, a great black wall of books breathed down the back of his neck. On the desk was a sheaf of papers to which he applied a silver pen which just so happened to catch the light as the camera shutter clicked, his tiny glinting sceptre.

How ferociously Glynn scowled in that photograph, as if he were engaged in the bloodiest act of creative engendering conceivable, though it is unlikely that he could have been writing anything much, really, not with that photographer buzzing about the room like a fly. The murderous frown must have been at the intrusion. 'Leave me alone,' he was scrawling across his papers, by the looks of it. 'Go away, feck off, get out.' Oh, to be there, not in Glynn's study, but any study, to be any writer in any study, to break through to that fictive space, the factory floor of the imagination. If there was a secret door leading to it, a revolving bookcase, a sliding panel, it had so far proved beyond my ability to locate it. I had tried, God knows I had tried, to find it by myself. Glynn would show us how to get there. Glynn, of all people, would know.

5

What's another year?

I never once saw the interior of Trinity in high summer, it has only now occurred to me. Never set foot within those collegiate walls outside of the academic calendar, despite having lived in Dublin for years, and despite the campus obstructing everything. Perhaps it was for this reason that Trinity never fully seemed part of the city to me but was instead an intermittent phenomenon, seasonal as a winter lake.

The clatter and blare of Dame Street died away as I emerged from the darkness of Front Arch onto the broad cobbled expanse of the quad. It was an impressive vista. Front Square and its environs possessed the tranquil air of a monastic cloister – an unsettling trait, depending on how you felt about ghosts. Trinity was built on lands confiscated from the suppressed Augustinian Monastery of All Hallows which had occupied the grounds since the twelfth century. The newest construction, the Graduates Memorial Building, was almost a hundred years old, and the oldest (not one of the original Elizabethan structures had survived) was The Rubrics, dating from 1700. The sole evidence of the twentieth century was the student body itself, and even they seemed relics of a time past, so aloof, so reserved was their demeanour. I was half an hour early.

I knocked on the front door of House Eight and pushed it open when I got no response. A notice was taped to the wall. 'Writing workshop top floor,' it read. Not Glynn's handwriting. Each door I passed on the way up the wooden stairs was shut, no trace of activity audible on the other side.

The workshop was not at all as anticipated. I'd expected floor-to-ceiling bookcases, as if books would propagate more books, words might self-seed. I'd hoped to step into that photograph of Glynn in his study, I suppose, but there were no bookcases, not even a shelf. The walls were bare as an egg. Plastic chairs and melamine tables were set out on the floor, no better than a staff canteen. A heavier table with side drawers was situated at the top. I placed my foolscap pad on a desk in the middle and glanced up at the clock on the wall. Thirty-three minutes to twelve. The clock was running late.

At six minutes to noon by the faulty clock, the group entered the building. Aisling, Faye, Guinevere, and Antonia. They were cutting it fine. The other three students had already turned up by then; one girl sat by the radiator under the window, the other next to the door. The guy with the ponytail and army fatigues had established a little dugout in the corner. We'd been sitting in silence for maybe five minutes when the door on ground level was thrown open. The sound of female laughter came drifting up the stairs, ascending the building as steadily as fire. Not Glynn then. My disappointment didn't last long. The group crowded through the door in boisterous pairs, talking, the whole time talking, all at once so as to confuse me. Four women. Two of them girls.

The presence of four silent strangers in the workshop ahead of them did not disrupt the flow of their conversation. The impact of Beckett's Protestantism and Joyce's Catholicism upon their respective writing styles was the discussion heading. Their cohesion, their bantering familiarity, was such that I assumed they'd known each other from before. What a surprise it was to learn some weeks later that they'd met on the way in the door. They gave such an impression of an organic whole that perhaps I never saw one without the spectrum of the other three. Even Guinevere. It proved a tricky process extracting her from their chrysalis, to the extent that in our private moments I sometimes sensed them listening in, waiting for me to put a foot wrong, poised to dive in and snatch her back.

A hush fell as the hands of the schoolhouse clock approached noon. All of us by then were seated. You would think Glynn was scheduled to appear with a puff of smoke when the big and little hands connected, never mind that the clock was slow.

'Jesus, I hate this kind of weather,' one of them murmured, the eldest. West Brit accent. Hard to miss it. 'For heaven's sake, just look at it.'

We turned our heads to the window, synchronised swimmers. A soft rain was falling on the shining slate rooftops. It was almost, but not quite, mist. An avenging angel in the distance brandished a sword before a verdigris dome. There was something immensely restful about this scene. The lack of living souls in it, probably.

'I knew it,' said the same woman when noon by the slow clock had come and gone. Antonia. Her standards were unattainably high. 'Glynn's not coming. I knew he wouldn't come. I just bloody knew it.'

The air seemed to go out of the room at this declaration. We had managed to fool ourselves until then, but Antonia was right. The chances of Glynn fulfilling a contractual obligation with an academic institution were laughable at best. His errant behaviour had been fussily documented over the years. He had made a name for himself by defaulting on contracts, ignoring writs, laughing off threats and generally bowling along with apparent impunity, capitalising on the extenuating circumstances allegedly occasioned by the artistic personality. There was nothing to be gained from suing a man with a print run of just a few thousand. Antonia dropped her head into her hands.

'I cannot believe I've been so effing stupid,' she said, 'coughing up good money for this.' Her words were met with rueful assent.

There was a discussion then, at least there must've been, though my recollection is that the four, my four, simply stood up and left. They filed out in pairs as before, and the workshop resumed its silence. I stood up and crossed over to the window to observe their exit. They reappeared below on Front Square and headed off in the direction of the Buttery, forming geometrical shapes as they moved along the cobbles – a parallelogram, a trapezoid, a diamond.

A lone seagull wheeled in a circle above the Examination Hall, its cries as distant as a star. I watched until the group had disappeared from sight, and then I watched the empty space that had opened in their wake, obscurely disappointed that they hadn't taken me with them. But why would they? They did not know me from Adam. Behind me, after a respectable period of time had elapsed, the other three students stole back down the stairs as discreetly as they were able, as if slipping away early from a funeral.

Glynn stood us up again the second week. Antonia maintained her position that she knew it, just bloody knew it, always had known it, that Glynn wasn't going to show up at all, ever, that we'd flushed our money down the jacks and landed ourselves with a pig in a poke. I didn't question how she could be so adamant, how it was possible to know in advance what Glynn – a capricious man at the best of times – would and would not do. It seemed natural that those around me should know more about Glynn than I knew. Everybody in Trinity was an authority on him.

'We should report him,' Antonia said. 'We should go this minute to the Dean of Studies, all of us.' She picked up her handbag.

'But we can't do that!' the one with the auburn hair protested. Faye. 'We'll get Professor Glynn into trouble.'

'Yeah,' the one with the black hair and white face agreed. 'Then we'll never see him.' Antonia hadn't thought of that. He'd outwitted her already. She reluctantly returned her handbag to the floor.

In the terrible absence of Glynn, I took to the library. Days on end I spent in the English section that October, arriving at opening time, staying put until the lights flashed last orders. On Saturday mornings, while normal students slept, I was in there on the off chance that the muse might creep up when no one was looking, as if inspiration were not a mental process but a ghost. If I could've slipped into that library in the dead of night, I would have, those early weeks, searching for a portal through which to access the metaphysical world of letters. I felt it as a constant alongside me, that world; fecund, poetical, but out of reach.

Week three. Glynn stood us up a third time. The group turned and left the workshop almost as soon as they'd arrived; a flock of swallows switching direction mid-flight.

The humanities library was located in the basement of the Arts Block. It had bare cement walls and orange carpet tiles. Figures wandered through the forest of bookcases; visible, occluded, visible, occluded. I saw Guinevere there from time to time, twirling a corkscrew curl around her finger as she read. Sometimes her lips pouted to form a particularly intriguing word, I couldn't help but notice. She had doubtlessly entered that serene state which so deftly eluded me. I didn't dare approach her. I didn't dare interrupt. At night, after they'd herded us out of the library to lock up, I crossed back over to the other side of the city, having failed once again to break through to that yearned-for condition, the contemplation of which had sustained me through those long quiet years in England.

One night I happened upon Aisling, sitting alone facing the wall in the Anglo-Saxon corner. It was her chemical hair that caught my attention as I passed, blacker than anything that occurred in the natural world and as magnetic to the eye as a car crash. On the edge of her desk stood a tower of books, stacked carelessly to the verge of collapse.

I padded back to my desk and sat there for a few indecisive minutes. The air conditioning exhaled down the back of my neck, too actual, too pulmonary. I couldn't shake the image of Aisling's precarious tower of books.

43

A minor adjustment was all it would take to put right. I could fix it. I could sort it out. It was a simple problem.

I stood up and headed in Aisling's direction, no notion of what I would say to her, but full of resolution. Would she recognise my face from the workshop? When I rounded the corner, the Anglo-Saxon section was empty. Spanning the length of Aisling's desk: a scattered fan of books. I don't know what precisely this scene reflected back to me, but panic ballooned in my throat at the sight of it. The deadened atmosphere of the basement was suddenly intolerable. I packed up my belongings and left.

New Square was deserted, not a soul in sight. The cobbles glistened in the lamplight and drizzle. I was nothing but a black shadow crossing the stones. I veered off the path and pressed my forehead against the façade of the Colonnades. It was as clammy as the wall of a cave. I would describe my state at that moment as borderline murderous. I had left it too late, you see; I saw. The years spent cherishing the aspiration to be a writer had wrapped it up and sealed it off, rendering it as discrete and inaccessible to the substance of my being as a pearl was to an oyster.

It was Glynn I blamed. He had lured me there, after all. He had enticed me to that bleak place only to abandon me to it. Had he materialised at that point, had he just happened to stray past, God forgive me, I'd have taken a run at him. The man wouldn't even have known who I was.

We met in House Eight for the fourth week. Guinevere drummed her fingers, Aisling inscribed the desk with the ornamental dagger hanging from her neck.

'How long can this go on?' Antonia wondered out loud.

Faye did her best to put a brave face on things so that the rest of us wouldn't lose heart. 'I'm sure Professor Glynn has a very good reason,' she offered. Antonia wanted to hear it.

The chairs we had assumed that first day had become set fixtures. The group sat up front in a row of four like the school debating team. I was stationed a few rows behind, by no means a jolly presence. One of the other girls was wedged against the radiator, but the second girl, the one who used to sit by the door, hadn't shown up that week. We never saw her again. The guy with the ponytail was still dug into his corner, the army-surplus jacket on his desk demarking his territory.

Antonia was complaining about Glynn; the usual drill. I wasn't paying attention to the specifics. I was thinking that I hadn't known loneliness like it before, despite my years in England. It was the loneliness of being in the company of the group, but not part of it. I gazed at them, at their baffling closed circuit of four. Aisling's hair was as black and blank as a hole in the universe, a rip in the fabric of reality.

Guinevere must have sensed me staring. I hadn't made a sound, but she turned around and met my eye and smiled. This was a smile of considerable sweetness. I smiled back and was still smiling long after she'd looked away. The group then packed up and left the workshop in that abrupt, symbiotic manner of theirs. The atmosphere in the workshop sagged. I was almost used to it.

And then, out of nowhere, seconds after their departure, the guy with the ponytail got to his feet. His name was Mike and he spoke without removing his eyes from the window. 'Lads,' said Mike, 'he's coming.'

45

6

Melmoth the Wanderer

We each had a favourite photograph of Glynn. Mine was the aforementioned *Irish Times* shot taken in his study, or 'The great writer at work,' as I had mentally subtitled it. Faye nominated the one taken in the early 1970s by the *Observer,* which was subsequently reprinted in the British broadsheets every time Glynn won a prize, and he was on a roll that decade, go on you good thing.What a rush of fondness that particular portrait generated. He could be a real charmer when it suited him, P. J. Glynn. The photographer must have been a woman. We were as familiar with his face in that shot as we were with the faces of our grandparents. You would swear that the man was not a complete stranger to us all. The jaunty go-heck of him caught by the lens appealed to Faye enormously. This was how she liked to think of him – relaxed, good-humoured, congenial, on the brink of astonishing literary achievement but making no great fuss of it.

He was pictured on what the caption printed beneath described simply as 'a Dublin street', leaning at an angle of around sixty degrees against the wooden jamb of what we decided was the door to Bartley Dunne's. By 'we', I mean, of course, 'they': the women. The women declared it the door to Bartley's, and so it became the door to Bartley's – the fiction-making process in action. I just went along with their reasoning. How they were so positive it was the door to Bartley's, I have no idea. No definitive means of identification were in shot. Just another of those arbitrary decisions the group arrived at which went on to enter the realm of fact. For all I know, they were right.

The composition of the image was immensely attractive. Faye kept a folded copy in an envelope as a bookmark, delicate as a pressed flower. The interior of the pub, what could be seen of it, formed a narrow column of black ink running the full length of the left-hand side of the frame. In the space between Glynn's tilted body, the door and the pavement stood a brilliant triangle of morning light, solid and true as an object in its own right. Glynn somehow always contrived to lure the eye toward the unseen. The triangle is just one example.

He had more hair then, and less flesh, and was dressed in old jeans and a plain white shirt. The shirt was open at the collar and rolled up at the sleeves, for all the world a man who'd logged a hard day's graft. Against the white cotton, his skin looked darker than we knew it to be, and his eyes looked black, not blue. 'Byronic' was the word Faye employed. His gaze was candid in the image, amenable even, lacking the customary scowl that appeared when photographers did. In fact, in that picture he almost looked pleased. I would go so far as to say happy.

What is not immediately apparent to the casual observer is that Glynn is dressed for a different season. You have to look at the photograph for a long time, and still there is no guarantee that you will notice this for yourself. I for one did not. Faye had to point it out. It was the telltale plume of white breath escaping from his mouth that had alerted her keen eye. 'See how cold it is?' she asked me, tapping the ghostly vapour with her fingernail. I dismissed it as an exhalation from his cigarette. Faye seemed prepared for this response – to have anticipated it, in fact, as if already she had learned to expect no better from me. 'What cigarette?' she countered, searching not the photograph, but my face. 'Show me where you see the cigarette, Declan.' It was unlike her to be so assertive.

I examined the petal-frail newspaper cutting again. Faye was right. There was no cigarette in Glynn's hand, though I could have sworn I'd seen one a second before. The other three had remained attentive throughout this exchange. If they'd been darting knowing looks around the table at my expense, these too had escaped my notice.

'Look at the background figures,' Faye continued in the manner of a tour guide discoursing upon a great painting, now broadening her frame of reference to encompass the pedestrians on the street. She had given her subject much consideration. 'Look at the way they're huddled up, Declan. They're absolutely perished.'

I could not confute her. The passers-by did indeed look frozen, buttoned into winter coats and wrapped up in scarves, some of them moving at such a clip that all the camera had captured was a blur of limbs. Glynn's nonchalant deportment betrayed no vulnerability to the cold against which the ordinary mortals around him struggled. How easeful he looked, the still centre of the image, as if it were perpetually summer in his domain. Antonia, of course, could well have had the measure of him when she pronounced him too effing plastered to register the elements.

This immunity to his surroundings seemed proof of something. It distinguished Glynn as fundamentally, intrinsically different to the rest of us. So entirely preoccupied was that great forehead with matters cerebral there simply wasn't room left in it to bother with minor details such as the weather. Transported is the word. This appealed to our notions of what a writer was. It was the condition to which we aspired. Glynn was everything in that photograph that an artist at the height of his powers should be, from the ink stains on his fingertips to the dishevelment of his hair. That was the Glynn we had signed up to see, and that was the Glynn we got.

The group backed up into the workshop when they heard the door on the ground floor slam. They resumed their seats with lowered eyes, their defection foiled. Glynn had put a halt to their gallop. I will not say I wasn't pleased to see them chastened. I threw a triumphant glance back at your man in the corner, suddenly my ally, but Mike didn't register my smirk. He couldn't take his eyes off the workshop door. The footsteps were getting louder.

We froze when Glynn at last appeared – you would think he had pulled a gun on us. He paused in the doorway to consider the room and its occupants. Glynn was never a big enough name for him. Hieronymus Bosch, he should have been called. Lucas Cranach the Elder. I was transfixed, as bad as the rest of them. His sheer tangibility was more than I'd bargained for.

He walked to the top of the room and pulled out the chair from the large desk, frowning at it as if it fell far short of his expectations. Still he hadn't spoken a word.

Finally he threw down his bulk and faced us. The silence at that point was absolute. It was not a formal silence, but a stricken one. We agreed later how alarming it had been the way he'd just sat there glaring at us like that, with such forthright disdain, such open contempt, and for such a protracted period of time too. The lot of us were in a rush to discuss him, to blurt our first impressions the second his back was turned, but while the man himself sat entrenched before us, we couldn't have opened our mouths if we'd tried to.

Glynn leaned back in the chair the better to get a good look at us. He folded his arms over his chest, which rose and fell soundlessly – he appeared to be panting, though he wasn't out of breath, not that we could tell. Faye said she thought he was having a heart attack, then thought she was having one herself at this prospect. From the outset, he commanded this level of rapt, almost fearful, concern. He was a spectacle we watched, a visual installation. We never knew what to expect.

Glynn's scornful gaze roved from one face to the next, sizing up who first to attack. Strange, how he singled the five of us out for special scrutiny, though there were seven students seated before him that first class. We like to think that he chose us. That's what we like to think. He did not speak for the longest time, just stared at each of us in turn. Impossible to know what he was thinking during this interlude. Glynn's mind was an object of fascination and some perplexity, a jellyfish washed up on a beach.

A jolt when his eyes met mine. To my shame, I couldn't keep from blinking. That unnervingly silent bullfrog inflation and contraction of his chest – was he doing it on purpose? Was it a deliberate act of intimidation?

There is every likelihood. My skin burned under the full force of his attention, but despite this uncomfortable proximity – intimacy, I almost called it – still I felt no closer to the artistic sensibility driving him, becoming instead only more aware of his remoteness, of the breadth of the gulf dividing us. I looked down at my notebook, my empty, unmarked notebook, unable to sustain his gaze.

When I raised my eyes again, Glynn had moved on. He was staring now at Guinevere, and Guinevere, more power to the girl, was staring right back. Aisling tilted her palms toward the great writer as if warming them at a fire. So she felt the heat radiating off him too.

The way he kept soundlessly panting like that, physically spent: I too wanted to be emptied out like him. Scraped clean of the seething mess within, granted the compensation of seeing it distilled into words, a life lived, an imagination quarried. Exorcisms, he had once called his books – demons that had been cast out to take form, hoisted up on bookshelves for all the world to see, a rack of carcasses in a butcher's window.

'What do you want from me?' Glynn finally demanded, the words propelled at us as if he'd dealt them a belt of a hurling stick. The question highlighted a troubling discrepancy, one we had failed to anticipate. Glynn's pre-eminence in our lives, the central role he had played, was such that, on some instinctive level, we expected him to recognise if not us, then our type. We had presumed he would understand innately what had driven us to his door, see that only he could help us with it and know it wasn't something that could be communicated in a sentence, not by us at least.

When Glynn got no response, he tried another tack.

'Why do you need me?'

'We don't need you,' Antonia snapped, averting her face and presenting Glynn with a wing of ash-blonde hair. It was the first instance I recall of the pronoun 'we' being used to refer to the group. *We don't need you.* The Anglo-Irish accent. Glynn won't like that, I thought. Turned out I was wrong. He did like it, had liked it very much.

Glynn grunted. I thought for a second that he was going to stand up and leave, seeing as we didn't need him after all. I think he thought so too. He spent a long while pulling at his earlobe. Antonia kept her face averted during this period; Aisling absorbed the bad vibes through her palms; Faye contemplated various avenues for making everything better, and Guinevere set her calm face in solemn preparation for whatever was to come. If Glynn left, he would not return, that much was plain.

'Why do you want to write?' he eventually asked, sighing to illustrate the excessive tolerance demanded of him by the situation. He nodded at the girl by the radiator, indicating that she should start. Sound choice, Professor Glynn. Selecting her had less to do with working from left to right than picking off the weakest first. Of the girl's startled response (we never got her name) all I remember is 'Well, um, because.' It seemed Glynn was correct in his initial assessment that here sat a shower of messers.

I didn't fare much better when my turn came. The question was designed to catch me out, to sift my dilettantism from his authenticity. Glynn had railed publicly against the notion that everyone had a novel in them, appearing to instead believe that he held the Irish monopoly on the form. This had earned him no friends

52

amongst that contingent who slept with draft manuscripts inspired by the War of Independence under their mattresses, that standing army of ten thousand or so, and counting.

Well we knew that Glynn could make words do whatever he wished them to, could turn our words against us with a flick of the wrist, and perhaps this accounts for the reticence and caution with which we navigated his question that afternoon. Except for Antonia. Her answer alone stood out that day, both for the content and stark gravity of her delivery. Sadness progressively descended upon the room with her every word, falling, falling, weighing down our bodies like a blanket of snow. When she was finished, it was difficult to move.

She spoke in brief cogent sentences and never once had to cast about for the correct term, knowing already which words to apply, as if they were laid out on the desk before her. She picked them up and put them down again as though talking us through a selection of historical artefacts. If Glynn's intention had been to send us skulking away in humiliation, well then, he had met his match. Antonia, face averted, nothing left to lose. I transcribe her answer, what I remember of it, in full, more or less, give or take:

7

Deirdre of the Sorrows

'I am thirty-nine years old now,' Antonia began, and lowered her head as if this were a shameful admission. 'My mind is full of fragments of roads travelled. I cannot remember the journeys themselves. I do not recall the destinations. On these journeys, it is always dusk, and I am always strapped into the passenger seat of a car, staring out the window. Someone to my right, a man, is driving. I assume it is my ex-husband, but I have no real sense of his presence. It could be my dead father. It could be a stranger. We travel along the road in silence. The only sound is the drone of the engine. It is warm inside the car, but outside it looks inhospitable, too inhospitable to survive the night.

'I have no idea where these roads are. There is nothing familiar about them. They are not within the environs of my home. Sometimes it is a rural landscape, other times suburban. Occasionally the region doesn't look Irish at all, but vaguely Soviet in character, some deserted province I must have seen in a documentary. These fragments don't present themselves in a chronological sequence, and are not linked to any particular person or event. If I could manage to glance down to see what I am wearing, there's some chance I might be able to connect the journey to a specific occasion. A hospital visit, a funeral, something grim like that. But I can't glance down. It is impossible to move my head. I've been staring out the passenger window for so long that my neck has set.

'All that remains of my twenties and thirties are these puzzling oddments, these disconnected recollections of staggered junctions, derelict outhouses, oppressive tunnels, road kill of indeterminate species. These fragments loom up at me without warning at any time of the day or night – at least three of them this morning alone. I am never safe from them. I could be making the bed or reading a book when, out of nowhere, I am confronted with a desolate road at twilight. These images leave me with a sense of profound emptiness, close to nausea in quality. There seems no end to the store stockpiled in my head. This is the mind I have been left with.

'Do you see?' she asked, suddenly addressing us, but thankfully not waiting for an answer. 'I have come to regard these snatches of roads as flashbacks from a kidnapping. The man in the driver's seat is my abductor. I was not, of course, abducted. It is merely how I've learned to interpret these images. The girl I used to be was bundled into a car and whipped away from her life. I am the changeling who took her place. She transmits these messages to remind me she's still out there.

'And now I find I am disappointed. I am a disappointed woman. What will sustain me through the long years ahead? The only good to be derived is that twenty years of this is enough to demonstrate the necessity to stop. It is time to plug the dam of wasted days. So, here I am.' She shrugged.

It appeared to be darker in the workshop when Antonia had finished speaking. Residues of her dusk roads had invaded the room, draining the colour from things, extinguishing the warmth. We saw them in our minds' eyes – her wretched thorny hedgerows snagged with shreds of plastic bags, her stagnant brown ditchwater, her rapidly dimming skies.

Antonia looked around calmly for a response, but got none. There was nothing to be said. What, I wonder, had she expected from us? We were so much younger than her. What did we know? She had moved beyond our frame of reference. However, she instilled an awareness that what had happened to her could as easily happen to one of us if we did not lead our lives with due vigilance, though to play that cautionary role was not what she had come for.

'I hate the word "journey",' Antonia concluded, and Glynn nodded. He nodded for a long time, apparently knowing what all this meant.

The second he was gone, Antonia began to tremble. Her lips turned purple as she shook with rage. 'Effing bastard,' she hissed, 'trying to demean us like that. Who the hell does he think he is?' A bubble of anxiety formed in the pit of my stomach. There was something about a grown woman's rage that I could not begin to cope with. Glynn would have been horrified too. He might have acted with a little circumspection had he witnessed her in that state, had he apprehended her terrifying volatility.

The three girls, naturally, knew exactly what to do. They sprang into action and were making soothing noises, stroking her arms, smoothing her hair, as I found myself being propelled out of that room with a velocity that I can only excuse as involuntary.

8

Strumpet City

I got nothing written in the library after that first work-shop. I couldn't concentrate on the page. A whole two words I managed to beat out during the long hours I sat in the chair: 'bearing' and 'virtue'. I keep the scrap of paper still. They weren't words I'd resorted to in the past, being terms from a different era, essentially, the courtly love period, perhaps. I am no authority.

Both were an attempt to evoke the same subject: Guinevere. The dullest throb of a notion had begun to form in my mind, innocently enough at first, and so inappreciable that it was months before I saw what I was up to, and months again before I admitted to it: that if I observed Guinevere, if I studied Guinevere, if I seized upon Guinevere, I would be able to write. As it so happened, I was not alone in formulating this plan.

I took down the library reference copy of Glynn's *Farm Animals,* a novel which, according to Dr M. J. Hanratty's breeze block of a biography, was originally submitted under the title *Apophthegm.* In light of the substantial length of this, Glynn's seventh novel (even with a dense word-per-page ratio, it ran to some seven hundred and seventy-two pages), the title was presumably employed in an ironic capacity. His publishers, whilst acknowledging the formidable power and importance of the work, and asserting their ongoing and unwavering support for Glynn's career, declined to publish the novel under that title, arguing that readers would be alienated by the use of a word they didn't understand, let alone know how to pronounce. 'An overabundance of consonants, Patrick,' Tobias Sweetman, the highly respected editor-in-chief of Prior Press, is reported to have told Glynn at a lunch held in Bloomsbury in the writer's honour. We can only imagine the alcohol-fuelled reaction. Glynn's artistic judgement had never been queried before.

When *Apophthegm* was politely but firmly ruled out by Prior Press as a title, Glynn's response was characteristically uncooperative. He submitted *Homophone* as an alternative option, followed by *Uaigneas,* then *Ocras,* the first two Irish words to enter his head, endeavouring to force Tobias to concede to his original choice. At least he'd addressed the preponderance-of-consonants issue, not that anyone thanked him.

Tobias, a fair man, and acting solely in Glynn's interest – a writer needs readers, after all, whether he likes it or not – didn't concede, and the novel was published in the summer of 1977 under the title *Farm Animals,* a 'last ditch compromise with which nether [sic] party was happy' (Hanratty, p. 655). Glynn's subsequent polemic, 'The Death of Art,' which appeared in the *Times Literary Supplement* (24 June 1977, p. 762) to coincide with the publication of *Farm Animals,* depicted Western culture as a steadily evaporating pond in a vast featureless desert in which words and concepts not instantly grasped by the masses (or 'pond life,' as he unhelpfully termed them) were pitched out onto the sun-cracked banks to thrash about and die.

The essay was similarly scathing in its criticism of a thinly veiled Tobias Sweetman, pillorying him as 'cowardly', 'womanish' (Glynn's lowest term of abuse) and 'woolly-headed', epithets which, by all accounts, were wildly undeserved. Glynn had committed the mortal sin of allowing his vicious streak to enter the public domain. Didn't he know they'd be waiting for him in the long grass? Didn't he care?

'It is doubtless that many authors have a nasty side,' noted the books columnist in the *Sunday Times,* 'but few display it so cheerfully.' 'Farm animal indeed,' remarked the *Observer.* Sweetman declined to comment on the matter.

Glynn's unprovoked attack marked the end of what had been a fruitful editorial relationship lasting some twenty-two years. Within eighteen months Sweetman was dead, and the general sentiment amongst the London publishing fraternity, according to Dr Hanratty's presumably authoritative sources, was that the Irishman had hastened the Englishman's end, a charge to which Glynn responded – when it was put to him in an interview in those blunt terms – 'Oh, so it's political now, is it?' The Troubles in Northern Ireland were at fever pitch. Glynn terminated the interview and left. Sweetman, it should be noted, had suffered an aneurysm, for which Glynn could hardly be held accountable.

Were he a less volatile man, or better equipped to grieve, or simply capable of taking good advice, Glynn might have been moved by the occasion of Tobias's sudden passing to compose another essay for the *TLS,* this time reflecting on the brevity of life and the foolish vanity of the ego – the two old friends had fallen out over a mere book title, after all, a weak one at that. Glynn conspicuously failed, however, to express his regret at Tobias's untimely death, leading to a deep-seated bad feeling toward him in the London publishing houses which endures to this day. Wherever Glynn went, the sound of slamming doors followed. Doors slammed by him, doors slammed on him.

Glynn's uncharacteristic taciturnity in the wake of Tobias's death was, as Antonia pointed out, his own choice. Nobody forced him to keep his mouth shut. No one had twisted his arm. 'He's old enough and ugly enough, etc.,' were Antonia's exact words, being a woman who favoured the use of abbreviations in speech. She adopted a heightened faux-naturalistic style when expressing herself, mentally passing her conversation through a filter that converted her initial choice of words into the colloquial dialogue of a contemporary novel. Perhaps it was an attempt to counterbalance the horsy vowels of her accent, about which she was defensive in our low company, you could tell. That's my theory at least.

Her self-conscious mimicry of the patterns of natural speech set me to thinking that Antonia was not revealing her true self to us but, instead, displaying some class of literary construct that she had concocted at home, demonstrating how all-consuming her desire to be a writer was, but nobody, if you listen closely, speaks the way characters in novels speak. Were you to transcribe an overheard conversation, it would read as contrived. The impression of verisimilitude created by a fine writer is an illusion, just as old masters succeed in making paint look more like skin than skin. Somehow, ineffably, the artifice transcends itself to become art. This uncommon ability to render the vision of the imagination onto paper or canvas or the bars of a stave is just one of those unquantifiable transformative powers with which the monumentally gifted, like Glynn, are blessed.

Farm Animals, despite the unhappy circumstances of its publication, always had the effect of recalibrating my mind, making me wish I could add my voice to its chorus, the way a great song makes you want to join in and sing. I opened it to the prologue. Some idiot had underlined and asterisked the opening sentence in red biro and scrawled *Cult of Self* in the margin. 'Shadows like rock pools,' I read, 'as cool and dark and alluring as–' It was no good. I snapped the book shut.

Even the opening paragraph, which I knew by heart, was beyond my scope that day. I could not begin to access Glynn's world, or the 'liquid suspension of the fictional environment', as he'd referred to it once in a keynote lecture delivered to an international conference on Irish literature in Stockholm. The full text was reproduced in a collection of essays I'd picked up for seven pence in a second-hand bookshop on Talbot Street otherwise jammed with Corgi paperbacks. The collection, *In Finnegans Wake: Irish Fiction after Joyce,* stood head and shoulders over its shelf-mates, high and solitary and most stern and, judging by the virginal condition of the spine, unread.

Although Glynn never acknowledged the influence of Joyce – he managed at that Stockholm conference to deliver a ninety-minute lecture on post-Joycean Irish fiction without mentioning the eponymous hero, such was the length of the Bloomsian shadow (Harold, not Leopold) that the big man cast over him – Joyce's artistic enterprise was as indelibly stamped on Glynn's imagination as Glynn's artistic enterprise was stamped on mine. In fact, *Giacomo Joyce,* Joyce's short prose-poem recounting his affair with one of his young language-school students in Trieste – a text I knew the moment I laid eyes on it would be one I'd return to throughout my life – could have been written by Glynn himself, such was the calibre of its erotic torment. 'Easy now, Jamesy! Did you never walk the streets of Dublin at night sobbing another name?' Yes he did, is the simple answer. Yes he did, and yes he would.

Though I intend the comparison with Joyce as praise of the highest order, it is not a compliment Glynn would appreciate. The truth of it was that Joyce would always have the following inalienable advantage over Glynn: that he had come first, that he was the original. Glynn could never fix that, no matter what he got up to, no matter how many stunts he pulled. Joyce was the primo-geniture of Irish fiction, but Glynn did not regard himself as anyone's baby, despite indulging in behaviour that strongly suggested otherwise.

I explained this theory to Antonia once, with not a little pride. 'Geni*tor,* not geni*ture,* for the love of God, Declan,' she scoffed, and inserted a cigarette between her painted lips. She flicked repeatedly at the crenulated wheel of her slim-line gold lighter, and cursed when the thing wouldn't ignite. Instead of producing the box of matches rattling in my pocket, I smirked at her difficulty, and Antonia fucked the lighter at my face. I ducked, and it clipped my temple, and though it hurt I laughed. A big theatrical *ha ha ha!* Guinevere shook her head. 'What's wrong with you two?' she muttered before walking off. Yes, there was a problem there right from the start; I don't know how I missed it. Antonia, to her credit, had me down from the outset as a halfwit, and who was I to criticise her judgement of character? I, who, in the end, proved to be the worst judge of character of them all.

The tang of rotting seaweed was rank on the air that night. The level of the Liffey was unusually low. A chain of mudflats broke the oily black surface of the water like the spine of a cresting sea monster. The drinking had started early, the flagons of cider were out. I picked a path through urine trails and splashes of vomit. It was Halloween.

I turned down Eden Quay and crossed onto Marlborough Street. The bike I'd bought the first week of term was gone. I'd come down two hours after getting it home to find it had been stolen from under the stairs, and no evidence of a break in. There was nothing to be gained by replacing it, I knew that. Same thing would only happen again.

Bonfires studded the north inner city as if it had been shelled. Some of them were as tall as double-decker buses. The locals had been constructing those bonfires for weeks. They had so little to do, and so much to burn. I steered close to the streetlamps and clear of the corporation flats. Lines of washing waved frantically from the balconies as if the rooms behind them were on fire.

Two teenage boys ahead of me on Sean MacDermott Street were carrying a large cardboard box. They ducked behind a gap in a construction-site hoarding. Shouts of excitement greeted their arrival. I stopped and pulled the loose board open a fraction. It was difficult to say how many children were on the building site. Forty or fifty at least, leaping in silhouette against the flames. They swarmed around the two boys with the box.

One of the boys reached into the box and pulled out a black and white cat. He held it up by the scruff of its neck, brandishing it so that all the children could see, before placing it on the ground. The children descended. Whatever procedure they carried out made the animal scream. They released it and stood back.

The cat shot free, but a fizzling spark was attached to its rear. I squeezed through the hoarding and ran for it. The creature raced along the base of the far wall, then the banger exploded out of it. The rocket scudded along the rough ground like a stone skimming the surface of water. The children laughed as they jumped out of its path.

One of the teenage boys started cursing. 'Yiz were supposed to put it in the other way around,' he shouted. 'Yiz were supposed to blow it up, ya stupid fucken spas. Here, show us it.' He gestured at the cat, which cowered beneath a wall too high for it to scale.

We dived at the creature, a pack of foxhounds. The children were more agile than me. They brought the flailing animal back to the boy, who seized it by a hind leg. The cat, a thrashing mass of terrorised muscle, must have bitten or clawed the boy, because he cried out in anger and pitched it on the bonfire. The small body twisted in the air before landing in the flames. Each of us fell still to watch. Every last child was quiet.

I was seized from behind and my face rammed against the hoarding. 'Ya fucken perv,' came the voice of an adult male, his teeth close enough to bite my ear. I hadn't noticed any men on the building site. I tried to get a look at him over my shoulder, but he kneed me in the kidneys and threw me down on the ground. I got onto my hands and knees. The cat was screaming.

A kick under the ribs flipped me onto my back. The two of us were face to face then. His head was shaved and leathery, burnished orange by the bonfire. He bent down and took hold of my collar. 'Filthy bollocks,' he spat, 'spying on the kiddies.'

His knuckles connected with my face, just beneath the eye socket, slamming the back of my head into the stony ground. There was a crunch. The stars floating in my eyes merged with the fireworks in the sky. 'Please,' I whispered. A girl was shrieking hysterically, but not for me. The wail of a siren approached.

The man punched me a second time, with greater force. 'Here, youse,' he called over his shoulder. There were more of them. I wrenched out of his grasp and scrambled for the hoarding. 'Get back here now,' he commanded me.

The sirens were almost upon us by then. The children rushed off the building site, and I joined their number. We flowed like rats through the gap in the hoarding. A stolen car screeched sideways around the corner, a garda van with lowered riot shield in close pursuit. Locals were out banging dustbin lids against the pavement. The children dispersed into the back lanes and flats, but three men were chasing after me. There was a loud *phht* not far from my ear, like a huge cat spitting, then a shower of sparks as the rocket collided with steel security shuttering ahead. A fire engine came hurtling along Gardiner Street, followed by an ambulance, and when next I looked over my shoulder, the three men were gone. I was running down a dark empty road on my own.

9

Amongst Women

The four, my four, the Square of Pegasus, the Northern Cross, were there ahead of me when I arrived at the workshop the following Wednesday. The furniture had been rearranged, on whose instructions, I never asked. The small individual tables had been pushed together into the centre of the room to form one large desk, around which nine chairs were placed. At the head of this expanse of reticulated tabletop, the bulky desk with the drawers was set. Glynn did not register surprise or even awareness of these modifications when he finally darkened our doorway, twenty-five minutes late. Two of the chairs were still empty. They were to remain empty for the duration of the class, and for the duration of the academic year. Already we were down to six in number: the four girls, myself and your man with the ponytail – Mike.

Antonia was first to read from her work. She'd written a disconcertingly ambivalent short story about a middle-aged man in the numbing wake of his mother's death. The man returned after a prolonged absence to his childhood home, which, since he was an only child and his father had passed away some years previously, had now fallen to him. He barely recognised the place, it was all so long ago. The son, unnamed ('The son scratched his head . . .', 'The son belched softly . . .', 'The son suddenly realised he was an orphan'), hadn't been close to his mother during her lifetime, had barely known the woman in fact, but after her death he kept finding dressmakers' pins around the house. This came as a surprise to him. He hadn't known that his mother sewed.

He encountered the first pin sticking out of the armrest of her favourite chair, and as he rolled the narrow metal cylinder contemplatively between thumb and forefinger, it occurred to the son that this unanticipated memento should move him to tears. He hadn't cried at the news of his mother's death, or at her funeral. Tears, however, did not come, and the son carried on watching *The Late Late.*

Antonia's prose entertained a certain amount of ambiguity as to whether the pins were intended as a symbol of the mother's creativity in the female domain, as in the burgeoning North American patchwork-quilt genre, or of her cunningly remonstrative spirit railing against an ungrateful and emotionally inert male; see Carter, Angela. My guess is that it was a gender thing. Glynn definitely looked uncomfortable. The pins appeared with increasing frequency, and in places the son was adamant they hadn't been the day before: a scattering of them on the mantelpiece, a sprinkling in the box of tissues, a lone embroidery needle lying in ambush between the sheets of his unmade bed. Mostly, the son located the pins by sitting on them. No matter how carefully he checked the cushions before lowering his apprehensive backside, a pin would surely prick the seat of his pants until one day his arse was pierced so deeply and so deliberately that tears of confused pain sprang to his eyes.

The son dropped his head into his hands and wailed. 'Oh Mammy,' is what he said. Dialogue was never Antonia's forte.

Once the tears started, there was no stopping them. The son wept until day became night became day again. His head changed colour several times (I'm paraphrasing). The pins stayed put in their pincushion after that. You had to hand it to Antonia. It was a very dramatic climax.

Aisling read aloud a poem, the content of which I recall in no detail – it seemed to erase its own shifting nature as soon as it was spoken, a palimpsest, I suppose you would call it – but each of us, Glynn included, registered the roiling aftershock of its dark inaccessibility, its staunch brevity, its confident deployment of the word *apotropaic* (adj. supposedly having the power to avert an evil influence or bad luck), introducing to Aisling's dynamic a radical element. She scared me, that girl. I think she scared herself.

She read the poem with such gravity that we knew in our bones it was the real thing. Not that Aisling's poem was the real thing – not one of us, if we were honest, understood a word of it – but that one day she would write poetry equalling her conviction. Her voice became progressively deeper, more incantatory, as she read, not fully emanating from her narrow chest but someplace altogether lower, smothered beneath those swathes of black clothes, as if an act of paranormal channelling were underway. She did not hold her manuscript in her hand, but instead left it on the table, her arms dangling limply by her side, her head hanging no more than a few inches from the page. You couldn't see her face behind that blue-black curtain of hair. She could have been anyone under there. This was no way to give a reading. We'd all attended Glynn's events. He had shown us how it was done.

Aisling did not look up for a reaction when the poem was finished, just turned the page a 180-degree angle, face down, as if it were attached to the table by a hinge. It seemed that she was closing a door, shutting out what had seconds earlier rampaged squalling amongst us. Despite its impact, that page occupied practically no mass, barely impinging on the room at all. It was so innocent, in fact, so blameless and white, and attractively tactile in that way paper is, that I experienced a moment of disorientation, having glimpsed the chaos encrypted on the other side. The round silence which followed her reading was broken by a small grunt of approval from Glynn, a small surprised grunt of approval.

Faye had brought in a short story about two little old ladies attending a piano recital in the National Concert Hall on Earlsfort Terrace. The first section detailed the pains the pair took getting dressed up beforehand, their appraisals of their reflections in the age-mottled mirrors which had once held images of their girlhood selves, the admiring glances they hoped their elegant (if dated) clothes and jewellery might attract. They separately, in their respective homes, envisaged the entrance they would make, imagined themselves in various social contexts, rehearsed the lines they might deliver upon encountering old acquaintances not seen in years. The two old ladies realised that they were nervous. Recent unspecified losses had shaken their confidence, and this trip to the concert hall was to be their first night out in some time.

The pair arrived early and purchased interval drinks –
one glass of white wine, a gin and tonic – before taking
their seats up on the yellow balcony. The seats were
excellent, commanding an impressive view, having been
booked well in advance under the guidance of the nice
man in the ticket office, who advised them to sit slightly
to the left if they wanted to see the pianist's hands (they
had nodded their heads: *yes please!*). The old ladies
looked around to see who else was in, and were pleased
to recognise more than a few faces, who recognised
them in turn. Yes, it was splendid. The world had not
changed as much as they'd feared. However – and there
was always a 'However' in Faye's work – as the two-
minute curtain call sounded, another couple, a middle-
aged man and his wife, arrived and hovered unhappily
over the little old ladies, who smiled sweetly up at them,
wondering if they were acquainted. Their faces didn't
ring a bell.

The couple looked at their tickets, then down at the
little old ladies, then back at their tickets again. There
were no empty seats left in the row. The man cleared his
throat and mentioned that the two ladies were occupy-
ing his seats. The little old ladies blinked. How papery
their powdered skin looked under the auditorium lights.
Faye deployed a deft simile to capture their fright,
though the phrasing escapes me now. Much bluster was
to follow. The couple showed the old ladies their tickets,
and, sure enough, this second set also read Row J, Seats
15 and 16. The old ladies declined to move. The middle-
aged couple continued to unhappily hover. A hush fell
over the rows behind. Two tickets for the same seat had
been printed by accident, and the concert was a sell-out.
What would happen next?

The middle-aged couple summoned the usher, a smart young woman, who, after a brisk examination of both sets of tickets, pointed out as tactfully as she was able that the old ladies' concert wasn't until the following evening. The little old ladies had to hurriedly collect their belongings and vacate the seats, as the recital was already late in commencing.

Faye's evocation of their humiliation as they were escorted to the back of the hall was as masterful as it was poignant. Applause met their exit as the soloist appeared on stage (a violinist! – how had they missed the absence of a grand piano on stage?). It wasn't until the two were travelling home in silence on the lower deck of the bus that they realised they'd forgotten their interval drinks. Each lady arrived at this discovery independently, but both made the decision not to mention it to the other. It was as complete an exposition of disappointment as I had ever read.

'Would it not be better,' Glynn suggested after some moments consideration, 'if the usher pointed out that the two tickets were for *yesterday* instead? In your version, the two little old ladies get a second chance, because they get to do it all over again the following evening.'

There was a sort of collective *aha* in the room, causing our chairs to creak beneath us. Aha, of course, perfect. That was the difference between Glynn and an ordinary writer, that ability to locate tragedy in the inappreciable details. Faye pencilled in his recommendation.

Guinevere then read an extract from *Hartman,* the novel she'd been working on for some months, the eponymous protagonist of which was an ageing American insurance broker with a cardiac complaint, failed husband twice over and parent to three outstand-ingly disaffected grown-up children, none of them his own.

This willingness to explore a complete stranger's messy and largely self-inflicted personal setbacks seemed less to me at the time an audacious act of imagining on Guinevere's part – a young Irishwoman narrating the inner life of a decrepit Bostonian about whom she could have known next to nothing: Guinevere hadn't even been to the States – than a touching act of compassion. Guinevere should have been more discerning with her pity and not squandered it on those undeserving few who could never get their fill of it, no matter how much she bestowed on them. I include myself in their number.

The extract she read was narrated in that effortless first-person narrative voice that flows so freely from the pens of the American prose masters, as if they didn't have to do any actual work to get their novels onto the page, merely show up and turn on the tap, or rather *faucet,* and of whom all, Guinevere pointed out to me one night in the pub, were men. Good stuff, I thought. Proper order.

I made no attempt to engage with the argument because I did not want to discuss other men with Guinevere. I did not want her to discuss other men with me. The sole exception was Glynn. Perhaps, she confid-ed in a confessional tone, this awareness of male prima-cy in the field explained the subconscious decision she must've made somewhere along the line to write in a man's voice. It was as much of a surprise to her as to anyone, she maintained, when this lemon-aertexed American golfer with his Pepto-Bismol started speaking the minute she sat at the page. 'The twentieth century novels of truly great stature,' she noted with little pleasure, 'come from the pens of male hands just as surely as sad songs are composed in a minor key.'

At this, Antonia practically sprang out of her seat. We hadn't realised she'd been listening. We hadn't realised they'd all been listening. Three appalled faces stared at Guinevere. 'Virginia Woolf!' Antonia proclaimed as an example of a female novelist of truly great stature, but the strained silence which ensued as she and the group struggled to produce another name indicated that Virginia, poor tormented, drowned Virginia, was the cautionary exception to the rule.

'I would like to believe,' Faye offered, 'that the names of great twentieth-century female novelists do not spring as readily to our lips as those of their male counterparts simply because we haven't heard of them.'

'So would I,' Guinevere replied flatly, her tone conveying that although she too would have liked to enjoy Faye's benign belief, the stark facts of the matter denied her that luxury.

'Am I doomed from the start?' Antonia demanded. 'Is that what you're saying? Is that what you're telling me? That I'm doomed in my literary endeavours from the outset because I'm female? That I may as well not bother?' The blood had drained so thoroughly from her face that Antonia's lips were the colour of skin, and her skin was the colour of bone. How unfamiliar she had suddenly become, and yet how genuine, as if the mask had finally dropped.

We were evidently in the grip of a serious crisis, and although I had no comprehension of the immense personal significance Antonia had clearly invested in the argument, the urge to defend Guinevere, who was sitting

73

listlessly by my side, was at that moment overpowering. 'Listen Antonia–' I began, the adrenalin surging through my body, but then Aisling slammed her pint down with such force that it splashed all over the table.

'Shut up,' she warned us, and we did.

There was something about Aisling's delivery on that occasion that made us pay absolute heed to her. The five of us drank in sullen silence until our glasses were drained. It didn't take long. Where was Glynn for all of this? God knows. And yet he seemed the very epicentre of the incident, present and amongst us in some auditing capacity, watching our five miniatures through a crystal ball, goading us into the expression of contentious opinions we didn't know we held so strongly, or even held at all. God forbid that we should disappoint him. We spoke our lines for him alone. They would filter back for his critical appraisal through one channel or another. Everything filtered back to Glynn, eventually. Everything bore his mark. I do not remember how that particular evening ended. Unsatisfactorily, I suppose.

And so Guinevere read to us her inspired solution to the quandary she said had plagued her (and plagued Antonia too, whether she admitted it or not): her novel narrated by a man. After a few sentences, we acclimatised to her light voice recreating that of an American male, until soon we were hearing not Guinevere's Irish accent, but Maxwell Hartman's East Coast burr. It crept up on you gradually, the cumulative impact of all that unassuming detail, the combined weight of those deceptively throwaway observations. It stole up, gathered round, had you surrounded, snug, until without warning it had come to life: Maxwell Hartman was in the room.

It was the polar opposite of Aisling's reading, which

foregrounded not the subject matter but the struggle of the artist herself. Guinevere receded altogether as a fictional character appeared in her skin, pressing his face into hers. There were times when it was clear that Guinevere could have done anything she wanted. Her use of the disappointed male voice generated a tragic resonance, but the real tragedy to my mind was that a young woman perceived an ostensibly successful and powerful businessman as so abjectly pitiful. Was that what got to me about Guinevere's writing: her ability to see through the male armoury to the shivering wretch underneath? Was that what made me come to her?

Mike adjusted his ponytail and read an extract from some class of crime fiction, some scrape about a good guy, a bad guy, a blonde and a bag of loot. The women didn't appreciate his efforts either, though Glynn bestowed upon him a hearty wink. And then it was my turn. I leafed through my manuscript in a harassed fashion for no good reason. It wasn't like the pages had scrambled into the wrong order behind my back. I was barely a paragraph into Chapter One when Glynn interrupted me.

'What happened your eye?' he demanded.

What eye, I wondered. There was no eye in Chapter One. Never had been. Or did he mean *I,* the first-person narrator?

Glynn raised his glasses to his forehead, awaiting an explanation. The lenses framed two rectangles of skin, as if a second, covert set of eyes was concealed behind the pink membrane, his mind's eye, his artist's eye, window to his imagination.

'Your eye,' he repeated, nodding at my shiner. 'What happened? Someone give you a dig?'

'Oh that,' I said. 'Yes.'

'Was it over a woman?'

'No,' I said apologetically.

Glynn peered at my black eye for another few seconds, then dropped his glasses back onto his nose to indicate that he'd lost interest. I shuffled my sheaf of papers as needlessly as before and returned to the business of reading out Chapter One. Anyone could see that it was about Guinevere, and that I wasn't up to the job. I listened to the lonely sound of my own voice losing conviction with every word. Soon it had dwindled to a barely audible trickle. I think this is how a parent must feel to discover that his child is not clever, or pretty, or even happy. The less said about the whole thing the better.

10

You scumbag, you faggot

The payphone in the corridor started ringing in the small hours later that same night. I was out of the bed and running down the stairs before I knew what was going on. 'Who's there?' I challenged the mouthpiece, as if the person on the other end had broken into the building. 'Giz woz ere' was scratched onto the coin-box casing. A light on the ground floor came on.

'Declan?' Guinevere's voice. I recognised it instantly. 'It's Glynn,' she said. 'He's in trouble. Can you help us? We're on Duke Street.'

It would take a good half-hour to reach Duke Street on foot, no matter how hard I ran. The fucker downstairs had stolen my bike. I pummelled his door with my fists on the way out. 'Give me back my bike, you prick!' I shouted, but didn't stick around for a response.

It was a freezing November night, no cloud cover, a rack of winter stars. A dog howled forlornly in the distance. Three knackers in silky tracksuits stood huddled at the entrance to the park. I pressed on. Guinevere was waiting on the other side of the river. I couldn't let her down.

The knackers lunged at me as I passed. They pursued me halfway up the street, white runners pistoning, then lost impetus and fell by the wayside. Their heart wasn't in it. The chase was just for show. I heard them laughing with bravado at my retreat, at the great triumph it denoted. 'Little Trinity gee-bag,' one of them shouted, then fired an empty can in my direction. It fell far short of its target. How did they know I went to Trinity? A life force I didn't think aware of my existence turned out to be monitoring my movements. It was as if the street-lamps had started to speak, or the gateposts nodded at my return.

A tall lone female was standing at the mouth of the service lane to Brown Thomas when I rounded the corner onto Duke Street from Grafton Street. My heart surged at the sight of her, and I waved. The figure did not return my greeting but unfolded her arms and threw her cigarette to the ground. The street lighting glanced off the crown of her head as she did so. Blonde bobbed hair. Antonia. My hand dropped to my side.

She didn't speak when I drew up, just checked her watch in irritation. You would think I had kept her waiting. 'Where's Guinevere?' I asked.

'Glynn, you mean. He's down here.'

She led me down the lane in silence. The others were stationed throughout it, Aisling first, so black that she merged with the background. I didn't realise she was there until she spoke. 'Hi Declan,' came her voice from the murk, the moon of her disembodied face materialising in the darkness. It was swaying slightly. Up ahead, amongst a pile of cardboard boxes and packing crates, bathed in the glow of a security lamp, lay the great man himself. Faye was on her knees ministering to him. Guinevere stood to attention at his head. It was the deathbed scene of a king.

Faye got to her feet when she saw me. 'He's taken a bit of a turn,' she said apologetically, brushing down her skirt.

'Hello Declan,' said Guinevere. 'Sorry to have called you in the middle of the night.'

'That's alright,' I told her. 'Any time.'

'Mike wasn't home, so we had to ring you instead,' Antonia clarified, in case there was any doubt as to their first preference.

They stood back to allow me to examine the body, which was in the recovery position on the ground. I nudged Glynn in the ribs with the toe of my shoe. No response. 'He's asleep,' I said. Aisling sniggered.

'We can see that, thanks,' said Antonia, and lit another cigarette.

'Problem is,' said Guinevere, 'he won't wake up.'

'Why didn't you call me earlier?'

'We thought we could handle it ourselves,' said Faye. Spurred sleech. I turned to look at her.

'Have you lot been drinking since the workshop ended?' That seemed like days ago.

Faye bit her lip. 'Afraid so. We've let Professor Glynn get into a terrible state.' Glynn's drinking became public knowledge when he was expelled from a Northern Ireland peace conference for singing rebel songs of his own composition.

'He's a grown man,' Antonia pointed out. 'He got himself into this state.'

I surveyed his length. 'Exactly how long has he been in this condition?' There was something about their anxious, solicitous tone that made me adopt a clipped, professional one. I'd gotten myself stuck in Mike's cop novel.

'I don't know,' said Guinevere. 'Two hours maybe?'

I nodded gravely, as if I were a doctor and this time span confirmed my worst suspicions. I wanted to punish them, I suppose, for leaving me behind. 'So what do you want me to do with him?'

'Fucking pick him up,' said Antonia. 'Jesus.'

'We can't seem to lift him ourselves,' Guinevere explained. 'He's a dead weight.'

'And we can hardly leave him out here in the cold,' added Faye.

I wasn't sure I understood their problem. 'Why didn't you just wake him?'

Guinevere shrugged. 'We couldn't. We've tried everything. Seriously.' Aisling sniggered again.

I moved around Glynn, hunkering down like a snooker player looking for a good angle. There was no good angle. Laid out on his side with his shirt untucked, exposing an expanse of haunch, Glynn's true bulk was revealed, and it was reckonable. There was at least a third more of him on the flat, a ship hoisted out of the water. The girls waited patiently for me to do something. Even Antonia gave me the benefit of the doubt. A stranger I was then to ageing flesh and had never been confronted with so much of it before, and of such a lifeless texture too, squeezed into goosebumped skin like sausage meat. I got down on my knees.

I tried to engage him in conversation, cupping my hands and calling down his ear as if it were the well shaft he'd fallen into. 'Hello?' I cried, then leaned back to check for signs of life. None. I bent over him again. 'Can you hear me, Professor? Do you think you could stand up?' That sort of thing. On it went. Stupid questions, the answers to which I already knew. Antonia made a tutting noise in response to each one.

'Look it, Antonia,' I told her, sitting back on my heels, 'this is hard enough without you standing behind me sneering.'

She tutted again.

'For the love of God, woman!' Glynn suddenly cried. 'Stop your infernal complaining. One of you: help me up.' I grasped his arm and hauled him to his feet. Guinevere inserted herself under his other arm for balance.

'The lovely Guinevere,' he murmured, drawing her to him.

'It's alright,' I assured her, swinging Glynn around so that she was out of his reach. 'I can manage.'

Glynn swivelled his head to regard me. 'Who's this clown?' he demanded but then decided it didn't matter, so intent was he on keeping up with the women. We stumbled towards Nassau Street, a three-legged race, the girls going on ahead to hail a taxi.

Guinevere opened the cab door and stood back to let him in first, but the man didn't understand what was required of him and gazed at the waiting taxi as if it were no concern of his. I tried to lower his intractable bulk into the back seat, but he wouldn't release my shoulder, so in the end I had to climb in first and ease him down on top of me. I inched him along the scalloped seat until there was enough room on the other side for Guinevere. She stuck her head in after us. I could barely see her over the mound of Glynn.

'Safe home now, Declan,' she said. The others chimed their goodbyes behind her. 'Wait,' I protested as the door slammed shut. I tried to wrench myself around to look out the back window as the taxi pulled away but was pinioned under the great slouched mass of Glynn, pressed hard up against me like a lover.

I tried to push him off, but he remained slumped across my shoulder. 'This isn't my car,' he observed mildly, then started to hum. *Ain't no sunshine when she's gone.* The first rumblings of resentment began to stir in my chest, as is so often the way with these things, but I said nothing, did nothing, just let it come down on me. The Irish are used to being rained on.

11

The Quare Fellow

We could not fail but notice, at the workshop the following Wednesday, that Glynn's voice had lost the antagonistic edge which had characterised previous classes. He commenced the session by speaking to us about the aloneness of writing, tacitly acknowledging for the first time that writing was a condition we shared.

Not loneliness, he clarified, but aloneness with the writing self. No amount of time spent alone with the writing self was too much, he said. You stay up with it all night as if it were your lover. You go through the details of your day with it until it becomes your closest friend. Your only friend, at times. Being a writer, Glynn believed, was like getting the keys to the city. You could go anywhere you wanted within the fictive space, do anything you wanted. To waste that freedom would be nothing short of irresponsible. Did we understand what he meant? We nodded. We understood. There were periods in Glynn's life – contemplating the various editions of his novels, for instance (translated into thirty-two languages now) – when he could enjoy a spirit of comradeship with his books, his fellow conspirators, that they had managed to pull it off together, that they had come this far, them against the world. These periods never lasted long. The great writer's face clouded. For a moment, we thought he was going to start telling us about his suffering. He took a breath, glanced at our expectant faces, but something held him back.

'I'll leave it there,' he said, getting to his feet.

The four girls jumped up and followed him down the stairs. I glanced at Mike to do something, stop him, but Mike just packed away his notebook. When was Glynn going to show us how to write?

The group left House Eight in a hexagon, for they had gained a fifth point. Glynn had joined their number. They had annexed Glynn. I watched them from the top floor, surrounding him like a bracelet, moving him across the cobbles with the sheer gravitational force of their presence. The five of them made their way to Front Arch. Glynn looked pleased. Bewildered, admittedly, as if he couldn't quite grasp how they were dictating his movements, but pleased all the same with the attention they lavished on him, willing to pay the price.

I came upon them a couple of hours later. It was the night we made the landmark discovery that all five of us had attended Glynn's Royal Irish Academy reading back in '81. Aisling had been celebrating her twentieth birthday. Now she was celebrating her twenty-fourth. It was our anniversary.

When I say I came upon them, I mean I followed them to the door of Bartley Dunne's, then returned a couple of hours later and wandered past their table in an abstracted manner copied from Glynn, as if my head was stuffed so full of poetic matter that there simply wasn't room left in it to accommodate the quotidian stuff, like looking where you were going. Glynn was singing come-all-ye's by then. The women had gone to his head.

It was Faye who spotted me, good old Faye. 'Look,' she said, pointing me out to the others, 'isn't that Declan?' A man could always rely on her type. She had seven cats at home, all of them strays, because she couldn't bear to see a fellow creature suffer. Her heart was too big for her own good. Her belief in the essential goodness of human nature was irrational and subject to manipulation by precisely the strain of badness she refused to accept prevailed in the world. All a man had to do was look crestfallen and she'd forgive him, no matter how heinous the transgression nor how hollow the assertion to reform. 'You know her husband beats her, don't you?' Aisling once whispered urgently into my ear while the two of us were standing at the bar waiting for our pints to settle.

'What! Whose husband? Jesus Christ Almighty!'

It hadn't been my intention to raise my voice. Aisling had caught me by surprise. The barman raised an admonitory eyebrow as he topped up our pints. 'Take it handy there, folks,' he warned us. Aisling glanced at the others in panic, though they were too far away to have overheard. 'Nothing, Declan,' she blurted, 'I shouldn't have told you. Forget I said anything, *please.*'

This wasn't the kind of information you could forget in a hurry, and Aisling knew it. Her face flushed red under all the white make-up, making her look stranger still. She had evidently just broken one of the group's secret confidences, one of those blood oaths with which their little cabal was ridden, and she grew so frantic, so distraught, as she fumbled first with her packet of cigarettes and then with her lighter, all the while begging me to forget she'd opened her mouth, that I backed off altogether to calm her down. Neglecting one to protect another. It was an insane situation, but there you go.

She finally got the cigarette up and running, and the two of us stood watching the other three conversing with Glynn as if nothing was amiss. *You know her husband beats her, don't you?* Aisling hadn't specified which of them was beaten, but it was hardly the time to ask. Faye was the only one who was married. Though Antonia technically had a husband still, in the eyes of the Irish State.

Faye, kind Faye, waved her hand and called my name as I was wandering through the red and black gloom of Bartley Dunne's, pint in hand. Imagine my surprise to encounter my fellow writing students. And the Professor too, as luck would have it. I stood there, smiling broadly at the lot of them.

They seemed pleased enough to see me, at any rate. Glynn interrupted his song to throw an arm out in welcome. 'Dermot!' he cried, knocking over his pint. The women had made him giddy. Guinevere stemmed the spillage by dealing a dam of beer mats with the air of one with much practice in this field. 'Sit down there now like a good man,' Glynn instructed me. I set my pint on the table and took my rightful place amongst them, the six of us crammed into a booth.

How delicate and colourful the girls were. It was like sitting in a flowerbed. I knew I was too big for them, too awkward, too crude. Didn't matter: I scrunched in tighter. Glynn leaned across. 'You've got your knees under the table now, so you have, ya boyo!' he winked. Aisling went to the bar to replace his pint.

'Did you follow us here?' Antonia demanded.

Guinevere laughed. 'God almighty, of course he didn't

86

follow us here. What sort of weirdo would do a thing like that?' *Ya fucken perv. Spying on the kiddies.*

'I often drink in Bartley's,' I told them.

'Do you have family in Dublin, Declan?' Faye asked, keen to introduce a neutral subject.

'No, I'm an only child.'

'Oh right. So do you go home to your parents at the weekends?'

'Ah no. The mother doesn't know I left England.'

Antonia lowered her drink. 'Your mother doesn't know you left England?'

'Yeah. She thinks I'm still in Leeds.' They were all looking at me now.

'But why?' asked Faye.

'She'd be really upset if she knew I'd given up a good job to do, well . . .' I gestured at the table, '*this*. So I didn't tell her.' Blank faces. 'She'd have thought Daddy would have disapproved,' I added, sensing more was needed.

Guinevere frowned. 'Your father doesn't know you're here either?'

'No, he passed away.' Daddy had been dead the past twenty years, yet despite his absence, no family decision was made without reference to him, without an agonised consideration of his feelings. Since he had been a quiet man, loath to complain, it had always been difficult to gauge what might have attracted his unspoken displeasure. There were no set rules. Like the Irish language, he had to be learned by ear.

'They were quite old when they had me,' I offered, talking to fill the gap. 'From a different era, really. More like grandparents, in fact.' I was as struck by this information as the girls. I hadn't looked at it that way before.

My ageing parents had treated me as politely and tactfully as a guest staying in their home. Ours had been a
reticent household, for the most part.

Antonia found it uncontrollably amusing that my
mother referred to her deceased husband as *Daddy*.
Really, she could barely contain herself. She repeated my
mother's words to stoke herself up again when her
amusement waned: *Daddy would have preferred to see
you settle*. 'Priceless,' she said, wiping away a tear. Faye
whispered to Antonia to for God's sake leave poor
Declan alone.

'Write it down,' said Glynn, 'Write it down.' He had
a tendency to issue words of advice twice, in order to
imbue them with the quality of axiom. A few observations regarding the state of mind of the artist might be
appropriate at this juncture, in the interests of posterity.
I hadn't seen him execute the office of Great Irish Writer
so movingly before. He sat amongst us in some class of
reverie, head tilted back, eyes shut, basking in the glory
of female company. His boyish good looks were extant
in sufficient measure to make you nostalgic for the hand-
some young poet he once had been, because it was poetry Glynn had started with, yes, it is true, all those years
ago when he was purer of mind and had less to say for
himself.

They say alcohol has spelled the ruin of many a great
Irish writer, but I maintain it is part of what made them
great in the first place. It lifts a veil, releases a man from
inhibitions, frees the creative spirit. Gazing at Glynn
across the table with that half-fledged smile on his face,
which expressed his contentment more completely than
any fully effected version, I was finally granted what I
felt was my first real insight into the internal layout of

the writer's mind. Were Glynn stone-cold sober, I would not have been afforded that licence. A July sunset on a rolling lawn is what I saw. Shadows on the grass as cool and alluring as rock pools. Glynn possessed a working knowledge of the stars which informed his writing, at times infusing it with a celestial dimension, other times foregrounding the staggering insignificance of man. 'There is a moment when you realise,' the stricken narrator notes towards the end of *Broken Man,* as he reflects on the sudden passing of his infant son, 'that the sun is not the sun, but a dying planet, expiring before your eyes.'

Dr M. J. Hanratty's biography mentions that Glynn never fully recovered from the shock of the death of his youngest child, Saoirse, who was killed by meningitis at the age of two. It was around then that reports about him beginning with the word 'troubled' proliferated in the papers. 'Troubled author Patrick Glynn was in court today to answer charges of drunk driving.' 'Troubled writer P. J. Glynn was expelled from an award ceremony in London's Guild Hall last night for punching a fellow contestant.' 'Troubled novelist Patrick Glynn is recovering from hypothermia in hospital tonight after being found in the water on Brittas Bay.'

But that was a long time ago, a different lifetime, a different Glynn. He had written three astonishing novels since Saoirse's death, one universally hailed upon publication as a masterpiece. His other daughter, Sofia, was grown and had flown the nest. His house was quiet once more, all strife and clamour behind him. That old grief had surely lost the power to pain him still, not when he had the inestimable consolation of art.

Glynn must have felt my gaze upon him. He opened

his eyes and squinted at me through narrowed slits, as if the sun were shining in his face, then winked and shut his eyes once more. The contented half-smile did not falter. It occurred to me that the man knew what I was thinking. I wondered whether he could glimpse the internal layout of other people's heads too. His work supports the possibility.

I had initially been sceptical the week before when our taxi drew up to that rundown shambles on Bachelors Walk with the redevelopment notices in the window. 'This can't be right,' I told the taxi driver, who maintained it was the address the women had given him. 'Are you certain this is it?' I asked Glynn slowly, in the measured tones of an adult speaking to a lost child. There had to be a mistake.

Glynn wanted to know exactly what class of ape I thought I was dealing with, that he knew his own fecking address, in the name of God, then he jammed an elbow into my stomach to launch himself as if pushing off a boat from a pier. Out of the back seat he waded, slow as a whale, one eye fixed on the pavement. He turned to toss a balled-up pound note into my lap with an unwarranted show of contempt. I waited until he had the front door open before instructing the taxi driver to pull away. Well so, he had a key.

Key or no key, it was difficult to accept that Glynn intended spending the night in that hovel. I'd had in mind for him a genteel old pile on the hilly outer reaches of Dublin Bay, either Aisling's or Guinevere's side. July sunset on a rolling lawn, shadows cool as rock pools. I saw that cliff house whenever I read his prose. The details were vague, but the atmosphere was unforgettable, as if I'd been brought there to visit as a child.

This is where the great writer lives. Shhh, don't make any noise.

There had to be a better reward for a distinguished life's work in letters. The building on Bachelors Walk was a bigger dive than my own. Small wonder he'd been reluctant to relinquish the Brown Thomas service lane. At least four women had been tending to him there. The house fronted onto a river, though, I had reasoned as the taxi progressed along the quays. A tidal river, at that, almost the sea. Gulls combed that end of the Liffey like any other stretch of coastline. Always happiest near water, Glynn. Perhaps he'd installed himself in the dilapidated digs in the name of research, it occurred to me then. I lowered my pint and looked at him. Perhaps he'd started a new novel. His first set in Dublin, right there on the quays. Jesus. Aisling nudged me from my speculations to murmur something into my ear that I didn't catch. She was too drunk to gauge the projection of her voice and just kept mumbling shyly, nodding dolefully into my eyes. They were all looking at me again, the girls. Antonia eventually couldn't bear it any longer and interjected. 'She's telling you it's your round, *Dermot*.'

Glynn sprang to life at the clink of the tray being set down on the table. He grabbed the nearest glass and raised it. 'A toast!' he proposed, but sank his pint before naming one, then stood up to regard us fondly.

'I'm off to write a novel,' he announced. 'Back in a tick.' He headed for the jacks.

Faye glanced around the table in excitement the second his back was turned. 'He's started, you know,' she blurted when she was certain he was out of earshot. 'He's started a new novel. He recited the opening line to me earlier when we were up at the bar.'

91

'How did it go?' Guinevere asked.

'*Now that the long evenings are upon me once again.*'

'Jesus,' said Aisling. 'Fuck.'

'His first set in Dublin,' I added.

'Does he have a title yet?' said Guinevere.

Faye nodded. '*Desiderata.*'

We marvelled at what a good title it was, wishing we'd thought of it first. And that opening line: such resonance. Five ideas sprouted in our minds.

'Did he say anything else about it?' Antonia asked.

'No, he just recited the opening line and asked me what I thought of it.'

'And what did you say?'

'I told him I thought it was beautiful. What else could I say? He just sprang it on me.'

We saw Faye's dilemma. 'Beautiful' was hardly complex enough a word for Glynn, but no adequate alternative was available at such short notice, not with so little to go on. It was a rabbit-caught-in-the-headlamps response, the literary equivalent of discussing the weather. The word had lost its currency. They were worn-out tools we'd been given to work with, cracked cups and saucers, tattered hand-me-downs, ruined through overuse. 'Beautiful.' How hollowly it must have rung in the great writer's ears. Same thing everyone said to him at every book signing, whether they'd read his work or not. How were we to prove to Glynn that we were any different? How was he to *know*?

The barman rammed the shutters down, and Aisling jumped in fright. The strip fluorescent lights shunted on, and she let her black hair fall forward to conceal her face, though we'd already seen the smudged eyeliner, the caked foundation. Difficult to miss it. She applied so much white stuff to her skin that it seemed she was try-ing to erase herself. She could have been anyone under that mask. We might not have recognised her without it.

I sat back from the table. My elbows were soaked in peaty brown stout. The pub was emptying out. The bar staff instructed us to finish up as they collected the last of the glasses. 'Alright now *folks,* make a move there now *folks,* have youse no homes to go to *folks?*' Roaring it over and over until it became unbearable. Where the hell was Glynn? He'd been gone an age. I felt inexplica-bly aggrieved that he had chosen to confide in Faye about his new novel. Judging by the sullen mood that had descended on our number, we were all mulling this same scrap of information, probing at it with our tongues like a piece of food trapped between our teeth; small, but extremely irritating.

It was me they sent after him to the men's toilets, jok-ing that I had my uses. No trace of the man. I came back out to find that our booth was also empty. Faye was waiting by the exit in her coat. She thrust my jacket at me before hurrying away, apologising that she had to run for the last bus. The other three had already left. The nation's finest, it turned out, had wandered off without telling us, as, we were to discover over the coming weeks, was his wont. We hadn't noticed him slipping away, sort of like the moment of death. The girls had drifted after him one by one. There wasn't a thing I could have done to stop them. I pulled up my hood and walked home to my hovel, as disgruntled as the worst of Glynn's narrators, as soured by my own plight.

I was barely in the door when a young fella in a silky tracksuit came panting up the steps behind me. He pushed past me into the hall, a pub-sized television set in his arms. I flattened myself against the wall to allow him pass. It was the fucker from the flat downstairs, the one who'd stolen my bike. *Giz woz ere.* 'Sorry,' I said when he stood on my foot.

He cursed, unable to throw a filthy look my way since his cheek was jammed against the milky grey screen. I watched him make his way up the stairs, half-blind and stumbling. What had he painted on his runners to get them so white? Tippex? The same stuff Aisling trowelled on her face? They were incongruously immaculate, considering the state of the rest of him; the stained tracksuit bottoms, the saggy black leather jacket, elasticated at the waist. Funny smell off him too. He drew up on the stairs.

'Here,' he said, unable to turn around within the narrow confines of the stairwell, not with that thing in his arms. I glanced over my shoulder. The hall was empty. The front door was shut. I looked back up.

'You mean me?'

'Yeah. D'ya wanna buy a telly?'

'No.'

He continued on his way without further discussion, the flex of the television trailing after him like a tail. Those Tippexed runners. They were familiar. I'd encountered them recently somewhere. I watched them pistoning up the stairs, but it wasn't until lying in bed later that night that I finally managed to place them. The knackers at the entrance to the park who had lunged at me last week. 'Little Trinity gee-bag,' the prick had shouted in my wake, laughing loudly for the benefit of his friends. He'd hurled a beer can in my direction, but it lacked the ballast to reach its target. He may as well have thrown a leaf. 'Little Trinity gee-bag,' he'd repeated, then laughed again, louder still, so pleased was he with this description.

12

I'm an ordinary man, nothing special, nothing grand

We greatly enjoyed the succinct biographical notes which accompanied reissues of Glynn's novels, never mind whether they were true. 'He lives in Wicklow and Havana.' 'He is a leading exponent of the rural post-modern in Anglo Irish Literature.' 'He retired from active service in the Irish Free State's Intelligence Corps when misdiagnosed with a wasting disease.' These notes, written in the third person by the man himself, were neither outlandish enough nor specific enough to leap out at the casual reader as blatant lies. It was Faye who disabused us of their veracity, showcasing the formidable research skills that would stand to her in her future career. Although he had joined the FCA in his youth, there was no Irish Intelligence Corps as such, and even if there were, the likes of Glynn would hardly have been enlisted, not with his criminal record, minor though it was.

We came to regard his biographical notes as demonstrations in miniature of the power of fiction. No sooner had Glynn published them than they entered the realm of fact. He had altered the world with a pen stroke, the very mark of a god. Lazy journalists rushing to meet deadlines parroted variations on them, covering their tracks as best they could be bothered with thesauruses. Thus 'Havana' became 'the Tropics', Glynn's alleged spell in the 'Intelligence Corps' became 'Republican spy', and his 'wasting disease' somehow morphed into 'rumoured syphilis'. Superb, as Antonia would say, then the horsy laugh.

These concocted fragments evolved into a colourful portrait that offered more of an insight into the man's playful spirit than a strict adherence to the bare nuts and bolts could have hoped to. For Glynn enjoyed parallel lives in his imagination, and it was his imaginative life above all else that those biographical notes sought to evoke, we concluded. What was a writer but his imaginative existence, after all?

It was true that he had been to Cuba just the once, and only for a week at that, but he never fully left it behind either. The place stole his heart, rendered him perpetually longing to return, escaping there on a regular basis in his daydreams, and so it could be said with some degree of conviction that part of Glynn *did* live in Havana, an important part, a substantial portion of his envisaging faculty, wandering down the narrow streets during the hot white noon while his earthbound self was tucked up in the *leaba*. We could all but see him in his crumpled linen, his jaunty fedora, seeking out the shade of the hibiscus or the respite of his favourite bar. Like a shaggy Irish wolfhound he would be, farcically ill adapted to the heat, an object of some curiosity and amusement to the locals, lying around panting in the shadows.

This notion of a doppelgänger, a southern señor Glynn, the Great Irish Writer in Exile, on tour, proved irresistible to us, particularly when it was raining. He understood exactly how to go about constructing his double, knew where best on the soft tissue of the mind to apply the electrodes to make his simulation of a man jolt into life and become one. The wrong imagery, and it mightn't take. But aside from his biographical notes being a masterclass in creative writing, it was their freedom that most appealed to us, this proffering of alternative versions of the self, just like that, with the insertion of an adjective, the souping up of a noun. For we were not there to continue being the people we had previously been, either. That was not our objective in enrolling on the course.

Glynn, or 'Professor Patrick Glynn, Writer Fellow', as the brushed-steel nameplate slotted into the door of his office in the Department of English read, finally appeared in the middle distance of Front Square. It was a cold bright morning in early December.

The walled college campus was divided into sections as distinct as the rooms in a home. Each section represented a different era in European architecture. Front Square, accessed via the Arch on College Green, was an eighteenth-century neoclassical tableau. The Arts Block, fronting onto Nassau Street, and towards which Glynn was presently headed, was a cement box homage to the nineteen seventies, the façade of which broke out in large weeping sores when it rained, as it often did in Dublin, lending the building a bleak, bedraggled appearance. It failed in its purpose to be a monument to the consolations offered by the arts and humanities, to act as a bulwark against the Irish winter. Small wonder we conceived of Glynn as being elsewhere. We rarely, if ever, pictured him in his office in the Department of English, despite it being his place of employment. As backdrops went, the Arts Block didn't live up to him.

Upon encountering the narrow passage between the 1937 Reading Room and the Colonnades (which wasn't all that narrow – it merely seemed so in contrast to the gracious expanse of Front Square) those approaching from the other side faltered and deferred right of way to Glynn, who proceeded without so much as checking his pace, nor registering the guard of honour of stalled students lined up on either side of the passage through which some minutes earlier I myself had slipped, unnoticed.

Glynn crossed the smooth worn cobbles flanking New Square. The gradient of the ramp leading up to the Arts Block appeared to cause him undue difficulty. He lost impetus and ground to a halt halfway up, as if the ramp were a taxing paragraph he would return to later, once he had mustered his resources. He leaned against the railing and checked his watch. Only thirteen minutes late: *Grand so*. He lit a cigarette.

That a literary colossus should struggle with a ramp was what you might call a paradox. From an elevated position, it was evident that Glynn was beginning to thin at the crown. He ran a protective hand over his hair, somehow sensing that it had become the focus of negative attention. He scanned the faces of the students milling about him, then squinted up in my direction, where I stood at a window on the third floor of the Arts Block, trained on him like a sniper. Could he see me? Hard to say.

Glynn stamped out his cigarette and finally gained the ramp. I lost sight of him until he reappeared at the far end of the English Department corridor, a full nineteen minutes late for our appointment.

'You wanted to see me, Professor?' It was a rhetorical question. I was reminding him, not asking him, because Glynn patently didn't want to see me at all.

'That's right,' he conceded. He'd asked me at the end of the last workshop to schedule a private appointment with him in his office later that week. I asked Aisling whether he'd issued the same request to the others. She told me he had not. Glynn unpinned the few notes thumb-tacked to his message board and unlocked the door, ushering me in ahead of him.

His office was the first disappointment. I had anticipated stepping into my favourite photograph of him, I suppose: bay window, mahogany table, tiny glinting sceptre. I had failed to deduce that a Georgian window could not exist in a modern building like the Arts Block.

'Have a seat,' said Glynn, indicating a tomato-red plastic chair, as he settled himself behind a metal desk.

It was uncomfortable, having him to myself like that. We had never been alone together. Wait, that's a lie. There was a preponderance of red biros on his desk, which I thought at the time was part of some intriguing system he'd devised to inspire himself, because everything was a big secret then, everything was alchemical and occult and enthralling. Glynn was frowning at one of the notes he'd untacked from his message board. It wasn't written on foolscap like the other notes, but instead on a pale blue sheet of watermarked writing paper, the kind of stationery used by old ladies and priests. He put his glasses on and sat riveted to the page. 'Be with you in a second,' he murmured.

He leaned over to root through a drawer in an agitated fashion, leaving the note face up on the desk. A few words – no more than three or four – were printed in the dead centre of the sheet in lettering compact to the point of illegibility. Jesus Christ, I realised, it was one of the famous poison-pen letters. Aisling had described them to me: the bond paper, the minute writing. They were arriving thick and fast by then. Glynn uncapped a fountain pen and grimaced as he flicked it. A spray of black ink shot across the desk. He checked his watch, then scratched a series of numbers along the base of the note – the date, probably, and time of receipt – before dropping both the note and the pen into the drawer and pushing it shut.

'So,' he said, placing his forearms on the table and interlacing his fingers: 'How are you settling in?'

I sat there like an actor who had forgotten his lines. I couldn't think of an answer. I reached out and rested my fingertips lightly on the cool surface of the metal desk, not far from the spray of black ink. Glynn had asked me that exact question before, years ago, in another life, I was certain of it. He wasn't Glynn, and I wasn't me, but we had faced each other then, as we faced each other now, caught in the same dynamic. Did he not remember?

The disorientation must have been written all over my face. Guinevere said you could read me like an open book. Glynn plucked at a button on the cuff of his shirt. 'It is not easy, I know,' he began, 'which is why I thought we might meet at this juncture, for a . . .'

He trailed off in search of the right word. That was a first – words failing Glynn. I wished the others had been there to see it. It was how he had opened his fourth novel, *Broken Man*: 'I am lost for words, Annabel.' And then appended a hundred thousand of them. On this occasion, however, the inarticulacy seemed genuine. He pulled a handkerchief out of his pocket and proceeded to polish the lenses of his glasses.

'For a . . .' he began again, and trailed off again, then put his glasses back on and cleared his throat. 'A chat, I suppose you might call it. It's just you haven't really been producing much new work, have you Declan? I'm afraid you appear to be struggling.'

I scanned the assortment of relics scattered throughout his office and shrugged. A crystal trophy, a granite one, wood, silver, gold; all displayed on his bookcase, from which also hung a medal on a ribbon. Honorary doctorates and black and white photographs of Glynn shaking hands with various dignitaries were mounted along one wall. Over his shoulder, through the window, was another wing of the Arts Block, offices the mirror image of the room in which we sat, festive fairy lights glowing in one. Christmas was less than three weeks off. House Eight was not in view.

A heap of brown leaves, I had noticed that morning as I'd walked along the railings of Mountjoy Square on my way in to see Glynn, had fallen into the shape of a skull. They can't have, I told myself, and went back for a second look. But there it was on the pavement: a skull. No two ways about it. A light-bulb shape, maybe three foot long, with cavernous eyes and leering twigs for teeth. What else could I do only gape at it, then go about my business as if nothing had happened? I didn't want to be late for my appointment with Glynn.

He had sent us away from the last workshop with a task. 'Right,' he'd said as we were packing up to leave, 'Next week, bring me in a sentence beginning with the words "All my life".' It was unlike him to issue cogent instructions.

Antonia immediately demanded that she be allowed start her sentence with 'All his' or 'All her life', but Glynn was determined to lead us up the garden path of the first-person narrator, and granted her no leeway. All she had to do was stick it into inverted commas and revert back to her beloved third person once the dialogue was complete, but I left her to figure that out for herself.

I had wanted desperately to get Glynn's task right. I'd sat down at my rickety desk in my rickety room and had written the three words at the top of a clean page. 'All my life.' You could tell a mile off that Glynn had composed them. It didn't even look like my handwriting any more. Something clenched in my chest, as if I was waiting for the crack of a starting pistol, and next thing I was paring the already pared pencil with a vigour that snapped the frail stem of wood in two.

I'd raised the broken halves to my nose and sniffed them. They had smelled of primary school. I'd stood up and sat down again in one fluid movement, then spread my hands out flat on the desk, surrendering custody of them. Glynn's partial sentence sat framed by my thumbs and index fingers. 'All my life.' I could think of nothing. Then the skull.

'I don't seem to be able to write, Professor Glynn.'

He nodded sympathetically. Hadn't written a whole lot himself, lately.

'So I was thinking about dropping out of the class.'

Glynn tilted his head in a manner that indicated I should continue, but I had said my lot. All I had produced in the seven weeks of attending his workshops were seven bits of Chapter Ones. It appeared I didn't have it in me. Guinevere Wren's smile, of all things, had tipped the balance – the realisation, rather, that this smile was not reserved for me alone. It was simply the way she looked at people. At the last workshop, she had read aloud a scene depicting the deep-seated alienation that poisoned the relationship between Maxwell Hartman and his eldest son. The group's reaction had been unanimous. We had praised the extract to the hilt. Her striking imagery, her lyrical language, the sincerity and complexity of the sentiment evoked – she had absolutely nailed it.

She'd received our encomia with a little frown – our approval appeared to perplex her. Her uncertainty only made us praise her more. We embarked on a sustained group effort to rid Guinevere of self-doubt, overturning every rock and stone in a bid to hit on something that might bolster her confidence. Even Glynn joined in. 'The electricity of poetic detail,' he murmured, without specifying which detail he had in mind. Any of them, all of them. Each one packed a voltage.

But nothing we said communicated our enthusiasm, and it began sounding as hollow to us as it patently did to Guinevere. We stepped up our efforts, but that ship was going down. Water was gushing in faster than we could bail it out. In the midst of our fervour – the five of us baying encouragement from the stands as if she were the horse we'd bet our life savings on – I experienced a moment of detachment. I looked at that lovely girl, her calm face silhouetted against the steely November sky, the praise showering down, staring at the stack of A4 pages in front of her as if it were the murder confession we were forcing her to sign, and I had never imagined that another human being could seem so remote. Remote from me, remote from herself.

Antonia, of all people, told me in the pub after that workshop that she had felt exactly the same. *How can anyone feel exactly the same?* I wanted to shout at her. It was the most inane thing I'd ever heard in my life, although I knew Antonia was only trying to be empathetic, or human, or something. She could not recall the specific trigger in Guinevere's reading, just the sudden onslaught in its aftermath of a sense of isolation so profound it had made her want to weep. Uncanny, how Guinevere had managed to summon into the room precisely the condition of alienation she'd been seeking to describe. It had pulled up a seat alongside us at the workshop table, where it had remained, slumped and odious, for the duration of the class, demonstrating the terrible irony that if you write well about something bad, you'll never have any readers. Where did that leave us? With very few options. Very few options indeed.

The shadow of the leg of Glynn's desk was rapidly fading from the floor. It could have been my own reflection I was watching disappear, the impact this dwindling had on me. A black cloud was occluding the watery sun. Glynn's office darkened with remarkable speed, as if a whale were swallowing us whole. I looked at the Professor with appeal and saw the same appeal in him.

'Dropping out?' he prompted me. 'Why?'

I shrugged. 'Because I feel so . . .'

The only adjective that sprang to mind was 'wobbly'. How could I produce the likes of 'wobbly' in front of the likes of Glynn? Words were at least as clunky as Glynn's collection of trophies, his bulky lumps of metal and stone which in no way communicated the literary achievements they'd been designed to represent. I didn't finish my sentence, merely shrugged again. Really, the intensity of the moods that used to sweep over me then.

The stoical nod with which Glynn received this information, or lack of it, indicated that nothing I could say would surprise the man. He had seen it all before.

Emotions that were new and raw to me had been endured by him years ago, in another life that was over now, and all he could do was nod with a recognition that was in itself a comfort. He stood up and went to his bookcase, his repository of infinite riches, his windbreak, and selected a thick red leather tome. *The Collected Works of William Blake,* his favourite British poet. *The Devil's Party,* Glynn's sixth novel, was loosely based on Blake's life. Parallels between the two men were not difficult to discern.

I watched as Glynn took down two more volumes of Romantic poetry and retrieved a metal hip flask from its hiding place at the back of the bookcase. He produced two teacups from his drawer and poured a generous measure of whiskey into each. He handed one cup to me and raised the other. 'So explosive, MI5 monitors the distillery,' he joked, but neither of us laughed. We sat in silence in Glynn's trophy room while the world outside darkened around us, and the whiskey warmed the world within us. Lights in the offices across the way came on one by one. Glynn poured himself another drop.

'You remind me of myself,' he finally commented. The compassion with which he offered this was almost paternal in quality. 'I won't lie to you,' he added, 'it's a difficult path we've chosen.' We. It didn't matter that everything recently written about Glynn read like a death notice. He kept writing writers' novels, that was the problem. Readers' novels were what was wanted. His career had been deemed moribund by those in the know, but still, I'd have done anything to join him.

'You wouldn't be feeling any better now?' he wondered when my cup was empty.

'I would,' I told him. It was the truth.

'Good man, good man.'

He returned the two teacups to the drawer and slotted the hip flask back in behind Blake, Byron and Shelley. I stood up, and he saw me to the door. Tacked to his message board was another pale-blue note. Glynn smiled weakly as he unpinned it. I lowered my eyes in embarrassment.

He gripped my shoulder. 'Look after yourself, Declan.' I didn't know what to say. He retreated to his den with the note. An image of a lily stem, of all things, flashed into my mind, a freshly cut lily stem with three closed buds that I had once contemplated in a glass vase. The buds would open because they didn't understand that their life supply had been severed, that they were already dead. I gazed at Glynn's stooped shoulders as his door swung shut and thought of that stem, think of it still, think of him still, think of us all still, flowering regardless.

PART II

Hilary Term

January

13

I don't like Mondays

The morning of the sixth of January found me sitting bolt upright at my desk in the flat on Mountjoy Square. I hadn't spoken in five days. A month had passed since the last workshop. My pens and paper were laid out in front of me, but I wasn't writing: I was *listening*. Several odd things had occurred in rapid succession. First, the animal cries. A dog started yelping at its upper register, its agony piercing the thin blue sky. It was coming from the back lane. Somewhere below, not far from where I sat, a bloody scene was unfolding. That I could not see it only made it worse. I would have given anything to make it stop.

And then, abruptly, the yelping did stop. The silence which ensued was more ominous still. I sat rooted to the seat.

Next came the rhythmic thumping in the sky, as if the wings of a huge bird were beating the air. It came from all directions at once, growing louder and closer. It took a long time for the helicopter to appear. That's when I clapped eyes on the gull. I hadn't seen it alight. A massive creature, big as a fox, but brazen, territorial, almost pugilistic in its assertion of its dominion, mounted on the spine of a roof. It had its eye on me, its glassy, lemony eye. It did not have to turn its head to regard me.

A shaft of low light illuminated the gull as purple storm clouds bore down on the winter sun. You could wait all year for such light and still not find it. I tried to take it in as best I was able. The gull was smooth, sculptural, declaratory, and showed no fear at all, just a – what could you call it? – a knowingness, as if it wasn't a bird in that round earless skull, exactly. No, not the consciousness of a bird in there, exactly.

The first plump raindrops slashed across the windowpane. A flash of sheet lightning, followed by a rumble of thunder. Something was expanding within me. I put down my pen. The gull was ululating by then, a wild, maniacal sound. A torrential downpour drowned him out. Then the doorbell rang. The doorbell, in that weather. I could hardly believe it.

Two men in navy suits and beige trench coats were standing on the doorstep under a green golf umbrella. The sky lit up theatrically behind them. 'Is Jesus in your life?' one of them asked me in a dapper London accent. Their trousers gleamed wetly like bin liners. 'You're having me on,' was the best I could manage.

I pushed past them down the steps, and the front door clattered shut behind me. 'Ah Jesus,' I cried – my keys were upstairs on my desk. The second man said something that I didn't catch and pressed a magazine into my hands.

The rain was lashing so hard by then that it bounced back up from the pavement. Cars ploughed hesitantly through the rising floodwater, waves rippling in their wake. The orange hulk of a double-decker bus was making slow progress along the North Circular Road. I ventured in the slipstream towards it. It was as dark as dusk, though the church bells hadn't yet rung the noon Angelus.

I could find no bus stop on that stretch of the North Circular, so I waved my Jesus magazine. The bus pulled in, and the doors retracted. 'Get in, get in!' the driver roared, like a man hauling bodies out of the sea. 'Where's your coat? Merciful hour.'

My shoes squelched as I climbed to the top deck. The rain was drumming hard on the roof. The bus braked, and I went stumbling forwards. There was an empty seat up near the front. I slotted myself in beside a man reading the *Star*. The windows had steamed up with condensation. The outside world was a mess of headlamps and tail lights looming through the dribbling greyness. 'Thin Lizzy' was scratched into the seat in front of me. 'Philo RIP.' The conductor came up and collected my fare. No one got on or off. We trooped along in a convoy of traffic as if we had all day.

I kept my eyes on the 'RIP', listening to the tinny *dumb dumb dumb* of someone else's headphones. Water rolled up and down the aisle of the bus, which surged forward and drew back again like an uncertain child. The idling engine hit a frequency that caused the windows to vibrate.

The bus performed a sharp swerve. We had turned away from town. I hadn't checked the destination before boarding. I sensed that we were passing a church – the pale grey mass filling the fogged-up window on the left formed, in my peripheral vision, a church. The intuition quickly developed into a conviction. A church, definitely, no doubt about it. I kept my head down so as not to invite further disorientation. If it were, say, a school, for instance, and not a church – I wasn't sure how I'd respond to that. Things were tentative that morning.

The woman in the front seat blessed herself. It was a

church. The water in my shoes had warmed up. These are the things I noticed. My teeth felt sharp in my mouth. I had never been so acutely aware of them before. Had never been aware of them at all, really, but suddenly it seemed all wrong, this army of sharp objects regimented across my soft pink gums. Tail lights the size of cartwheels flared in the front window as the lorry ahead applied the brakes. The bus pulled in to allow a squad car to speed past, followed by an ambulance. Passengers craned their necks to get a look at the blur of flashing blue lights. Murmurs rippled through the top deck. We were no better than worried cattle.

The flashing blue lights disappeared when we took another corner. The chain of approaching headlamps on the far side of the street was replaced by a low lichen-green expanse. I stared at it for some time, trying to make it out, before realising that it was the Liffey. We were travelling along the quays. I jumped off at the next stop. The water in my shoes became cold again.

I stumbled up Westmoreland Street against the driving rain, colliding with pedestrians, apologising without looking up from my feet. I was almost hit by a car while crossing Fleet Street – I'd run straight into its path. *Sorry,* I mouthed at the driver, bloated and deformed behind whirring windscreen wiper blades. If I could just make it to Front Arch and get out of the thunderstorm. That's what I kept telling myself as I blundered along. If I can just get under the Arch and take shelter for a while. The weather will be more clement on the other side.

It was no such thing.

The lights in House Eight were out, but the door was unlocked. Up the wooden stairs I ran and threw open the door to the workshop. It hadn't been disturbed over

Christmas. The murky shadows of raindrops trickled down the white walls like – I don't know. Like something inimical. The creative imagination failed me that day. I couldn't come up with a single simile to elevate those oozing shadows. They were nothing better than their grimy selves.

Glynn would not have fallen at that hurdle. He wrote about Irish rain as if no other rain in the world was quite like it, quite as desolate, quite as disabling. How bleak that room was without him, and without the group. I touched a radiator. It was cold. 'Jesus, Mary and Joseph,' I whispered – the touch of cold metal was the final straw. I stood there shivering and dripping, not knowing where to turn, a man who had reached the dock only to find that his ship had already set sail, after the great struggle to get there, the blind rush across the city.

'Who's there?'

The voice, a woman's, had come from downstairs. I went out to the landing and leaned over the banister. Faye was standing at the foot of the stairs. She put her hand on her heart when she saw me.

'Declan! Oh, thank God, you scared us. Come down – we're all in the kitchen.'

The kitchen? There was a kitchen? I joined Faye at ground level and followed her around a corner, down another flight of stairs into the basement, whereupon she opened a door into a gaslight yellow room. And there they were, the girls the girls the girls, sitting around a table drinking tea. How did they know to be there? They just knew. They sensed the state of emergency too. We weren't due in until Wednesday.

We sat around the kitchen table clutching mugs as

intently as hands at a séance. I placed my copy of *The Watchtower* in the centre. There was one small window in the room, sealed shut with layers of old gloss paint. It faced onto the twelve-foot wall that separated Trinity from Pearse Street and was level with the cobbles outside. We looked out through weeds and security bars. A Superser heater wheezed away in the corner like a dozing grandparent. It was as if we'd always been there.

Guinevere was relating how she'd woken up that morning weeping for no good reason. Uncontrollably, she added. Difficulty breathing. Funny, how the mention of suffocation brings out the symptoms in the listener. We took deep breaths and nodded in sympathy. It was stuffier than the bus in that basement. Aisling's chain-smoking didn't help.

'I don't know why I'm so upset,' Guinevere shrugged. She attempted a smile, but it didn't take, which only made things worse. We were in the same seating arrangement as for the workshops, I noticed. It was no time for banal observations.

'Poor pet,' Faye murmured, in that calm, sympathetic way of hers which was soothing to us all. I wanted her to say it again. Guinevere was paler than usual that day. As white as a page, I remember thinking. But not as white as Aisling.

And then, when Guinevere finally got herself up and out of the house, a jumbo jet had flown overhead at too low an altitude, while a motorbike simultaneously accelerated past without a muffler, making that awful sound – 'You know the one like a lion's roar?' We nodded. 'Except it seemed that the roar had come from *within* the biker's helmet, as if some mythical half-man, half-beast was inside.'

'Oh fuck,' said Aisling. 'Chimera.'

'I know it sounds stupid,' Guinevere continued, 'but what with the jet engine reverberating in the sky, and that violent roar warping the street, I suddenly found I couldn't take another step, so I pretended to root around in my bag in search of something, when, in reality, I was crouching against the wall.'

'Crouching against the wall!' she repeated incredulously, and had a go at a laugh, her voice pitching upward.

'Poor pet,' Faye repeated.

Aisling was peeling strands of her hair in two. 'Do you think the rain's going to stop?'

Faye squinted out the little window. 'Not for a while yet.'

'Anyone catch a forecast?' These were my first words to the group that year. Hadn't even said hello.

No one had caught a forecast.

Faye asked for one of Aisling's cigarettes. I didn't know she smoked. 'Something weird happened to me too this morning,' she said quietly. Faye wasn't one for talking about herself. She was more what you'd call a listener.

'It's no big deal, just, my doorbell rang, but when I opened the door, not a sinner was there. The garden was empty, and the latch on the gate was in place. No one could ring the doorbell, then run away and latch that gate in the time it took for me to answer. It's a fecky little device, the latch. You see, you have to-' Faye demonstrated with her fingers how to get the latch in place. These mid-air gestures made no sense without the context of the latch itself. She may as well have been playing a zither. 'Anyway,' she concluded, seeing the futility

117

of her explanation, 'it can't be done that quickly. And the garden walls are too high to jump. I can't explain how it happened, but when I closed the door, I sensed a presence in the hall with me.'

'Is it here now?' Aisling asked.

Faye rotated the ashtray, first clockwise, then anti-clockwise, her head tilted in concentration as if it were the combination wheel to a safe, Pandora's Box. 'She,' Faye softly corrected Aisling. 'She's a she, this presence, not an it.' Aisling shuddered extravagantly.

'I do not believe in ghosts,' Glynn had written in *Hibernia,* 'but I can see how the misunderstanding arose. A longing so fierce as to be almost corporeal, an inability to come to terms with loss.'

Antonia, who had remained withdrawn throughout, abruptly got to her feet. 'Why is everybody whispering all of a sudden?'

We didn't register how low the volume in the kitchen had fallen until Antonia reprimanded us. The impact was the same as switching on the lights in the middle of the night. We winced at her and blinked.

She pulled on her coat and picked up her handbag, muttering that she needed some fresh bloody air. You would think we'd been intentionally depriving her. We listened to her trip-trapping above our heads, huddled in our bunker watching the ceiling, on the other side of which a phantom Antonia paced, one who deviated qualitatively in nature from the woman who had just stormed out. A crack in the plaster splintered across the ceiling, dramatic as a shooting star. What a day we were having.

'Are we hiding?' Aisling asked. Same thought on my mind too. I was beginning to think like them.

The front door to House Eight slammed so hard that the four of us recoiled. Aisling spilled her tea. There was nothing to mop it up with. 'I suppose we had better go after her,' Faye sighed, getting to her feet, and Aisling joined her, pocketing her cigarettes in case the situation called for them. Guinevere didn't move.

Those wide grey eyes stared at me like a wild animal when the others were gone. That is what she reminded me of at that moment: a pair of eyes I had once caught sight of, looking out from the cover of ferns. I had stopped in my tracks. The eyes had locked with mine for a beat, long enough for it to strike me that we were essentially the same. The same, when it came down to it, but in a different vessel, I told myself – or not quite told myself – it was not as direct as all that. Just a piece of stupid nonsense that entered my head. Why this compulsion to forge a connection with something that wants nothing to do with you? The thing had turned and fled, after all. 'I don't like it down here,' Guinevere confessed. Tears started streaming down her face.

'Hey, what's wrong?'

'Nothing.' She shook her head. 'Just . . . nothing.'

I stood up and clasped her shoulders. The force of her emotions. A shaft shot out of her into the heavens, another down to the molten core of the Earth. I felt the true magnitude of her, caught a glimpse of her dimensions. All I can compare it to is how certain places, certain historical sites, connect you to the events that unfolded there centuries earlier. It is a poor comparison, but it is all I can offer. It is the closest I can get. She raised her face. I placed my lips on her tear-stained cheek, and then I kissed her mouth.

Footfall on the stairs – we pulled apart. They were

coming to take her back. Guinevere wiped away her tears, and I returned to my seat. We turned our expectant faces to the door. It was Aisling who burst in, noticing nothing. 'It's finally stopped raining,' she announced.

14

The Butchered Boy

The rain had stopped alright, but the north wind had picked up, and it cut right through to the bone. I stood around Mountjoy Square for the guts of two hours, waiting for someone to come home and let me in. My keys were in the ashtray on my desk, my jacket slung over the back of the chair. I shouted through the letter-box and pumped the doorbell like a Morse code button, but the building didn't rouse from its darkness.

I took another turn around the park to keep warm. The wind roared overhead in the crowns of the trees like an ocean liner powering towards me. On the far side of the square I was grabbed from behind and shoved into the railings and wet shrubbery. A flash of metal as some-thing sharp was thrust into my face. I blinked to get it into focus. A blade? No. It was a hypodermic needle.

'Give us yer fucken wallet,' I was instructed in a flat Dublin accent. The man held me up by the scruff, as if impaled on a pitchfork. He banged me against the rail-ings. 'Now!'

'Okay, okay,' I said, reaching into my back pocket. I held up my wallet. 'Here.' The needle was withdrawn and my collar released. Laughter. I turned around. It was the knacker from the flat downstairs. I recognised his white runners.

'Classic,' he said, slotting the needle like a pen into the breast pocket of his leather jacket. 'Ya shudda seen yer face.' He nodded at my wallet. I was still holding it up. 'Put yer money away,' he told me grandly, as if I'd been insisting on buying him a drink and he wouldn't hear of it. He rubbed his palms together. 'Aw, I was crackin me hole.'

I didn't respond. Couldn't. The world had stopped at the sight of that flash of metal, and it hadn't fully started up again.

'Wha?' he demanded, interpreting my silence as criticism. 'Fuck's sake, relax, it was a joke.'

'A joke,' was all I said, and gently enough at that, simply repeating the word, explaining to myself that I was no longer in danger – that all it had been was a joke! – but he marched right up and bared his teeth in my face as if I'd insulted his mother.

'Joke!' he shouted in rage, jaw clenched, tendons pulsing. His body, I knew without laying a finger on it, would be as hard as nails under that tracksuit, and not because he was strong but because he was pinched, sucked protectively around the pit of his stomach to the point of concavity. *Joke* was an instruction, not an observation, meaning, in effect, *laugh*. Laugh, he was shouting into my face, *laugh you prick, or else*.

I laughed. He joined in as if I'd cracked the joke and it was a job well done. 'Giz,' he said, extending his hand, and then proceeded to walk me home in high good humour, as if the pair of us had been out on the lash. 'Ya shudda seen yer face,' he kept saying all the way around the square, shaking his head in amused recollection, though Giz patently hadn't seen my face, on account of it being shoved in a bush.

His head swivelled from side to side when he walked, as if crossing a busy street. It seemed part of his gait. It made no difference where he was, indoors or out. He did it while climbing the stairs to his flat, checking left, then right, left, then right, perpetually on the lookout. The condition was chronic, and contagious. Soon I was checking my back too.

He unlocked his door and switched on the lights. 'Go on ahead,' he instructed me. 'Be witcha in a minute.' I couldn't find the right words to decline and stepped inside. He shut the door behind me.

There were no books on his bookshelf. I ran a finger along the spines of his collection of video nasties, which was extensive. He was urinating noisily down the corridor. There didn't appear to be a bed in the room. Looked like he slept on the couch. No sign of my bike, either, that I could see. My hair was still wet from the shrubbery. I found a leaf snagged in it, which I tucked into my pocket, I don't know why. Scared of offending him, I suppose; scared he'd decree the leaf accusatory on some level, a reproof for what he'd done earlier. Hard to tell what would set him off.

I raised a corner of the grey wool blanket which was nailed over the sash window. Giz had a fine view of the square, for all the good it did him. His communion photograph was displayed on top of three television sets, stacked high in the alcove like a totem pole. I took the picture down to examine it. The standard-issue cloudy-sky backdrop, brown and gold cardboard frame – there was an identical one of me at home on the mother's sideboard. The seven-year-old Giz was dressed as a miniature man in a three-piece off-white suit. Black shirt, white tie, red rosette, hands pressed together in simulation of prayer, a rash of blotchy freckles across his nose. The camera had caught him with his eyes squeezed shut. A new set was drawn on his eyelids in red marker, crooked like a Picasso. The toilet on the landing flushed. Giz entered the flat and plugged in the two-bar heater.

'That's funny,' I said to him, 'my eyes were shut in my communion photo too.' I don't know why I said this. It wasn't true.

'I made a hundred and eighty quid that day,' he said. 'How'd ya get on yerself?'

'I don't know. Twenty, I think.' More like half.

This pleased him. 'Retard.'

A plastic bottle in the shape of the Blessed Virgin stood on the windowsill. Her crown screwed off like a toothpaste cap. She was half full of holy water that had gone fibrous with age. On the floor was a tin of beans, one of sweet corn, and a box of Coco Pops – food that came in pellets and didn't need to be cooked – all lying empty on their sides. Under the table was a Scalextric set. One link missing.

Giz swiped a section of the sofa clear of crisp packets and bedclothes and indicated that I should sit. I didn't disobey. He pulled up an armchair and set about rolling a joint. This procedure demanded his full concentration and most of mine. We did not speak for the duration. A religious ritual might have been under way. His nails were bitten so close to the quick that his fingertips ballooned over them, tiny bald scalps. Homemade black dots tattooed his knuckles, the workmanship poor. He took a lump of gum out of his mouth and placed it on the table where it sat like his brain; small, grey and chewed.

There was a whirring sound in the corner followed by

a mechanical clunk. We were plunged into darkness. The electricity meter had run out. 'Fuck!' Giz shouted, '*fuck!*' He kicked the coffee table and something hit the floor. The bars of the plug-in heater glowed like a Sacred Heart. I scooped a palmful of coins out of my pocket and picked out the five-pence pieces as best I could see them in the residual light.

'Here,' I said, holding them up, stacked like gambling chips, but he was already out of the armchair, knocking things over in his wake. 'I've more upstairs,' I added for no good reason. There was no disguising the fear in my voice.

Giz crossed the room in silhouette and grabbed something from the shelf. It glinted orange in the dying light of the heater. He climbed onto a chair and got to work on the electricity meter, ratcheting away at it as if jacking up a car. The glow from the heating elements was fading rapidly, as was the outline of Giz. He expanded towards me in the darkness, loomed inches from my face.

The lights flickered on again. Giz shrank back to his regular dimensions, angry and compact. He cast the butter knife aside and jumped down from the chair, sighing like a man knocking off the night shift. I began to laugh, with relief I believe. I had seen strange forms in the dark.

The two-bar heater began to hum convivially once more, resuming its interrupted conversation. Giz picked up the ball of chewing gum and put his brain back in. 'Where was I?' he asked, standing hands on hips over the conjoined Rizla papers. He sat down and bent to his work again, childlike in his absorption. I watched him at his labours.

Somewhere along the line I stopped fretting about

how to get out of there and settled into the couch as the joint passed between us. The buzz and fizzle of the two-bar heater was the very sound of cosiness. I pointed at the section of ceiling that supported my bed. 'There's my bed,' I told him, as if introducing Giz to a member of my family. 'And that's my desk.' I indicated the space by the far window.

Giz screwed his eyes up against the smoke. 'I know.' Of course he knew. He'd broken in once. Nothing to steal, but buckled the door, scribbled his name on the wall. 'Here, d'ya wanna buy a Sony Walkman?'

'You're alright, thanks.'

He nodded as if he couldn't blame me.

'Tell us,' he said later, 'how's your book?'

He made it rhyme with *puke*. He'd sunk so deeply into the armchair by then that his knees – cobalt blue and shiny in the silky tracksuit – were higher than his chin. A muscle in the hollow of his jaw flexed.

'Me buke,' I repeated, testing the pronunciation, trying it out for myself. When had I told him about me buke? He was holding the flame of a match to the tip of his cigarette but couldn't get it to ignite.

'Giz.'

'Wha?'

'Wrong end.'

He took the cigarette out of his mouth and saw that he'd been trying to light the filter. He held it up for my inspection. 'Wrong end,' he told me, then we laughed for, I don't know, an hour. His shaved cuttlebone skull. It was a head-butting head.

When the doorbell rang downstairs, an hour or so again after that, Giz went to the window and raised a corner of the blanket to look out. He cursed when he saw who it was and pulled on his leather jacket. 'I'm expectin a client,' he told me, and I nodded to indicate that was fine by me and shoved up on the couch. It took a few moments to cop that Giz was throwing me out. 'Aw, slick,' I said, like he'd outfoxed me fair and square in some game of wits we'd been playing. I hauled myself to my feet. It was cold out there on the sagging corridor. For some reason, we shook hands before parting.

15

How can I protect you from this crazy world?

A full forty-eight hours elapsed before the north wind finally dropped. The flag mounted over Front Arch collapsed, flayed and crucified upon its pole. The sun shone fiercely throughout the day. I do not remember it faltering for so much as one second. The flash floods had receded, leaving tidemarks of detritus behind. We had gathered upstairs in House Eight in advance of the first workshop of the year.

Something looked different after the storm, we agreed, but not even Faye's keen eye could identify precisely what. The terrain seemed smoother, the edges had gone off things. 'That tree is new!' Aisling exclaimed, pointing to the great oak behind the Campanile. It was like returning to a childhood room after an absence of years and finding it altered in scale, though you know it to be the same. The room hasn't changed; you have. Our surroundings hadn't changed; we had. The storm had changed us. We had weathered it together. We had come out the other side.

Glynn, too, we found altered. His funny walk was immediately apparent that first class after Christmas, even from a distance. When I say funny, I mean the opposite of funny. There was nothing remotely funny about it. Faye had been sitting by the radiator under the window when she abruptly stood up and put her hand to her mouth. The novel she had been reading slipped from her lap, landing with a slap on the floor. We crowded at the window to see what had upset her. Faye did not have to tell us. You couldn't miss him. There he was on the far side of Front Square, reeling in our direction.

Antonia folded her arms after we had watched this spectacle for thirty seconds or so. 'How long has that been going on?' she demanded. She sounded cross with Glynn, as if he was deliberately putting it on to annoy her, testing her patience and pushing his luck. The world was one big trial designed to antagonise her. To this end, no stone had been left unturned.

Nobody answered Antonia's question. Nobody had an answer. It was the first any of us had seen of him that year.

We observed his erratic progress from our bird's-nest vantage, five wan faces behind a pane of glass, five hearts in five mouths. A sentence had formulated in my mind of its own accord, and, once it lodged there, it would not be dislodged. The phrase wasn't one I had consciously composed but seemed rather to arise as a natural accompaniment to Glynn's spasmodic procession, each syllable attuned to the jerky movement which had inspired it: *Something is now broken that cannot be fixed, something is now broken that cannot be fixed.* Uncanny, how precisely it fitted the rhythm of Glynn's gait, as if it were the beat he was dancing to.

The storm had washed the cobbles on Front Square as clean as riverbed pebbles. Glynn's hobble wasn't regular enough to count as a limp, being instead palsied, random and mortifying. Something had happened to his brain, not his legs. He trundled across the cobbles, perverse as a supermarket trolley, limbs accelerating with no increase in pace. We were used to him drifting along lost in thought, musing in the medium of poetic metaphor. *Something is now broken that cannot be fixed, something is now broken that cannot be fixed.* His actions were timed so perfectly to those words that it seemed he could hear me, or that I was controlling him, or that we, rather, were controlling him, standing up there, agents of fate, drawing him to us, our puppet. 'I can't bear this,' Guinevere said.

Glynn must have been muttering away to himself, because students were turning around to look back at him in surprise, then smirking to each other. How could we have stopped them, answer me that? How could we have shielded him from their ridicule? Not everyone saw past his faults, as we saw. We saw so far past his faults that we barely saw him at all. We were dying for him up there. That is the only way to describe it. The five of us were dying up there for Glynn, wanting him safe inside with us where he was treasured, no matter what his state. I never loved Glynn more than at that moment, if love is the acute compound of tenderness and anxiety for another that I believe it to be.

Glynn's short journey went on for an eternity. He didn't glance up at the window to check for us. He knew we would be watching. We were always watching. Everyone slows down to gape at car crashes. *Something is now broken that cannot be fixed.* There was no way out of that sentence.

Eventually Glynn entered the shadow of House Eight and cleared our field of vision. It wasn't until he was out of sight that we started breathing again. 'We're all ballsed now,' said Aisling.

We took our seats at the workshop table and waited for him. Waited and waited and waited. Faye's head was in her hands throughout this period. What was he doing down there? And so quietly too. After an extended interlude of silence from the stairwell, the girls elected me to go down to investigate. I'm sure they heard him calling me everything under the sun before turning on his heel and storming out. You would think I had mortally insulted him. 'Professor Glynn,' is all I had said, but the sound of his own name proved a step too far. He had swiped the air in fury at it, batted it away like a swarm of bees, telling me that I made him sick, that we all made him sick, that he couldn't stand the sight of us. The whiskey fumes were enough to fell a pony.

I made my way back upstairs and admitted myself into the workshop as unobtrusively as I was able, shaking my head apologetically as if they were a waiting room of expectant relatives and my role was to break bad news. A flamingo-pink disc of a sun was shining at the tip of the Campanile, tinting the workshop windows rose. The sun couldn't, of course, have been shining at the tip of Campanile, not at that hour of the afternoon, not at that elevation, but I distinctly remember looking up to see it suspended in the sky, glowing through the soft haze like something from Miami.

'I'm sorry,' I told them gravely, 'I'm afraid he's gone,' and then I took Guinevere's hand in mine without a second's thought. I led her away from there, as if love was a simple thing and freedom was a possibility and an old man's troubles weren't ours. Who did I think I was?

16

Alive alive oh

Glynn spoke at length during the lecture he delivered to
– ah, how can I be expected to remember the where and
the when of it? All I'm good for is parroting variations
on Glynn's words, in this instance his description of his
love not just for the physical world but for the world of
physics. I'd nodded my head in fierce agreement before
I'd even heard what the man had to say, that is the class
of fool I was then. It was no less than tribal. Glynn was
a country I'd have borne arms to defend. Show me
where the cudgels are kept, and I will take them up for
you.

Physics delineated the natural world from a stand-
point that was new to him, Glynn told us almost shyly,
not being a man of science, here amongst a hall of them
– he gestured at the audience at this juncture. Earlsfort
Terrace, I have it now. I was halfway through my engineering degree. That's why the girls weren't there. Few
women, if any, were present that evening, and it sort of
took the wind out of Glynn's sails, sort of knocked out
his stuffing.

He'd stepped up to the lectern on the hangman's plat-
form and cleared his throat more than once before
commencing, a man summoned to give an account of
himself. I was sitting on my own in the back row of the

lecture hall, looking down on him from a steep incline. Long thin planks ran the length of each row by way of a desk, into which various names and dates were inscribed, including my name, including that date: the night I first saw Glynn in the flesh.

The invisible forces acting upon the human psyche was his topic, as seen from the perspective of the creative mind. It was neither the time nor the place. Physics lent him the methodology and terminology to explain those forces which were working upon us when nothing appeared to be happening, Glynn explained. He made reference to that old school textbook staple, the balanced see-saw, for the love of God: not motionless because it was at rest, but because two equal turning forces were acting against one another. He paused and looked around the hall to allow this to sink in. The example might have impressed a class of junior-freshmen English students, but it was never going to constitute the revelation to the School of Engineering that it evidently constituted to Glynn. How thoroughly he had miscalculated the situation; so it seemed at the time. Someone in the audience sighed. Staff members were out in force. What joker had deemed it appropriate to invite a novelist to address an engineering faculty in the first place?

'This is not wood,' I remember him proclaiming, rapping the wooden lectern with his knuckle for dramatic effect. 'This is energy in a static form.' He had not the slightest clue what he was talking about, it was obvious, but still he made the effort, undeterred, striving to forge a link between his world and ours – the burden the artistic imagination is cursed with.

Load, thrust, potential energy, torque, he continued,

throwing about words and ideas he found attractive but didn't understand. All of them tearing us this way and that, he went on, exerting pressures on the body that were invisible to the naked eye, so that even though he was being hurled around the Earth's atmosphere by centripetal force, still he was accused of sitting around on his backside all day doing nothing. Glynn all but winked, earning himself a low ripple of laughter for his efforts, a low rumble of gruff amusement. *Sitting around on your backside all day doing nothing.* I don't know why he felt obliged to poke fun at the writerly endeavour, his life's work, on that occasion. There were plenty happy to do it for him, and plenty more happy to listen. Oh Glynn, did you have to make it so easy?

Despite having imposed a liberal interpretation upon forces which did not sustain a liberal interpretation, and despite his flawed grasp of the laws governing the universe, I still kind of knew what Glynn was stabbing away at down there in his oblique, unscientific, analogical way, a diagram of a rotary wing from a previous lecture chalked on the blackboard behind him. Questions were invited from the audience, but none were forthcoming, and the applause that closed the event was by no means ardent.

It is almost certain that I was alone in that lecture hall in experiencing a moment of enlightenment. I wanted to speak up to let Glynn know that at least one of those blank faces lined up before him had grasped something of what he'd been trying to communicate to us that night, but I didn't budge from my back-row entrenchment, and the department head led him away. Physics, Glynn mistakenly believed, had equipped him with the vocabulary to depict something else entirely, something that wasn't physical at all, or quantifiable, or even describable, but which he still, despite these multiple impasses, managed to evoke in his novels. Here we run into representational difficulties of our own.

Glynn was onto something ideational, something the audience before him lacked the curiosity to understand, it being a phenomenon of no interest to the practical mind. There are extrasensory faculties at work that cannot be adequately explained. It is not my intention to sound so portentous. Stare at someone hard enough and they will feel your gaze. Keep staring, and they will turn around to identify the source of it. Glynn perceived those forces that whirred about us, and whirred us about, when we appeared to be at rest. He saw those pulsations spooling from our fingertips like dragonflies through the air. It is difficult to explain. I have a memory of a walk I took along a country lane. It was late May, or early June, one of those still, momentous evenings brimming with promise, when life finally seems on the brink of commencing and all is yet to play for. Meadows unrolled on either side as I descended into the valley, the seed heads of the wild grasses tipped gold in the setting sun. I had nowhere to be that night.

The lane below curved around an outcrop of rock and disappeared out of sight behind the grove of flowering whitethorn which had so strongly scented the evening air. I sensed the presence of a small party of people on the other side, making their way up the hill. I had caught a strain of laughter on the air, gaiety, a thrumming. As I rounded the corner into the shadows of the grove, I prepared to encounter faces on the other side. The other side, however, was bare.

I paused in the middle of the lane in confusion. The

shafts of sunlight piercing the dun shade quivered like plucked strings. That thrumming was everywhere; the valley, the meadows, the hedgerows, on the breeze. The whitethorns were loud with the drone of bees, but it was more than that. Something had been interrupted.

This wavering, I propose, approximates on some level to the condition of being Glynn – living with that swarm of nascent activity alongside you, that charge of potential energy, that flux. I am applying scientific terms to artistic ends, using the technique propounded by the master. Except that upon rounding the corner, instead of almost encountering them, as I almost encountered them, Glynn saw the faces of the people in his path, their colourful clothes, their longing for each other revealed in their gait, desires divulged by subtle tilts and inclinations. Sometimes they even took him with them, off on their summer adventures. Where did they all disappear to? Into which Kavanagh poem?

The world, when I picked up Guinevere's hand and led her out of the sun-pink workshop, was not the same place it had been that morning. There was a before and an after. We saw not just pavement, city and sky, but future tenses swirling around us. The wet surface of Dame Street glinted silver as we emerged from the Arch, blinding Guinevere with the glare. I shielded her eyes with my hand before leaning in to kiss her.

I picked her up outside City Hall and twirled her in the air. Guinevere Wren was no weight at all. She laughed, her coiled hair streaming out behind her, and I realised I could not be happier. It was not possible to be any happier. She was the difference between the sun shining and not. 'Put me down!' she shrieked, but I couldn't bear to. Though I'd walked that street a thousand times without her, our first walk together would eclipse all previous walks. I knew that even as the journey was unfolding. Dame Street would never be detached from my memory of walking it, practically running it, hand in hand with Guinevere. She was taking me to her room.

The sky seemed terribly high up later that day as we lay on our backs looking out at it from her tangled bed. The rush of air had gone to our heads. It was deep blue and dotted about with small white scudding clouds. They were perfect clouds, spot on, I couldn't have asked for better. Round, plump, *flocculent,* the kind you'd like to fall asleep on. A tear had formed in the corner of Guinevere's eye. It was the most beautiful tear I had ever seen, an absolute credit to her. I didn't know whether to mention it or not. A butterfly had once closed its wings to me, barely a butterfly any more then, really, no better than an old brown leaf. I'd nudged the thing with my foot, expecting it to flutter away and reveal its pretty colours once more, but the tiny scrap clung tightly to the path and my boot destroyed it.

The tear swelled and spilled down Guinevere's cheek. I turned back to consider the panorama of sky. It took all my restraint not to try to prise her open. I wished I knew more about types of clouds, about the atmospheric conditions necessary to sustain those small white pillowy ones. And I wish I'd known more about the conditions necessary to sustain Guinevere. I never thought to ask.

17

The Book of Evidence

It had started again, as if the coming together of Guinevere and I had tipped a scale, setting some vast rusty mechanism grinding back into motion, unleashing those turning forces Glynn had discoursed upon that evening in Earlsfort Terrace. He was writing once more. A heart that had been still a long time contracted and squeezed out a beat just as we'd given up on it. Glynn was a master of cliffhanger timing.

The discovery was made the following Wednesday. Guinevere had deemed it inappropriate that she and I arrive at the workshop together, so I had been dispatched ahead. We had kissed goodbye on the doorstep of the labourer's cottage she rented in the Liberties. She shared it with a theology student who was never there but who showed up in the dead of the night to move beer cans around as proof of his existence, in case she stopped believing in him. On the windowsill of the cottage next door was a pot of leggy geraniums, the stalks brown and segmented like earthworms. A child's small bike had been abandoned two doorsteps up, the back wheel still spinning and the front door ajar, leaking a smell of institutional cooking onto the cul-de-sac, which was called a square though it was no such thing, just two rows of terraced redbrick cottages truncated by a wall.

Guinevere and I had spent the week in bed.

Her face had a newly hatched moistness without make-up. She was wearing a powder-blue dressing gown and not much else besides. I could tell, from the way she kept tightening the knot on the belt, glancing up and down the length of the cul-de-sac, that she felt exposed standing out on her own doorstep, an animal that had strayed onto open ground. 'Cold, isn't it?' she asked me.

I did not take the hint. She performed a shiver. Her feet were bare on the stone doorstep. Still I would not let go of her hand, tracing my fingertips across her palm, stooping to kiss the faint blue veins lining the inside of her wrist – anything to detain her. I wanted to watch her get ready for class. That's what I was angling for. I wanted to witness her moments, all of them. Her showering, her dressing, the pinning up of her hair. Whatever it took her to become the Guinevere she presented to us in class – that would be my subject. Not one drop of her time would be wasted were she to spend it all with me. I tried to explain this exciting new project, but Guinevere just laughed, pulling her hand from mine and retreating into the cottage, protesting that she didn't want to be late.

Aisling was sitting alone at the bottom of the staircase in House Eight, swathed in her widow's weeds. I clocked her before she clocked me. Sometimes it was hard not to stare at her. Her head hung low between her knees, looking too large, too burdensome, for the pale stem of her neck, which was exposed as if for a beheading. A leather cord was knotted at her nape. Aisling hung weird artefacts around her neck – not the skulls and horns the regular Goths purchased from the wind-racked stalls on

O'Connell Bridge but antique medical instruments, phials of dark viscid liquid, little brass dial things saying Yes or No, mummified bits of Christ knows what. Where did she even find them? They were not from this century. It was an eerie world she went home to, that contained such oddities strewn throughout it, and her harvesting them like toadstools in a forest. There seemed no end to her supply of peculiarities. Amulets, I suppose you might call them. The manner with which she constantly toyed with them, turning them over and over in her left hand as if seeking their counsel, her eczematous fingers spinning like the legs of a spider, imbued them with a sentient status.

Her long hair had pooled between her Doc Martened feet on the linoleum floor, so black it looked synthetic. She often presented herself in alarming configurations, her bones a bundle of sticks she'd tossed into the air and allowed to collapse into a pile any which way. This was done unwittingly, as far as I could tell. It was simply her nature, the casual disregard with which she treated herself. She was more careless with her own person than even Glynn.

You would think we'd have acclimatised to her endless rag-doll positions, the broken-winged bird shapes, but, if anything, they grew progressively more upsetting. Normal girls didn't sit like that, as if a joint were dislocated, a central sinew severed. The aura of calamity surrounding Aisling didn't drop its guard for a second. I longed to return to my thoughts of Guinevere. They were a warm bed on a cold morning.

Aisling's head lashed back when I touched the door handle, as if it were no door handle at all but one of her drifting tentacles. I, for my part, recoiled as if stung. The two of us looked at each other in momentary alarm, but she relaxed when she saw it was only me. Who had she been expecting?

She stood up, slinging her canvas army bag over her shoulder, and blocked my entrance. 'What's going on?' I asked when she motioned for me to turn around and go back out. I was forever having to ask them what was happening. They were forever having to interrupt themselves to explain. Aisling narrowed her eyes at the sky, deciphering more there than the weather. I foolishly glanced up too, as if warplanes might crest the horizon.

'It's Glynn,' she said. 'He's holed up in his office.'

We set off for the Arts Block, the miniature magnifying glass swinging from her neck warping the matter on the other side, an evil eye. It was a bitterly cold afternoon, even for early February. Frost coated the tracts of cobbles still trapped in the shade. Aisling wasn't dressed for the cold and was soon hunched up against it like a greyhound, all shivering spine.

She offered me an unfiltered Major, and selected one for herself with a suit-yourself shrug when I declined. I couldn't bear to watch her inhale those builders' smokes into her tattered lungs. The orangey-yellow nicotine stains on her fingers were a source of pride to her, for some reason. She had brandished them at us one night in the pub, holding them out to be admired like an engagement ring, as if she couldn't quite believe her good fortune and wanted to share it with us, though they were the colour of old men's feet. She gave one of her terrible racking coughs, hoarse as the cry of a hooded crow, and so raw that I felt the pain myself. She pressed her palm against her thorax in an attempt to subdue it. This stratagem didn't work.

The other three were already waiting when we rounded the corner onto the corridor of the English Department, stationed in manneristic postures of stylised concern, a bible scene. Guinevere had somehow contrived to get there ahead of me. Aisling left my side, and they made way for her. The light flooding through the window behind them picked out the folds of their garments, the contours of their bodies. Had they any conception of how striking they looked when placed together in such a formal arrangement, staggered like peaks in a mountain range? They took my breath away. It was to do with their silence as much as anything else on that occasion.

All that was missing from the composition was the big man himself, towards whom the four women were inclined so that it was all about him, and no one but him, though he was not present. You had to give Glynn his due.

'What's going on?' I asked again, my voice an uproar in the church-quiet corridor. They shushed me by waving their hands and putting fingers to their lips, scared I might disturb Glynn, whatever he was up to. He should've been in the workshop with us. They seemed to think he wouldn't suspect they were there, listening at his door in their default state of rapture, but Glynn always knew where to find his audience.

I hesitated before approaching. There were times, as I went stumbling through their doll's house, knocking things over in my clumsy wake, smashing their bone china and matchstick furniture, when it seemed I was too big for them. They didn't know what to do with me. I could read it on their faces, particularly Faye's, who was smiling that tolerant, sympathetic smile of hers that

I had no liking for when it was directed at me. She could take her benevolence elsewhere. Guinevere was strange and separate once more. I knew that if I took her hand and tried to lead her away from the pack, it would not work this time.

Faye beckoned me over to listen at Glynn's door. I pressed my ear against it. He could be heard muttering away to himself inside, low-level malcontent grumblings. 'It's been going on for hours,' Faye whispered. She had been about to knock on his door that morning when she'd overheard him. 'When I eventually did knock, he roared at me. "Feck off, I'm working," he shouted. We think he's finally writing the new novel.' *Now that the long evenings are upon me once again.*

'Jesus,' I said, and the four of them nodded. The last we'd seen of Glynn, he could barely walk. Now this.

'Blake!' he suddenly exclaimed. We looked at each other in delight, as if a baby in the womb had just kicked. Even Antonia looked intrigued.

It had long been Glynn's habit to talk to himself. That was nothing new. He told a reporter once that he was indeed aware of it but made not the slightest effort to censor himself, since he regarded it as a component of the writing process externalised. Glynn was full of fighting talk in interview situations, tending to interpret questions about the creative act as attacks upon it. Sometimes he was right. These occasional unintentional articulations on his part, he informed the journalist, were not the first sign of madness, but rather evidence of what he called his 'imaginative fertility', but which another well-known Irish author of similar vintage rechristened his 'imaginary fertility'. In fairness, he'd been asking for that one.

143

Fragments of Glynn's internal monologue regularly escaped his lips when he thought himself alone, or had forgotten we were still there, or knew we were still there but didn't care, or was trying to impress us with his scope of reference – by us, I mean the girls. So many ideas clamoured for attention in his brain that he can be forgiven if the excess spurted out, like lava. This, however, wasn't thinking aloud so much as arguing. '*Blake!*' he insisted once more, in a tone of high exasperation, as if his own company were being wilfully obstinate, which it probably was. We could just see him behind that door, amongst his books and accolades, pacing the length of the room which could never contain him, gesticulating impatiently at imagined opponents. Something was heard to fall over.

The Blake invocation was of central significance. That Glynn based his sixth novel, *The Devil's Party*, loosely around the life of William Blake has already been mentioned. Despite its eighteenth-century setting, Glynn acknowledged in a radio interview that *The Devil's Party* was his most autobiographical work. 'To date,' he added tantalisingly.

The radio signal did not broadcast the wink we agreed he almost certainly appended. A great man for the winks, no more than his protagonists, leaving you neither here nor there. Was it all a big joke, or what? Is that what he was trying to tell us? He enjoyed toying with people, pulling their legs, seeing how far he could push them. You could practically hear him gearing up sometimes, cracking his knuckles, flexing his digits, rolling up his sleeves. I do not wish to reduce him to a series of ludicrous traits, merely acknowledge that he had more than a few. Which of us is without flaws? Vanity was

Glynn's great weakness. No portrait of the man would be complete without a reference to his ego, which he dragged around like a ball and chain. It stunted his progress, begat the funny walk. That's why he got on so famously with us: we worshipped him, plain and simple.

Of his eight novels, *The Devil's Party* was our favourite, and not just because the main character was a writer. Antonia cited an early minor work, *Gorsefire,* as her favourite, just to be obtuse, but *The Devil's Party* was the one she could quote at length, as I lost no time in reminding her. On the inscription page was an extract from Blake's great prose work, *The Marriage of Heaven and Hell:* 'The reason Milton wrote in fetters when he wrote of Angels and God, and at liberty when of Devils and Hell, is because he was a true Poet and of the Devil's party without knowing it.'

A key element of the Glynnian endeavour fell into place while I was sitting out there on the corridor, concerning the iconography of evil. Glynn did not publicly admire Blake because it was safe to – Blake was well dead and therefore no longer posed a threat to his ball-and-chain ego, which, though cast in heavy metal, was as fragile as glass. It is a sorry indictment, Antonia had more than once pointed out to us, that most male writers would rather choke than praise the competition. No, Glynn admired the poetics of Blake for the same reason that Blake admired the poetics of Milton, namely, for its depiction of badness. Milton infamously evoked evil not as a deviation, but as human. The mind of Lucifer was more accessible than the mind of God. It was divinity he found remote.

A distinctive characteristic of Glynn's work was his use and reuse of the same four rogues throughout the eight novels. Not half enough has been made of this in the academic domain. Glynn's protagonists encounter the same villains over and over, from novel to novel, as if trapped on the same carousel. There was Malachy, P.J., the Dogman, Flood. All four featured in *The Devil's Party,* lifted from fifties parish-pump-politics Ireland and transplanted wholesale to Georgian England, unchanged but for their outlandish and anachronistic period costumes with which Glynn clearly amused himself (cod pieces, skullcaps, cuckolds' horns). They played marginal, inessential roles, neither advancing the plot nor developing the characterisation, hardly needing to be there at all, really, from a technical point of view. The Dogman was merely sketched into a crowd scene, little more than a leering flash of teeth, yet distinct as a painter's signature.

Seen from this perspective, Glynn's approach is comparable in its symbolisation of evil to that of the British medieval mystery plays. Belsabub, Sattan. Bonus Angelus et Malus Angelus. Diabolus I and II. Stock characters, waiting in the wings to posture and speak their lines with an ironical sneer before retiring to loiter backstage until the next novel gets underway. Not that this was a simplistic vision, far from it. It was rather an insight into the absolute intimacy Glynn felt with evil. He knew his demons on a first-name basis. Their commerce was almost neighbourly.

Evil was a local occurrence. It ran into you in the bookies, shot past you in the backseats of taxis. In *Farm Animals,* the narrator, O'Dea, reads about the Dogman in the court pages of a regional newspaper whilst sitting in the waiting room of a dental surgery in Gorey, queuing to get a rotten molar extracted. Entirely coincidental, spotting the Dogman's mugshot like that – O'Dea would have preferred to scan the GAA fixtures, but the scrofulous young fella with the scabby kneecaps had appropriated the sports section.

That Glynn referred to his villains as he might the weather – that is, in passing – leads the perceptive reader to draw the conclusion that Glynn had drawn the conclusion that one can never escape one's demons but must instead learn to live with them. So he turned them into background figures: Malachy, the Dogman – Diabolus I and II, thus rounding off his moral universe, the depth and complexity of which was renowned. Personify the bastards: oldest trick in the book. Finally, I'd spotted one of his invisible wires.

'Would you fucking keep it down?' Antonia snapped at me.

I wasn't aware that I'd opened my mouth. 'Sorry,' I said sarcastically. Inside Glynn's room, something hit the wall and shattered. Glass. Aisling had been jabbing at a carpet tile with the tip of her biro, trying to slay it, but she looked up at the sound of this crash.

'You've interrupted him,' she said darkly.

The lock on Glynn's door disengaged, and he pulled it open to find the five of us sitting on the corridor floor. He glared down at us, frog-faced, dog-jowled, then stepped over our limbs without comment, none too steady on his feet. From that low angle, the distension of his gut was hard to miss. His trousers were buttoned tightly under it, the straining waistband pushed down around the groin where his girth was narrowest.

Aisling jammed her foot in the door just before it clicked shut. The others didn't notice. They had climbed to their feet to traipse after Glynn, stiff as passengers disembarking from a long-haul flight. Aisling looked at me, wordlessly rotating the magnifying glass suspended from her neck. The second the others rounded the corner out of sight, we slipped inside. It was almost dark by then.

Glynn's office had the stifling pall of a sickroom. He'd been holed up in there for some time, possibly overnight. The most extraordinary booze-fumes polluted the air, and a cigarette smouldered in the overflowing ashtray. Aisling dived on something.

'It's here,' she said. 'Jesus Christ!'

'What?'

'His red notebook.' I must have frowned my ignorance. '*The* red notebook,' she clarified. I still didn't know what she was talking about.

She held it up briefly before placing it on his desk to rifle through the pages. I got to work on the contents of the wastepaper basket. We worked quickly in the gloom, unable to turn on the lights as the staff in the offices opposite would see what we were up to. Shards of glass crunched underfoot – the remnants of a whiskey bottle, judging by the gold foil collar, and not one of Glynn's crystal trophies, as we'd feared. Another whiskey bottle was stashed in the wastepaper basket, buried beneath a snowdrift of crumpled paper balls. The bottle was drained. I smoothed the paper balls out one by one on the floor. On the top of each page was scrawled a single scored-out word. ~~Storm, fire, funeral~~; that sort of thing. I can't remember the others. They added up to nothing. Anyone could have written them. I crumpled the pages up again and tossed them back in the bin.

I took down his *Collected Works of Blake* to find a bottle of Baby Power's pressed hard against the back of

148

the bookcase, its hands raised in surrender, caught in the act. This bottle too was empty. I removed *Paradise Lost*. Getting harder to read the titles in the dusk. A naggin of Bushmills, not a drop in it. I started unshelving volumes at random. Whiskey bottles riddled Glynn's bookcase like dental cavities, like shadows on his lungs.

I pulled open a drawer in his desk. Ink jars, rulers, sellotape, a stapler. I rammed it shut and grabbed the next handle down. Letters sprang out of that drawer like a jack in the box, it was packed so tightly. I gathered those that had fallen. Bond paper, pale blue, the stationery used by old ladies and priests. A few words were written in copperplate in the dead centre of each page, the lettering so tiny I had to hold it to my nose. *You will pay,* read one. *Mark my words,* read another. *There is always a price.* At the base of each note, the time and date was scratched in a different hand. Glynn's.

'Look,' I said to Aisling, 'the poison-pen letters,' but Aisling wasn't listening.

'It's the demons,' she said, still bent over the pages of Glynn's red notebook. Her black hair had fallen forward, concealing her features. She was invisible in the darkness in her funereal clothes. It was like looking into a vault. Not until she raised her white face to me, which was contorted with distress, did I see where the voice was coming from. 'It's weird fucking drawings of the demons, Declan,' she practically whimpered. 'The ones you were talking about.'

'*Me?*'

'Out there on the corridor. Belsabub and Sattan, you said. Diabolus I and II. He's drawn pictures of them. Look.' She held up the pages of the red notebook to me, but what could I see in the dark?

'Come on,' I told her, 'we'd better go before we lose him.' I couldn't think of anything else to say. It was the best that I could come up with. We shoved everything back where we'd found it and got the hell out of there. Glynn's door locked shut behind us. Aisling clapped a hand to her mouth.

'The cigarette,' she said. We'd left it smouldering. The two of us stared at each other in mute concern, then Aisling started to laugh – this mad, hysterical, unhinged laugh, to which there was no reasonable response.

18

An puc ar buile

The goat is mad

Coronas of mist encircled the Victorian lanterns as we raced across the black sweep of Front Square, the cobbles slippery and glistening in the drizzle, Aisling a shadow flitting by my side. We caught up with the others just before they disappeared under the Arch. They hadn't noticed our absence, so preoccupied were they with Glynn and his raucous tumult, squalling above his head like a flock of gulls. His funny walk was back.

Glynn blundered out onto College Green and headed up Westmoreland Street. We trudged along after him, docile as a herd of livestock. We're lumbered with him now, for better or for worse, I remember thinking. It was too late to abandon him. He led us to the nearest pub. If he was surprised, upon turning around, to find the five of us lined up behind him, he betrayed no sign of it. But then, he was hardly capable of discharging a look of surprise, the whiskey-sodden state of him.

Glynn's work, in keeping with the great tradition of Irish fiction, is littered throughout with scenes fuelled by alcohol, of which his male protagonists partake liberally, enabling Glynn to introduce new characters through old ones: his men turn into different people with a few jars on them, sometimes aggressive, sometimes maudlin, effectively doubling his cast. What a frugal individual he was. Nothing went to waste.

Alcohol was a narrative device he leaned on heavily, employing it to fulfil the function more traditionally executed by the conceit of the dream. Inebriation freed Glynn's novels to roam in whichever direction he wished, unconstrained by logic or the limiting principles of plot development. It liberated Glynn's work so much in fact that at times it seemed he was working within the fantasy genre. He wrote about chaos as if it were a real place, like Nighttown in Joyce's *Ulysses*. Which is why, I suppose, when Glynn took a drink, it was a literary event. He located an empty table and sat at the head of it. We filed in on either side of him.

I tried to catch Guinevere's eye. She hadn't acknowledged me since I'd left her cottage that morning. Glynn must have noticed this one-way exchange, so plastered that he had acquired a bird's-eye perspective on matters that didn't concern him. I think he wanted to be young again. That's what I suspect. He raised his glasses to his shiny forehead, observing the two of us with his artist's eye, before leaning over to speak into my ear in the same low rumbling growl that had gone on all afternoon in his office.

'You ever seen footage of human gestation, Declan?' he wanted to know. I shook my head. 'The little wriggling sperm trying to penetrate the big white ovum?' He sat back to try to get my face into focus. Couldn't. Didn't matter. He leaned in again. 'Because that's what you're like, Declan. You're like that little sperm, banging your head over and over against their battlements, whining for admittance.' He scratched his head, then examined his fingernails to see what he'd dislodged.

'That's lovely,' I said. 'That's just lovely. That's a really lovely image you have of me there, Professor Glynn.'

'No, no, no, no,' said Glynn, nudging my arm with the rim of his pint, leaving a strip of foam on it. He was more the Dogman than himself at that moment, the way he smirked lopsidedly into his stout before sinking his teeth in it. He was enjoying himself, enjoying his troublemaking. 'Not you *personally*, you fecking eejit, Declan. This is a paradigm that applies to all male–female relationships. You – meaning: us, banging our heads off the walls; and them – meaning: the women, imperturbable, impassive, oblivious.' He gestured at the group. 'Look at them,' he remarked caustically, as if the four girls proved his point for him.

He was yellower than usual. Were we aware at the time of just how yellow he was? To a degree, perhaps, in the back of our minds. He had never exactly radiated rude health. It was only when I came upon an old photograph taken around that period that I grasped the full extent of his discolouration. There we were, the six of us, sitting around a pub table. Not that pub, not that night. Don't know who held the camera. Some passing drunk – picture's crooked. How young we looked, with the exception of Glynn. Astonishing, that we missed the ogre in the corner, the *memento mori,* the ghoul, his arms thrown genially around us, smiling for the dickybird, on the brink of expiration. It brings a lump to my throat. Four of us are flushed as pink from booze as Glynn is drained yellow. Aisling's skin is so powdery white that the snow-glare practically blots her features out. She is two heavily kohled eyes staring out from an all but mouthless face. It was as if the camera had recorded not our likenesses, but our auras.

Glynn swirled his pint and knocked back the dregs.

'Latin me that, me Trinity scholar,' he concluded. A smattering of buff matter clung to his lapel. Something glinted at the base of his leg – a thin metal strip. I pretended to tie my shoelace to get a closer look. There was a smell of polyester trouser down there.

It was a staple. I sat up again. Professor Glynn had stapled his hem. Marjorie had turfed him out. It only dawned on me then. The group had probably known all along. That's why he was living in the dive on Bachelors Walk. Not for research purposes. Marjorie had sent him packing. That wasn't her name, by the way. Her name was a fine one: sophisticated, elegant, proclaimed in italics on the dedication page of his eight novels – no *to*, no *for*, just the six letters of her name, a cry directly from the heart. Marjorie was the name we assigned to her. It was the name she deserved, we decided – or they decided, rather – the girls. Marjorie or Mavis or Gladys. Gladys Glynn. They didn't like sharing him with other women.

Glynn stood up to absent himself. 'I'm off to write a novel,' he announced. 'Back in a tick.' He only had the one joke. We watched him lumber towards the men's toilets, ungainly as a bear.

'At least he's writing again,' Faye offered, forever seeking the silver lining. Was that the night Aisling told me her husband beat her? *You know her husband beats her, don't you?* It must have been that night. I can't tell them apart any more, especially those long diabolical ones.

'Yeah,' said Guinevere, 'you heard what he said about Blake.'

Aisling mumbled something in response. She used to do that a lot – just mumble, forgetting that the outside

world was a full remove away and that she was therefore required to project. There were times, I think, when
all she could hear were the sloshing sounds inside her
own head.

'Would you care to repeat that?' Antonia demanded.
This was her first line of defence: undermining her opponents using their own words, leaving them wondering
what they'd let slip to inadvertently indict themselves.
Her ex-husband was a senior counsel.

Aisling repeated herself so clearly and carefully this
time that there was no mistaking it. 'I said, "He didn't
say Blake".'

Antonia folded her arms. 'So what did he say?' Ever
the sneering tone which, for all her brains, she never
managed to connect to the world's overwhelmingly negative reaction to her.

Aisling mumbled again, her facial muscles as limp as
an arm that had been slept on.

'Sorry?'

Aisling got to her feet and stood over Antonia. 'Glynn
said "Fake"!' she yelled. A hush descended on the pub.
We were going to get thrown out.

Aisling collapsed back into her seat in a lolling slump,
an unattended puppet. Her chin rested on her chest as if
her neck were broken, revealing a stripe of light hair
along her parting. Underneath the mad make-up, the
mourning weeds, the black dye, she could have been a
Guinevere.

Glynn returned to the table and set down a clutch of
whiskey tumblers on a tray. He doled them out with the
matter-of-fact efficiency of an Irish mammy, mindful to
demonstrate that favouritism was not in practice and
that complaints would not be entertained. You could tell

he'd grown up in a large family. 'There's no names on them,' he asserted, his Arklow accent that bit thicker than usual. None of us had eaten, but we didn't let that stop us.

'The problem with the contemporary novel,' he told us as he resumed his seat at the head of the table, having apparently given it some thought at the urinal, 'is that beginnings are more important than endings. This is because advances are calculated on the basis of the first thirty pages, and readers rarely get beyond the first thirty pages anyway.' He glared at each of us in turn in case this was an avenue we were contemplating ourselves and seemed disappointed when no one challenged him.

He went on to expound his theory regarding the inverse proportion between literary output and humility. Some writers published more because they had less humility, he argued. Those clowns who were prolific had no shame at all. He cited his main contemporary as proof of this phenomenon – twenty-one novels and counting. Those who barely published at all any more had let their natural God-given modesty get the better of them. Glynn rolled his eyes mournfully at his tumbler at this point. It was an insidious attempt to solicit sympathy from the women, and it worked. 'But Professor Glynn!' Faye interjected, as he was hoping she might, 'Don't be so humble – your work is wonderful.'

His sleeping-tablet habit was escalating. He was up to three a night by then but was never quite asleep at night, and never quite awake in the morning. This, I got from Aisling, who had sprung back to life and was muttering animatedly into my ear, the magnifying glass around her neck revolving in her hands like a small planet on a wooden axis. 'Could the sleeping tablets possibly explain his demonic visions?' she asked me. They were more vivid than ever now. Aisling seemed to think, after ransacking Glynn's office together, that I would understand what she was talking about. I most certainly did not.

'He's seeing demons?' I repeated incredulously, interrupting her flow.

Aisling looked panicked. 'Shh, he'll hear you.'

I glanced at Glynn. He was deep in sparring conversation with Antonia. ('What bright spark allowed women into Trinity anyway?' he grunted. 'Who on earth admitted the Catholics?' she countered.)

'Is that what he told you, though? That he's seeing demons?'

Aisling nodded.

I shrugged and drained my glass. 'Well, he must have been speaking metaphorically, that's all I can say.'

'You were talking about them too. Belsabub and Sattan.'

'I was talking about medieval English mystery plays.'

'But you saw the drawings in his red notebook.'

'They were just doodles.'

'You don't understand, Declan,' Aisling insisted. 'I *recognised* them. I *recognised* the demons in the red notebook. I've seen them too, the very same faces. They aren't doodles: they're portraits.'

Demons. Even the word. Glynn shouldn't have burdened Aisling with that guff. Of all of us, she was the one who least needed reminding that a powerful imagination was as much a curse as a gift, that the world could tip into chaos without warning, and that it didn't get any easier with age. Her world view was fragile, and Glynn abused his position in his endless, ruthless search for an audience, knowing – what with her being the most impressionable – that Aisling would also prove the most receptive. And the least critical. Aisling or Faye. They wouldn't be up to the like of him.

Faye set down another round of pints. Glynn reached for one without thanking her. 'Why do you do this to me?' he entreated Antonia in an uncharacteristically plaintive tone of voice. The pair of them had been huddled over each other the past ten minutes, his arm thrown along the back of the banquette, and she sitting in the crook of it. Antonia threw back her head and laughed, cruelly and with relish, as only she could. Glynn raised the pint to his lips and drank deeply without removing his eyes from her throat. There was something unseemly about the look of gratification on his face. Antonia revelled in the attention.

He started talking in the low rumbling growl again. Antonia had to lean in to hear him. His belly was almost lewd in its tumescence, a great egg cradled on his thighs. How was he getting fatter, when we never saw him eat? You couldn't help but stare at him, whether you wanted to or not, like a skip full of discarded furniture. Articles you'd no more take into your home yet still you found yourself pausing on the kerb to peer in, urging yourself to move on but unable to.

Glynn was hell bent on finishing whatever it was he had to say to Antonia. Nothing would be permitted to interrupt his soliloquy. That is the problem with first-person narrators, the overbearing, unadulterated self-absorption. No wonder Gladys had dumped him.

'Stop it, for God's sake!' Antonia cried, unable to take any more. Glynn retracted his arm and sat back, a smirk of satisfaction on his face. Oh Christ, I realised, he was fucking her. I can't say precisely why I felt so sure of it. Nothing that would stand up in court. Aisling dropped her pint on the floor. She simply let go of it, and the glass smashed on the tiles, splashing all over our shoes. Guinevere stooped to pick up the broken pieces.

'Don't,' Aisling warned her.

Glynn glanced at Aisling. The depth of her voice had unnerved him too. Difficult to gauge how far you could push it with her. She was an Emily Dickinson fan. Glynn called for a fresh pint, then they settled again, himself and Antonia, circling each other like caged lions, and us, carrion birds, circling them.

Aisling steadily drank the fresh pint Glynn had ordered, as if it were a grim task he had set her. You had to admire her determination. He and Antonia were locked into some class of battle which was simultaneously hushed and frantic. Their facial expressions were those of people screaming, but we couldn't hear a thing. They screamed underwater. We in the cheap seats found it immensely disorientating. 'Something bad is going to happen,' Faye said quietly.

At that, Aisling banged down her emptied pint glass and left. Islands of creamy froth slid towards the bottom of the glass like snowflakes down a windowpane. How had she drained it so quickly, the size of her? Her exit was marked by the crunch of broken glass. She was absent from the table for some time.

Faye slipped into the seat she had vacated. 'We're worried about her, Declan. Did you notice her little finger?' I shook my head. 'She stuck it into a pencil sharpener while we were sitting there last week and . . .'

I put my arm around Faye when she started to sob. She couldn't apologise enough as she dabbed the tears

159

away with a tissue, but they kept welling up and spilling down her cheeks as if a pipe had sprung a leak. She was unable to stem them.

When Aisling returned, her hair was beaded with mist. She didn't say why she'd gone outside. The tip of her little finger was indeed bandaged up. I don't know how I'd missed it before. Now that my attention had been drawn to it, I couldn't tear my eyes away, couldn't keep from wondering about the maimed nub of flesh inside. She bought a round and joined us at the table, looking about herself mildly. It was hard to know which of the girls to worry about most. Guinevere, for one. She had kept her distance all night. What had I done to offend her? She leaned forward to place her drink on the table and I glimpsed a white slope of breast inside her shirt. Desire surged so cataclysmically through me that they all must have noticed, they all must have sneered.

Guinevere looked at Faye. 'Whatever happened to Mike?' she wondered.

Faye frowned. 'Who?'

'God, yeah, Mike,' said Aisling. 'Your man with the ponytail.' She laughed. It was as if we had imagined him.

'You stupid bitch,' Glynn suddenly spat at Antonia with no small degree of venom. We looked at him in shock. A door in the cabin of the plane had burst open during flight. An entirely different element had been introduced, one against which we had no defences. We sat there in horror, buckled into our seats, waiting for instructions: an oxygen mask to drop, a parachute, *something*.

Glynn got up and lurched away, almost knocking over the table. We steadied it with our hands. It was clear that he was gone for good this time – he had taken his pint.

The four of us turned to Antonia for an explanation. She tossed her blonde head and smiled.

'Well, I don't know about you, but I've had a perfectly lovely evening,' she informed us, opening her handbag and dropping her cigarettes and lighter into it. She clicked the bag shut and tucked it under her arm. 'Honestly, I have to get going,' she insisted, as if we'd implored her to stay.

'Did you shag Professor Glynn?' I asked her straight out, a feed of pints lining my belly.

She reached forward to slap me hard across the face and then laughed gaily, a connoisseur of ambiguity. She was aristocratic, I'll give her that. Haughty and cruel and balletic. She swung her coat over her shoulders. 'Goodnight, all,' she sang, a forced lightness to her voice. I wouldn't have been remotely surprised had Antonia turned around one day and addressed us in an entirely different tone of voice altogether, as if she were possessed, or dispossessed rather. Her natural voice would be deeper, slower, more resigned. Maybe I could have warmed to her then.

Were I a real writer, I would narrate a scene describing Antonia's solitary journey home to the leafy suburbs of south County Dublin at night. Our influence would wear off as the train stations shunted past, and she would become less glossy, more subdued. What did she have to go home to? No one, nothing, an empty house. Small wonder she was out with the likes of us until all hours. Small wonder she was out with Glynn.

She'd get off the DART and walk the few streets to her unlit period seaside home with its rose garden and bay views. If you couldn't write there, where could you write? The house had a name, which I no longer recall.

Something genteel and Anglo. I can see the black font, but not the word itself, painted in duplicate in block capitals like a trespassing sign as I passed through her twin gateposts that one time. The crunch of gravel on her driveway delineated the point at which the mark had been irrevocably overstepped. I found I couldn't turn back.

That house was too big for Antonia. It was a large family home. She had cheated it of its purpose. It needed children, dogs, an adult male. She rattled around on her own inside, constituting a temporary anomaly in its two-hundred-year history. It wasn't designed for a separated woman in early middle age in the late twentieth century. Little, you could argue, was. The house was waiting for her to pack up and leave so it could resume a more suitable tenancy, she had once told us. But she wouldn't give in to it, no, she most certainly would not. It wouldn't get the better of her, she averred, knocking back a gin and tonic, a one-woman microcosm of the Anglo-Irish ascendancy still trying to hold the fort. We didn't like to think of her going back there to brazen it out on her own, not after Glynn's vicious attack. *You stupid bitch*. What had possessed him?

Antonia would unlock the lacquered front door onto an empty hall, through which she would pass without switching on the lights, ghostly in the tarnished mirrors. Down to the basement kitchen she would descend, the old servants' quarters, to sit at her pine table in the darkness. I imagine she was tired, more tired than we were, being that bit older. The second she sat down, the mask would drop. *Voom*, like that, a dead weight. Onto the floor it would land with a clatter, the night's dirty work, a sack of stolen loot.

162

I have no idea what Antonia's real face looked like, except that it was smaller than the one she allowed us to see, less haughty, more pinched, and it ached from the effort of exerting self-control, and control of others, all day. When I think of her alone in her beautiful home, surrounded by her beautiful possessions, all that family silver and china but no family, I think of a Christmas tree in January with the fairy lights unplugged. It was not the image that she strove to project, but still, after all these years, it is the image that persists.

19

Mise Glynn an file

I am Glynn the poet

It had stopped raining by the time Professor Glynn came barging out through the double doors of the pub onto the arse end of Fleet Street. He took a moment to regain his bearings, looking up the street, then down, then up the street again, then down again, an eyebrow cocked sceptically as if it were all a big ploy to catch him out and he was having none of it. He turned around to read the name of the pub over the door and snorted: a likely story. As if he'd sink to drinking there. He was still clutching his pint.

Events that evening had not unfolded to his satisfaction. They rarely did, but that somehow never lessened the torment, never prepared him for the series of crushing disappointments that inevitably lay in store. Glynn was not an adaptable man. He complained bitterly about the evening's proceedings, for all the good it did him – no one was listening any more. Stout sloshed all over his wrists and sleeves as he gesticulated angrily, for the great writer was still driving home his points, determined to win the argument, to assert his moral position (that she *was* a stupid bitch), though the opportunity for doing so had long since passed. Glynn was out in the cold.

He consoled himself by gulping down what remained of the pint, then stooped to deposit the empty glass in a doorway rank with piss. He missed the pavement. The glass fell over and rolled into the gutter, where it shattered. Glynn looked away regally as if it were nothing to do with him, then unzipped his fly and contributed to the filth, the general squalor, the reeking cesspit that was Dublin City at night.

At the junction of Fleet Street and Westmoreland Street, the bould scribbler checked his watch only to discover that he wasn't wearing one. He studied his bare wrist for a protracted period, then orientated himself to the right to contemplate the Liffey and O'Connell Bridge, leaning back as if this flat vista were a mountaintop of sublime proportions, too staggering to view at such close range. Whatever he saw placated him. Must have been the familiarity. The Mighty Glynn swayed gently, a man hearing strains of music on the breeze. There was a warm smell of hops on the air and he inhaled it deeply. His state of outrage appeared to have abated. He even seemed contented, briefly.

Glynn grunted and thought the better of going home. He consulted his bare wrist again, and it told him that the night was young. He turned his back on the river and set off in the opposite direction, making his way up Westmoreland Street with ostentatious care, raising his knees too high in the air as though the pavement were a flight of stairs. What a barrel he had become since gaining that extra weight over Christmas. Every pound of it had amassed around his middle, taut as a pregnancy, only higher. His limbs looked comically thin by comparison, shuttling up and down with the thirst. An awful cross to bear, the thirst, and Glynn a martyr to it. God knows, he wasn't the worst off that night, and closing time wasn't for another hour yet. It was the week before the annual deprivations of Lent, and the city's drinkers were going at it hell for leather.

Outside the public toilets on College Street, Glynn collided with a group of young fellas dressed in silky tracksuits. Oblivious Glynn hadn't been looking where he was going and couldn't see more than a foot or two in front of himself in any case, having left his glasses on the pub table. He was blithely navigating his way to Bartley Dunne's by ear when *bang*. The youths had colonised most of the public area, and the unexpected obstacle they presented sent the writer flying.

He reached for the nearest one to keep from losing his balance and caught the lad by the hips. Big mistake. The young fella shook him off with excessive force. 'Get off of me, ya sick prick!' he roared, 'ya filthy puff, ya dirty bollocks, I'll fucken burst ya!' His friends goaded him on. 'Fucken burst the poofter, go on.' Several pedestrians turned around to detect the source of the commotion, but only so that they could avoid it. Nobody came to Glynn's aid.

Aghast Glynn, blinking at finding himself in the centre of a ring of hooded teenagers who were baying words at him that he didn't understand, was wholly at a loss as to how to respond. He stood beneath the statue of Thomas Moore, mouth agape, rocking on his heels, until the one he had allegedly *molested* stepped up to his face and hawked a big gob of spit into it.

Glynn crumpled before the teenager in a gesture of feudal submission, clawing the clotted fluid from his face as if it burned. 'State a ya,' the young fella pronounced in lofty judgement over the writer's bent back. The rest of the youths laughed and congratulated one another on the calibre of the joke. Nice one, deadly, your man's a fucken spa.

The writer in the end provided little sport, remaining crouched in a stained heap on the pavement. He wasn't even worth a kick. The gang quickly lost interest in him. No, there was more to it than that: they quickly became embarrassed by him, keen to distance themselves from the grown man huddled into a ball, making a holy show of himself in the middle of College Street, clutching the back of his head as he rocked gently and gently moaned, the fucken bleedin mentler. Nothing to do with them.

Glynn slipped off once the gang moved on. He no longer merrily high-stepped but shuffled uncertainly forward, the heels of his hands pressed into his eye sockets as if they had been gouged. It seemed that he was crying, and maybe he was. Emotions had been running high all night.

He dodged a bus and made it to the other side of the street where he clamped a hand to a black rail of Trinity, holding on to it to steady himself like a commuter on a train. It took him some time to regain his composure. He was unused to such rough treatment, unaccustomed to interacting with people who made no allowance for his gift. A jewel glinting up from the bottom of a rock pool is a jewel only for so long as it remains there. Pry it from the mossy stones and it becomes a piece of broken glass once more. The same applied to the great writer. Out on the street, he looked like any tired civil servant trudging home from the office, any disappointed husband or bad father. Detached from the context of his staggering achievements, Glynn was just another old drunk in a city rotten with them.

Eventually he released the rail and struggled on, a swimmer submitting to the powerful currents of the street. He was swept around the corner with the flow of traffic from Pearse Street, all the time glancing fearfully over his shoulder. Indeed, he was being watched, but not by the little knackers. They had decamped to the Abrakebabra at O'Connell Bridge.

He headed not to the nearest pub, as might be forgiven under the circumstances, but straight back into the Republic of Trinity. He'd only lasted a few hours on the outside. This hasty retreat was an indication of just how thoroughly the attack had rattled him. He hadn't seen it coming. Crime in the work of Glynn was perpetrated by the same old rogues and was thus predictable, manageable, even comical, part of the natural cycle of things. He depicted it almost as a form of tax, from which no one was exempt, except of course the artists.

No artists' exemption was available to the professor in the wake of the assault on College Street. It had come from a quarter he barely knew existed. Glynn was essentially a man from a different era, although he hadn't recognised it until that young fella stepped up to hawk a big gullier in his face. *State a ya. Fucken bleedin mentler.* The large wooden doors at the entrance to Front Arch had been bolted over at that hour, and Glynn had to step through the hatch cut into one of them. No gougers would gain admittance there; the night porter would personally see to it.

It was mercifully dark within the seclusion of the college walls, but not so dark as to be unapparent even from a few hundred feet away that Glynn was shaking hard. The flame he applied to his cigarette strobed with the tremble of his hand. From that distance, it could have been a firefly. He sought refuge under the Campanile. Glynn was now standing on the former site of the high altar of the All Hallows Priory, whether he knew it or not. The ruined priest at the ruined altar; it was a compelling image. On a better day, Glynn might have gotten a short story out of it.

He was invisible under there except for the glowing tip of his cigarette, which smouldered about his person like a tiny fiend. They were never far from his side, the demons. You couldn't throw a stone. Glynn ventured out and wandered for a time between the statues of old provosts before settling down on a wet bench beneath a tree outside the Rubrics. The black and silver branches of the old oak were jewelled with glistening raindrops which splashed down on the great writer from time to time, though he didn't seem to mind. He shook his head softly at his thoughts, which can't have been happy, then checked his watch: still missing. It was ten past eleven.

Even with the august backdrop of the eighteenth-century collegial architecture lending him ballast, Glynn was not restored to his former self. He fell forward into a slump, cutting a despondent figure on the deserted lawns, like one of the wretched characters in the novels of his late career. It was getting increasingly challenging to tell him apart from his protagonists these days. Perhaps this was a difficulty of perception Glynn experienced too. Who was he if not the voices of his books, and what were they, only inventions? He had been accused of self-parody in the recent past in a provocative article about life imitating art published by a young academic from a lesser educational institution seeking to make a name for himself. Good luck to him.

Glynn's mood of resigned acceptance didn't last long. The icy temperatures must have gotten the better of him, because he jumped to his feet and took off across the cobbles again. How quiet the campus was at night, and what a racket he made there. You could tell from the way he twitched, all elbows and knees, that he was entering a state of mounting agitation, his excess fury converting to kinetic energy. He must have resolved to commit his thoughts to paper, because he rushed along New Square towards his office, a man with a deadline to meet.

Unfortunately, the Arts Block was locked at that hour. Glynn rattled the long vertical metal handles of the glass doors in anguished protest as if they were the very bars of his cage. At least he was free to express his rage there without fear of retribution. It was hardly an adequate consolation, all the same.

He gave up and crossed over to the Berkeley, jerky as a hen. Two nights had passed since he'd slept in his own bed, in any bed at all. By then he had found himself in the company of some imaginary companion, one who was annoying him. He had to reprimand that individual more than once, but still they didn't get the message. Glynn tried repeatedly to shake them off, pulling his arm away, swiping the air. 'You're a persistent fecker!' he was heard to cry into the darkness of the rugby pitch. He did not stick around for a response but instead lashed up the steps of the Pav in his metal-tipped shoes, slamming the door behind him. At least he was back on form.

He lashed back out again seconds later, having got no satisfaction. Last orders had already been served. He paused at the top of the steps to gaze at the heavens and contemplate his plight before tackling the steep grassy bank. Here, he practically went on his hole. 'Someone could fecking well kill themselves on that,' the writer pointed out as soon as he had uprighted himself. He looked around for a response, but his companion had deserted him. Glynn shrugged in resignation. This did not surprise him in the least. That was what you were dealing with. Everyone let you down in the end. Besides, he was used to being alone, though he wasn't alone, not half as alone as he thought himself.

He set off across the sports ground again, his metal caps destroying the wet pitch a second time. What did he care? What was it to him? You could see him rehearsing the arguments in his head. As a proud Irishman, he had no respect for the rugby, it being the coloniser's game. Glynn took pleasure in proclaiming divisive opinions when drunk, relished nothing better than starting a good pub fight, and did so as if it were his national duty. He never got a rise out of the girls.

The destruction of the pitch, it is to be hoped, allowed him feel less impotent for a spell. He held dominion over a soggy rectangle of grass, and he tore up and down it with the righteous indignation of the oppressed. That was Glynn all over. Never did know which side his bread was buttered on. Never managed to learn.

I hadn't anticipated that he'd double back on himself like that. He turned his head and looked right at me, where I stood hands in pockets under a tree. We stared at each other for a beat – hard to say which of us was more taken aback. I thought I'd been rumbled, but in the scale of odd things that had already loomed in and out of Glynn's blurred field of vision that evening, my lone presence did not strike him as especially perturbing. He may as well have dreamt me. I didn't move a muscle, and, sure enough, Professor Glynn dismissed me and set off on his travels again. Where was he off to next? There was only one way to find out.

The other three slipped out from behind the tree when he had loped on a safe distance. We watched his departing figure. 'Do you think he saw you?' Aisling whispered. I shook my head, and they believed me. God knows what possessed them to invest faith in my opinion. The poor things, they were shivering, faces white as ghosts. Blue, in fact, in that light.

Glynn navigated his way back to Front Square, now plodding and sullen, having reached the conclusion he inevitably reached after a hard night on the batter: that there was nobody out there to help him. Instead of heading for the Arch, he veered off to House Eight and admitted himself in the door. After thirty seconds or so, a light on the first floor came on. We looked at each other in surprise. Not one of us had seen that room lit up before. It existed in our minds only as a locked door.

Glynn appeared in the window. He stretched his arms above his head and drew the edges of the curtains together, erasing his silhouette from view. It was the gesture of a god. We waited until the light was extinguished before relaxing our guard. Past midnight by then. Faye crept forward and posted his glasses through the letterbox, wrapped in a cocoon of tissues. Quiet in there, she reported. Not until we were certain he was safely delivered did we call off our vigil. And how was he when you found him? future biographers would ask us. Fragile, we would tell them, but we did everything in our power to protect him. The girls might catch their death, but no injury would come to Glynn on our watch, we would see to it. If they'd hit him, those gurriers outside the public toilets, if they had harmed so much as a hair on his head, we'd have come down on them, the four of us, like a ton of feathers.

20

The Stolen Child

Glynn had little time for children and, according to his wife, showed next to no interest in his own. She would say that though, wouldn't she, Gladys or whatever she was called. Gladys or Gloria or Glenda Glynn. Her accusation rings hollow in light of the fact that so much of Glynn's work could be defined as childlike in character. This assertion may strike the attentive reader as a contradiction – children are rarely depicted in the work of Glynn, and when they do feature it is to appear out of thin air and catch you in the act, Mammy's little double agents, no more than a plot device, really, a way of forcing events to a crisis. The exception was his own child, Sofia, the one who lived, or Cassandra as she was christened in the text, accursed daughter. Sofia Cassandra appeared just the once, but oh how memorably.

No, by the term 'childlike', another meaning altogether is here intended. Glynn's writerly imagination was childlike in its intensity, rendering its surroundings as fresh as if experienced for the first time. He was never found wanting when it came to the profound. When personages of national importance passed away, it was Glynn whom the press canvassed for a quote, Glynn who appeared on the *RTE News,* his patrician hair nodding compassionately. He was the closest we had to a poet laureate. The urbane jadedness endemic in the work of the next generation got short shrift from him. It was true that his work had gone out of fashion lately. He would have been the first to admit that.

Glynn had spoken eloquently about the nature of the imagination when we first came together as a group without knowing it that filthy wet night in '81. He evoked it as unknowable and majestic as a star and went on to rue its woeful undervaluation in our society. A number of audience members nodded their agreement at this assertion. The imagination was a faculty shed by most children once they hit double numbers, Glynn continued. It evaporated with exponential momentum until nothing was left by adulthood but a silty tidemark outlining what once had been. It was a sad irony of the human condition, the great writer pointed out, that the taller we grew in feet and inches, the smaller we shrank in scope. It wasn't an irony at all, of course, we knew that; it was a paradox.

Glynn proposed the theory that same evening that future generations would evolve the imagination out of their genetic make-up altogether. It would come to be regarded as freakish as an atavistic limb – people would pay an admission charge to squirm at its workings. He lambasted the pre-eminence accorded the so-called 'real world'. No parent would encourage their child to become an artist in the real world. Money didn't grow on trees in the real world. But what were we without our sense of wonder? he asked the audience. Take the child-like imagination away, and what was left? What was the point? Why should we bother? Did anyone know? Anyone at all? His questions were met with silence.

The theories propounded by the great man that night

provide insight into his refusal to grow up. 'I don't want to be an old man,' he had complained midway through his bender the previous week, speaking as if this fate was peculiar to him alone. It's quite possible his staggering solipsism allowed him to believe it was. It can be appreciated how an artist might feel constricted by the quotidian world with its emphasis on pounds and pence. 'Banal' is a word they reach for often, and never with reference to themselves, employing it instead as shorthand for the rest of the world. Western society had been infected by what Glynn called 'blandular fever'. It was the artist's duty to swim against that current, he informed us during a workshop. Was he talking about us though, or yet again about himself, when he used that loaded term 'artist'? We never knew where we stood.

What cannot be as readily appreciated is the artists' persistence in perceiving themselves as alone in their persecution by the quotidian. This is a monumental failure of the imagination on their part. Spouses and children, specifically, could not possibly comprehend their predicament. Spouses and children, they appear to think, do not suffer like they suffer. No one, they think, suffers like an artist suffers. They believe themselves not made for this world, but worse than that: they believe that others are. The question is, why do they marry, why do they procreate, why do they inflict themselves on the human beings around them if they harbour such low opinions of them? Making certain that someone's around to take care of them? Securing a captive audience?

A young woman was making a terrible scene in the middle of Front Square, oblivious to the looks she was attracting. She'd have drawn curious glances even had she kept her counsel, so out of place did she look on the college grounds – an ungainly figure dressed in ungainly clothes, like something got from the nuns. Her floral skirt kept inflating in the breeze, revealing solid, mottled legs. A sudden gust blew the hem up as far as her thighs.

So visibly distressed was the young woman by then that she didn't appear to notice the exposure. Glynn did though. He noticed the girl's thighs, and he noticed those around him noticing, his colleagues and students, the odd tourist. He couldn't screen the girl from their prying eyes, although you could tell he dearly wanted to. Nothing he said or did placated her. She didn't seem to hear him.

'Do you think she's maybe deaf?' Faye asked.

Antonia shook her head. 'No, she isn't deaf.'

Glynn gestured towards Front Arch and made to place a guiding hand on the woman's shoulder, seeking to escort her off the premises. The woman shied as if she thought he was about to hit her. 'Oh no,' Aisling whispered, chewing at her cuticles, peeling them off in strips with her teeth. A fazed Glynn retracted his hand. That was a first: Glynn looking embarrassed. We didn't think him capable. Odd, that he didn't storm off, his standard cop-out. What hold did this person have on him?

The woman's skirt blew up to her thighs again, and again she failed to notice. Her white nurses' shoes were yellowing at the soles like geriatric feet. Ankle socks, at her age, white cotton ankle socks folded over at the hem – the woman had strayed out of her depth with Glynn. She was too young for him, apart from anything else, far too young and gauche. The five of us watched closely from the workshop window. What had he gone and brought upon himself now?

Glynn's voice, though raised, unfortunately wasn't raised enough to make out what he was telling the girl, even after we'd opened both windows. He had the courtesy to look sheepish, I'll give him that. I would go so far as to say guilty. Good enough for him. Served him right. Might put manners on him in future.

'She's not exactly his type, is she?' I observed.

Antonia turned from the window to regard me with withering disgust. Truly, she outdid herself. 'You are obscene,' she said. 'That isn't his lover. That's his daughter.' She returned her attention to the sparring pair below. 'Bet she's the one sending the poison-pen letters.'

I looked down at the woman in the quad again, at her flowery dress, her fleshy knees, her permed hair, her sloppy dismay. She was crying now, big blotchy tears that didn't hold a candle to Guinevere's. She wiped her nose with the back of her hand and Glynn produced a rancid hanky, which she declined. This was Sofia? This was Cassandra? No, I remember thinking. Not possible. She departed too radically from the image held aloft in my mind. Glynn had written about her with bewildered tenderness in *The Common-place Book*. She was his strange fairy child, his troubled sprite, and I was half in love with her.

Glynn cupped his daughter's shoulders. She submitted to being held in this manner, if not quite embraced – he tried to draw her to him but she cowered and he immediately desisted, knowing better for once in his life than to push his luck. She was almost as broad as him, the poor graceless girl. Those ridiculous, matronly, ill-fitting clothes. Where had she gotten them? Not from her mother, that was for sure. Gladys was a striking, statuesque New Yorker who wore her silver hair in an angular bob, hardly the drudge we made her out to be. We demonised her to suit our purpose, which was to lionise Glynn. We required a figure of grand proportions in whom to invest our faith and therefore glorified Glynn as a tragic hero, or tragic anti-hero at least.

The breeze plastered Sofia's hair across her face. It stuck to her tears and snot. She permitted her father to disentangle it, and he carefully tucked it behind her ears. The wind whipped it straight back into her eyes again, and she lowered her head in defeat. How had Glynn engendered this shambling, big-boned creature? Nothing by his hand was this crude, this unworked. She was his only child.

The four women were hungry to construct a narrative, a family saga, out of every tiny gesture Glynn and his slovenly daughter exchanged. Their attention was almost predatory. It was a wonder the intensity of their combined gaze didn't set the Glynns on fire. I, on the other hand, no longer wanted to know. It was a shattering disappointment that Glynn's offspring wasn't the match of him. Such a disappointment, in fact, that I felt cheated. My overriding need to believe in some transcendent essence had been dealt another blow. There was no unquenchable spark of brilliance. It had petered out by the time it reached Sofia. She resembled her father only in stubbornness.

A strange thing started happening then: my disillusionment with Sofia began to infect my high opinion of Glynn, dismantling him before my eyes like a degenerative virus. Had his unquenchable spark of brilliance petered out by the time it reached Sofia, or had it petered out also in the man himself? Was it possible that Glynn was now every bit as ordinary as his daughter? Had we been hasty in our appraisal? He hadn't written in so long. He hadn't written in years.

Sofia's shoulders sagged in capitulation as she conceded Glynn a little suppose-so nod. The fight had gone out of her by then. Conflict was not her natural disposition. She didn't take after her father in that regard either. Glynn still held her upper arms and was speaking entreatingly to her slumped form. He wished she'd stand up straight for once in her life and kept rolling her shoulders back to try to straighten her frame, but she just slouched forward again. Twice he gently shook her, trying to rouse her, to no avail. Sofia kept her eyes on the cobbles.

His dishevelled girl swayed on her feet as if her father's words had lulled her into a trance. She reminded me of Aisling at that moment, the way she lost herself. Glynn tipped a finger under her chin, attempting to raise her face. This level of intimacy proved a step too far. Sofia snapped out of the trance and shoved Glynn with both hands so violently in the chest that he staggered backwards. Her face was marbled red and white.

'I hate you, you cow!' she screamed. *You cow;* there was no mistaking it. The only words we'd caught from the entire exchange.

'Deary me,' said Antonia, folding her arms with satisfaction. Sofia's outburst had hit the spot. Antonia loved that sort of thing – not other people's distress, but their botched mismanagement of it. Made her feel better about her own life, I suppose. At least Antonia knew how to conduct herself during a dramatic crisis. So she liked to think.

Sofia turned and ran away like a walloping great child, flat-footed in her white nurse shoes, bumping into students along the way before disappearing under Front Arch. Glynn just stood there watching her recede, the rancid hanky still in his hand. Faye said it was enough to break your heart. Mmm, I murmured along with the others, but I was glad to see the back of her.

Suddenly the women crowded around Guinevere, who was standing with both palms pressed against the wall, leaning her weight against it. With her eyes shut like that, and her lips drained of blood, her face was as colourless as a death mask, as Aisling's.

The other three elbowed me out of the way and lead her to the door. 'What's happening?' I asked, but none of them answered. 'It's okay, chicken, we've got you,' Faye was coaxing her. I followed them out to the landing. They were helping her down the stairs.

'What's wrong with her?' I asked their descending backs, as if Guinevere couldn't speak for herself. 'Is she going to be okay?' I trailed down the stairs in their wake, yapping at their heels. They entered the women's toilet. I grabbed Antonia's wrist just before the door closed behind her. 'What the hell's going on? Tell me.'

'It's her period, fuckhead.'

The door slammed shut in my face, leaving me standing alone in the empty corridor. Quiet out there, after the commotion. It was as if they'd passed into the wall. That door was as good as a wall to me. I could not pass beyond it. A plate sticker of a matchstick woman warded me off like a skull and crossbones. The triangular skirt and spherical head seemed less a representation of womanhood than a delineation of man's limited understanding of it.

I could hear them inside, murmuring, crooning, their voices pitched low to deliberately drive me mad. What rites and rituals were under way in there? It should have been a question mark depicted on that plate sticker, or a set of quotation marks containing nothing. A pair of mirrors adjusted to reflect infinity. A pentangle, a sprig of hemlock, twigs bound into a bundle. The circle and triangle didn't begin to cover it. Fuckhead, Antonia had called me.

Glynn rounded the corner, catching me with my ear pressed to the door. I jumped back to find him at the far end of the corridor, battle-scarred from his skirmish with his obtuse, abstruse daughter who had just called him, of all things, and in front of everyone, a cow. You couldn't make it up. On his face was the same expression I felt written all over my own, a combination of resentment and disbelief.

He angled a weary eye at the isosceles triangle on the plate sticker, then down at me hovering below it. Big white ovum, tiny wriggling sperm, whining for admittance to the female toilets. A no-win situation, if ever he saw one. He placed a heavy hand on the banister and a leaden foot on the stair. 'Are you right?' he asked me gruffly, but fondly enough all the same. I nodded and followed him up.

Woe was general all over Ireland

'Here Comes Everybody,' Glynn said glumly when the four women finally joined us upstairs, having taken their sweet time. Aisling had embarked on a novel. That was the day's big news. She distributed a partial manuscript to each of us when her turn to read came.

It was like one of her poems, only more so. I had not the slightest notion what it meant. There were over thirty characters in it, as far as I could make out. It shuttled back and forth in time through major civilisations: Hellenic, Celtic, Mycenaean and one wholly imaginary one – at least, I think it was wholly imaginary. It was written in a compulsively rhythmic Dublin street argot which was part observed, part invented. The Peamount Tuberculosis Hospital functioned as some class of portal. Sickness was a major trope. 'It's part one of a trilogy,' she told us after she'd read out the first five pages. Her reading was met with silence.

When queried by Glynn, Aisling described the novel as the application of the apparatus of string theory to the traditional murder-mystery genre with a view to elucidating the chaos rife in our daily environment, from which there is no escape.

'I see,' said Glynn, leafing through her manuscript, pausing to read paragraphs at random. He was frowning. 'And you've been working on this all year, have you?'

'Em, no,' said Aisling. 'I started it this week.

'This week?'

'Yes. Monday.'

Glynn flicked to the end of the manuscript. Two hundred and sixteen pages in length. In three days. Two days, actually – Aisling had been with us since half eleven. He raised his glasses to his artist's eye to peer at the girl. How stark she looked in the vivid company of the others, a black and white photograph in a roomful of colour, a figure from a past century transplanted to the modern age. 'Have you been sleeping, Aisling?' Glynn asked with a kindness we didn't know he had in him. Aisling smiled shyly and shrugged, as if she wasn't really sure. Her eyes were dark and glossy.

Glynn invited her to read a little more, though I wished he hadn't. I was rapidly losing my bearings, such as they were. How had the girl managed to write so much in two days? It wasn't physically possible. *Syncope,* the novel was called. Even the title was a reproof. I had no idea what it meant. Had she made that word up too? I glanced at the faces of the others for guidance. They gave nothing away, as usual.

Aisling leafed through her manuscript and settled on a passage about halfway through. We opened our copies to the designated page as if it were a hymnbook. This extract was entirely different in character to the novel's opening, consisting solely of dialogue. Dialogue was my terrain. It was the only thing I was good at, the only thing the girls ever praised me for. Even Antonia had assented, sort of. ('Have you considered trying your hand at a screenplay instead?' was how she phrased it,

meaning she thought my descriptive prose was crap.)
Turned out Aisling had a natural flair for voices which
far outshone mine. This was a gift her poetry had kept
firmly hidden under a bushel.

Her switch from poetry was both abrupt and wholesale. Her first prose endeavour did not even have the
safety net of being a short story. It was a shot at a novel
and therefore possessed all the latent threat of a novel,
all the danger, all the potential. A trilogy at that. Aisling
had dived off at the deep end. I couldn't get a handle on
the words in front of me. The piece was so good that I
was unable to quantify it. All I discerned from hearing
her read was that I was no good, I should give up.

She read in her customary way, to which I was unable
to grow accustomed: head lolling broken-necked over
the page, arms dangling lamely by her side – what in the
name of Jesus was wrong with her? The curtain of hair,
blue-black as a magpie's wing, concealed her face and
the source of her voice, which was ventriloquial at the
best of times but now seemed to be emanating a whole
yard shy of her. I got it into my head that it was no
longer Aisling under there. Were I to part that heavy curtain, I did not know who – or what – would look back
at me.

Aisling's second reading was met with another silence
from us and an impressed nod from Glynn. The fictional space should never be cosy, he had recently warned us.
Glynn didn't rate Dickens for the same reason he didn't
rate Mozart. Not enough doubt. Didn't reflect the
world. That's why he responded so positively to Aisling's
piece that day: it was doubt incarnate.

'Well so,' he said, sitting back in his chair to indicate
that the discussion was now open to the table. He waited

for our reaction. So did Aisling. But what could we say? A meteor had crashed through the ceiling, and we stared at it smouldering away on the desk, wondering where the fuck it had come from. And what the fuck it was. This was not matter as it existed on Earth. There we were, the rest of us, plodding around trying to hone our similes, conjugate our adverbs, and Aisling had just invented – well, what? What had Aisling just invented? My biro rolled across the desk and fell through the gap that had appeared between our tables. I made no attempt to retrieve it.

'Page ninety-six,' Antonia eventually said, seeing as no one else was prepared to get the ball rolling. 'I have a problem with your use of *meta-*. You've used it as a prefix. *Meta-* is not a prefix. It's a combining form. A combining form is a linguistic element used in combination with another element to form a word, e.g., *bio-* equals life, *-graphy* equals writing, hence "biography". Neither element is a complete word in itself.' As openers went, even I could have done better.

'Okay,' said Aisling. She didn't know what point was being made either, still less care. Antonia waited for her to pencil her comment into the margin, but Aisling didn't seem to grasp what was required of her and looked about the table benignly, as though our faces constituted pleasant if unremarkable scenery. She may as well have been drifting down a river in a punt. Perhaps it was the lack of sleep.

'You should have used *para-*,' Antonia said. '*Para-* is a prefix, so you can append it to a complete word. Hence, in this case, it would be "paranotional". Which isn't a word either, obviously, but it's grammatically more accurate than "metanotional", as you've used.' Antonia had

185

been drinking so much black coffee lately that her teeth were marled brown.

'Thank you, Antonia,' Aisling said but still didn't reach for the pencil. We stared at it, lying there like a loaded pistol, willing Aisling to pick it up and put us out of our misery.

Faye swallowed tensely, the room so quiet we heard her ligaments wrench. My eyes made the sound of the drip of a tap every time I blinked. I tried to stop blinking. No good. Guinevere kept her head down, and Glynn, his mouth shut. It was entirely his fault, whether he admitted it or not. He had single-handedly engineered this crisis. *You stupid bitch,* he had spat at Antonia, introducing a different element, bursting open the cabin door, then storming off and leaving her to brazen it out on her own, humiliated in front of all of us.

Though it was possible he no longer recalled the incident, Antonia would never forget it. There had been something of the jack-in-the-box about her ever since. Our every word was construed as potentially antagonistic, an insinuation of her damaged status, another twist of the handle. *Did you shag Professor Glynn?* Wallop. Fuckhead, she had called me. The spring-loaded mechanism was getting tauter by the second. The leering head would explode across the table. It was only a question of time.

'Did you listen to a word I said?' Antonia demanded.

Aisling scratched at the powdery eczema coating the back of her hands. Her knuckles were bleeding, the blood pink and watery. Words tumbled into her as into a black hole when she was in that frame of mind. They met with no resistance, just kept falling, never to connect with their target. There was no point in even saying them. I don't know why Antonia couldn't see that. The two of them were caught in some sort of inversely proportionate closed energy system. The tenser Antonia got, the more languid Aisling became. She was sinking into her chair, melting into a pool of faded black fabric. Antonia shook her head. 'There's a name for people like you, Aisling,' she said carefully. She indicated the manuscript. 'People who write this sort of thing, dismissing the rules, abandoning the signposts.'

'And what might that be?' Aisling asked. 'What's the name for people like me?' So she had been listening all along.

Antonia flicked her blonde hair. 'Icarus,' she said. 'You're sailing too close to the sun. You are going to crash and burn like Icarus.'

Nothing. No reaction at all, not a flicker. The black hole had been reinstated. Antonia sat there looking at Aisling. Aisling sat there looking back. The rest of us held our breath and waited. Something bad was about to happen, as Faye would say, or Aisling, or Guinevere, or even myself. We were all primed for catastrophe by then. We could all see it coming. By leaving Antonia wounded, by cornering her, Glynn had forced her to this, to attack Aisling, who could least sustain it, who was sailing too close to the sun. What was it those poison-pen letters had warned him? *There is always a price.* But when had Glynn ever listened?

'Where were we?' he asked, but nobody answered him. Nobody said a word.

22

This boy is cracking up, this boy has broke down

'So what's going on?' I said to Guinevere after the workshop. It was with some difficulty that I had managed to separate her from the pack. They reluctantly agreed to go on ahead without her after she'd promised she'd be along soon. The second they rounded the corner out of sight, I steered her down the damp lane running alongside Bartley's. She had her back against the wall. 'What was all that about earlier?' I demanded. 'In the women's toilet?' She didn't like my tone.

'Nothing, Declan.' She looked down at her arm. I saw that I was still holding it, and let go. She massaged it as if I'd hurt her. It was a quarter to five. The setting sun was shining thinly upon the tips of things, picking out the sharp edges which had sprung up around us. There was no guarantee that the fine spell would hold.

'Why didn't you answer me when I asked you before the workshop what was wrong?'

'Jesus,' she said, 'you make it sound like I felt sick on purpose.'

'Right,' I said. 'Okay, fine. Just, you made me look like a complete dick in front of the others, that's all.' Fuckhead, Antonia had called me.

She blinked. 'Why are you being so obnoxious?'

I looked up at the sky, what was visible of it from the

narrow lane, and laughed in disbelief. 'Why am *I* being so obnoxious?'

She sighed as if I was wearing her out. 'Don't do this,' she said quietly. She was still massaging her arm.

'Do what?'

'You know.'

'No, I don't know. Tell me. Oh wait: you never tell me anything. Sorry, I forgot.' An oniony smell of sweat hovered on the air. I realised with a surprise that it was me.

The lane was littered with weeds and broken glass. Guinevere looked up and down the length of it in desperation, but there was nowhere for her to run, no one to appeal to for help. 'Why are you trying to upset me?'

'Why am *I* trying to upset *you*?'

'Yes, why are you being like this?'

'Why am *I* being like this?' It was like some sort of foreign-language exercise in pronouns.

'Stop it!' She had never raised her voice to me before.

No, something inside me said, *no, I will not stop.* 'Stop what?' I asked flatly, warming to my subject. A twisted life form had pierced the forest floor, a coiled stump of fern – primitive, flowerless, beckoning. My black thoughts extended their fronds around Guinevere. Spores hung all about us on the air.

'Listen to yourself, Declan,' she said in wonderment, her head tilted to one side as if she were reasoning with a rational human being, one possessed of empathy and kindness.

'No, *you* listen to *your*self.' An unspeakable resentfulness had overtaken me. I had never known its like.

Guinevere couldn't seem to register what she was dealing with and persisted in treating me like a grown-up. 'I think you should apologise to Antonia,' she advised me.

'*I* should apologise?' This, I could hardly credit.

'You're the one who suggested she'd shagged Professor Glynn.'

'So everything's my fault now?'

'That's not what I'm saying. Antonia is very upset about the whole thing, and I think you should have a quiet word with her. Sort things out before the situation escalates.'

I threw back my head and laughed again. 'Here we go.'

'I'm glad you find this so amusing.'

'Yeah, so am I.'

'There's no point in even talking to you.'

'If you say so.'

'You're doing it on purpose.'

'Doing what?'

'For fuck's sake!' she cried in frustration. She said, I said, she said, I said. It went on for ever. It was dark before we knew it. People were going about their business on the street beyond. You would think it was a normal evening like any other. Guinevere bit her bottom lip. My answers were just inversions of her questions, she complained, wiping away the first of the tears. I observed her as if she were trapped in a vacuum: mouth moving, no sound, a specimen in a jar.

'You seem to be enjoying this,' she noted.

'Dunno, am I?'

I was as good as lying at the bottom of a well by then, listening to the distant sounds of life going on above me. I had become a small man trapped inside a large man's suit of armour, too short to see out the eye slits. It is difficult to explain. Yes, extremely difficult to explain. Even looking back on it, it seems terribly remote, hardly me at all in fact, as if, no more than Aisling, I had temporarily drifted away from myself, leaving the whole show behind.

'What's wrong, Declan?' Guinevere implored me. 'Has something happened? You can tell me.'

'Dunno,' I mumbled again.

This was less than the truth. I was not good enough for Guinevere, and she, with her remarkable powers of perception, would see through me sooner or later. From the way she was now studying me, it was evident that this process had already begun. I had never attained my heart's desire before and had revealed myself, in the having of it, to be unworthy of it, undeserving. I had exposed myself as an essentially unsympathetic character. Cardinal sin in a novel, they tell me.

Guinevere's protestations continued undiminished, and unheeded. At one point she pummelled my chest to get my attention, and I wondered, in my abstract, sullen way, whether it was warped of me to find those punches arousing. Didn't matter any more, one way or the other. Talk to me, she kept insisting, as if such a thing were still possible. We had gone beyond all that. She said that I was being selfish, that I was being a selfish bastard. Who was I to disagree? The girl was shivering from head to foot. We had been standing in that dank lane for hours.

'So that's it then?' she finally asked after an extended period of silence had elapsed. Though she had phrased it as a question, I deliberately interpreted it as a statement.

'Okay,' I shrugged, like it was fine by me. 'If you're sure that's what you want.'

She sharply averted her face as if my breath reeked,

which it probably did. Then she started to cry again. I kept my hands in my pockets. Her tears were not the usual picturesque variety, I noted sourly. A blast of sea smell hit my nostrils, as pungent, as evocative, as childhood. I looked about for the source but could not identify it. Where was all this fatalism coming from? We were in Glynn terrain now.

'So here we are,' I said, and felt for one exhilarating moment that I was over her and that there would be another Guinevere. That she was one in a sequence of extraordinary women I would love, and who would love me. I must have been in shock. I was young then and had no comprehension of the significance of proceedings, no grasp yet that such encounters were unique and unrepeatable, instead regarding all that occurred as preludes to the main event. Life was an entity due to commence at some point in the future. That's what I used to think.

'Here we are,' I said again and felt that surge of liberty again. Fainter this time, I couldn't help noticing. It was a satisfying enough moment all the same. I wasn't confined to the muted surroundings of my own head, for once. I was living at last, sort of. Here we are, still standing, having come out the other side. I shouldn't say we. I was speaking for myself. Didn't ask Guinevere what was running through her mind at that juncture. Nothing good, by the looks of it.

She dried her tears and stared at the ground for some time. Those lashes of hers. So long. I wondered if they edged the objects she looked at, set things off like a picture frame. No wonder she wrote from such an elegant perspective.

'Are you happy now?' she asked me quietly.

When I did not reply, Guinevere turned and walked

down the lane to rejoin the civilised world. She held her head high and not once did she glance over her shoulder. I watched until she had left my sight. She had the most beautiful back.

On I blundered across the city without her, as if it meant nothing, as if there would be no consequences, as if I wasn't leaving tracks of blood in the snow. *There is always a price.* A good hour passed before it dawned on me that the scene in the lane with Guinevere conformed almost identically in spirit to one Glynn had written over a quarter of a century earlier in *Prussian Blue.* I laughed, but not for long. The specifics were different, but the dialogue was broadly the same: dismal, repetitive. The narrator had broken a girl's heart because he was a stupid bastard. Then he'd gone out on the batter.

There was a time I would have attributed these uncanny parallels to Glynn's unrivalled ability to distil the real world into prose, but that time was over. It was my behaviour that demanded a critical appraisal. I had internalised Glynn's imaginative landscape so thoroughly that I could no longer tell where he stopped and I began. 'You're worse than him,' Guinevere had said. I wasn't even aping the big man himself – it was worse than that: I was aping characters from his novels. And Glynn's novels never had happy endings. Everyone knew that.

I sat on my little soldier's bed and looked at my knees, viscerally regretting the absence of a trace of Guinevere in that room now that it was too late. A pillowslip she had slept on to press to my face, a towel still carrying the faintest hint of her scent. Should have thought of that. Should have thought of a lot of things. She had requested once to see where I lived, but her request had been denied. I hadn't wanted her to witness the room's meanness, as if she was the sort of girl who would think less of me for it, and so I had hidden it away from her like an embarrassing parent; an embarrassing, forsaken parent. A long slash of seagull shit streaked the window, calcium white and acidic.

Jaunty and shipshape, I had decided when I first laid eyes on that room. It was one of many lies I had to tell myself. Just like Van Gogh's sunny bedroom in Arles, I had affirmed as I'd looked around, forgetting that Van Gogh's painting was a work of optimism, not realism. No sign in it of the chaos he daily endured. His belongings all hanging neatly on pegs, as if that would suppress it. Same amount of pegs as objects to be hung. Not so much as a patch of shadow under the bed. Not even a speck of dust. No evidence of his demons at all. Where were they hiding? Under which loose floorboard, behind what crack in the plaster? Because they were there, alright, lying in wait for him. Who was he trying to fool? Himself, I suppose, most of all. Within one year of painting that cheerful yellow room, with its sturdy little bed and pillows for two, the artist had gone and topped himself.

'Alright Deco?' said Giz when he answered my knock on his door. He didn't seem in the least bit surprised to see me standing there. It was as if he'd been expecting me. 'How's it goin?' he asked, 'What's the story?' As if I would know. Me, who never wrote any story, me who never got past page five. Giz made sure before unhooking the security chain that I had money in my pockets this time, then he named his price.

I sat into his couch and smoked until I was juddering

from side to side when I closed my eyes, though my body was still as stone. Giz sucked lighter fluid through a balled-up sock. His bedsit was as grey as a rotten lung. I found myself gasping for breath all of a sudden and clawed at the armrest in panic, but it was no good. Giz was too far gone to notice or help. 'Are you happy now?' she had asked before turning her back on me. Are you happy now?

23

Lowry Lynch has horse's ears, Lowry Lynch has horse's ears

A bell was tolling on Front Square. Graduates filed out of the Examination Hall dressed in black gowns and tasselled mortarboards. Commencements. 'Look at them,' Antonia scoffed. Glynn was two hours late.

'Why are they called commencements when it's all coming to an end?' Faye wondered.

I had no idea either what I would do once the course was over. Only a few months left, and nothing to show for my time. Then what? Back to England? Back to the factory, empty-handed? I looked away from the window.

'What good will it do us anyway?' Aisling asked. 'What use is their stupid scrap of paper? How will that secure us a job?' It was an unexpectedly practical line of thought for Aisling. I'd never have guessed that such considerations entered her head. 'I don't want to end up on the dole,' she added. Her fears were met with silence. I hoped her parents were wealthy.

It was dusk before the lord of the prose finally materialised under the Arch. Don't know why we'd bothered waiting. A reluctance to go home, must have been. He made his way across the cobbles in our direction, roaring drunk yet still managing to keep a glad eye out for admirers. The graduates and their families had disbanded by then. Glynn was out of luck.

'Oh, the rotten bastard!' Antonia cried when he veered past House Eight and diverted to the Buttery. He had seen our five faces bearing down and thought the better of it. Antonia grabbed her coat and ran down the stairs, the others in close pursuit.

They had him surrounded by the time I arrived. He'd only made it as far as the side of the Dining Hall. Antonia was upbraiding him while the others stood at her side, silently lending their support. Glynn didn't like it one bit. He didn't appreciate being corrected by a shower of women. He growled and broke free of the arena of girls, then turned his terrible eyes on them. Red and white, they were; half mad. The girls instinctively drew back.

He panted fiercely at us through his nose, a bull working up to a charge, but then he winced sharply and tore at his ear. At first we thought a wasp had stung him. He shuddered and whimpered in an agonised paroxysm, clutching the side of his head, shambling about in a small circle, tripping over his own feet. Never had he looked more like a derelict.

The writer crumpled before our eyes, emitting a shocking moan. Aisling shook her head pleadingly, as if that would make it stop. I felt a bolt of terror that I would in good conscience describe as mortal, for Glynn, it appeared to me at that moment, had entered a realm beyond common mortal experience. Whatever afflicted him was invisible to the rest of us. There was nothing there, as far as we could see.

We formed an arc around his torment, stricken observers. No one could help him, no one knew what to do. That was the worst thing about it: we could only stare. The tears were stinging my eyes. Glynn's palm remained clamped to his ear, trying to shut out unwanted voices. The demons. They were here.

He finally straightened up and lowered his fist, holding it out like a conjuror for the big reveal, ensuring he had our full attention. His arm trembled with the strain of clenching his fingers so tightly. Glynn threw us a grisly leer – victorious, scornful – before flinging the contents of his hand away with a force that nearly knocked him off balance. A glimpse of outstretched fingers silhouetted against the electric-blue dusk, then his hand dropped to his side.

Glynn stood winded in our circle, half the man we knew him to be. He had exorcised his demon, cast out his succubus, with the terrifying complication that we had *seen* it. Something three-dimensional had shot from his fingers and fallen into the shrubbery. We had heard it land. I looked to the others. They too were transfixed. Glynn delivered a final jubilant scowl – he seemed to have taken pleasure in the whole macabre spectacle – before lurching down the ramp to the Buttery.

'Fuck,' I said when the double doors clattered shut behind him, 'what the hell was that?'

They didn't answer. I glanced at them again, pale blue and black-eyed in the dusk. Aisling was rotating the crystal amulet hanging from her neck, her fingers spider-spinning.

'What the fuck just happened?' I was worn out with petitioning them, sick of the sound of my own whine. Tiny wriggling sperm, big white ovum. Fuckhead, Antonia had called me. 'Jesus Christ, one of you. What did Professor Glynn just throw into the bushes? Aisling? Faye? Tell me.'

Guinevere inclined her head toward Aisling. This

motion was so slight and so slow that it was sinister in the twilight, a statue coming to life. What good murderesses they'd have made. They continued to ignore me, though it didn't appear deliberate, more that they'd tuned me out, which was worse. As if, like Glynn, they were now functioning on a different plane altogether, one on which I was no longer audible, so thoroughly had I been dismissed. I could have shoved the lot of them over in frustration. Down they'd have toppled in a sprawl of limbs, a heap of porcelain dolls.

The four girls descended on the shrubbery, stooping to work the bare brown bushes like a paddy field.

'Let's just go,' I urged them. 'You'll find nothing in the dark.' Of course they'd find something. They'd find everything. They missed nothing, those women. 'Jesus, come on. What's the point? It'll have escaped by now.'

Aisling straightened up sharply. 'It'll have *what?*'

'Go home, Declan,' said Guinevere. 'You're only impeding us.' It was the first time she'd addressed me since our break-up. *Are you happy now?*

The others kept their faces averted, and Aisling lowered her eyes and returned to her work. So they'd heard. They'd discussed the break-up behind my back. Don't know why that came as a surprise.

Their strained silence was punctured by a loud hiss. Faye stumbled out backwards from the shrubbery with a cry of pain. A small black sinewy creature darted along the base of the wall, snapping undergrowth in its wake. Aisling gasped in alarm. 'Your arm, Faye,' said Guinevere, 'it's bleeding.'

The girls crowded around to inspect the damage, what could be seen of it in the flicker of Antonia's lighter. Must have been the feral cat, they decided from the pattern of the claw marks. They'd named it Sylvia after their favourite author. You'd see it crouched in the shadows watching the outside world in fright, if you knew the right places to look. They'd taken to leaving food out and reporting on its appetite and general appearance. I'll bet they even made it feel special for a while, the unfortunate trembling mite. Who'd watch out for it when the course was over? That's what I wanted to know.

Because it was so slight, barely able to defend its corner, the girls had assumed that Sylvia was female, though the cat could as easily have been a young male, I once pointed out. They didn't hear me, so I'd said it again. Still no response. They'd moved on to more pressing matters. I should have thrown myself on my back and bawled it in frustration: 'This wretched suffering creature on which you take pity could just as easily be a young male!' They'd never have listened.

The group resumed their search. Faye poked around with her good hand, finding it difficult to accept that Sylvia could have done such a thing to her and making excuses for the animal. That was Faye all over. Didn't live in the real world, was unable to assimilate the idea of badness into her outlook. Got it, Antonia finally said without inflection, without her customary air of condescension. Night had fallen by then.

The girls climbed out of the shrubbery to examine their quarry, their skirts wet and clinging to their legs. On the palm of Antonia's outstretched hand lay a small curled trilobite. 'It's his hearing aid!' I stammered with relief, 'oh thank God for that!' but they'd tuned me out again. Faye would have to explain it all to me later, in that patient primary-school-teacher way of hers, and I would sit by her knee, listening and nodding attentively, obedient as a Labrador, as good as gold. I hoped. Go home, Guinevere had told me, you're only impeding us, and not one of them had contradicted her.

'I suppose we'd better bring it back to him,' Aisling said.

Antonia slowly tipped her palm, and Aisling caught the small salmon-pink plastic moulding in her cupped hands. 'He's all yours,' Antonia informed them. 'Go in there and tie his shoelaces. I'm washing my hands of him. Goodnight.'

She headed for the Nassau Street gate, shoulders thrown back in full Valkyrie mode. I watched her glide across the cobbles, steady as a ship on her stilettos. You could see why Glynn had fallen for her, all the same. No one could deny she had class. 'You have to admire her sometimes,' I conceded, turning back to the group, but they had already deserted me.

24

School for Scandal

I caught up with Antonia on the ramp to the Arts Block. She appraised me with an arched eyebrow. 'Look who it is,' she said without slowing her pace. Her causticity suited my frame of mind. I was in the mood for her.

'State of Professor Glynn,' I offered, believing it was a topic she'd rise to, but Antonia would not be drawn.

'Glynn is not a professor. That's an affectation he picked up in the States.'

'But it says *Professor Glynn* on his door in the English Department.'

'No it doesn't. Go back and check.'

We emerged onto Nassau Street and stood at the kerb, side by side with nothing to say to each other. A convoy of double-decker buses trundled towards us. Antonia was standing too close to the edge. There were so many buses, all of a sudden, that it became farcical. Just as it seemed a gap in the traffic might appear, another came heaving around the corner.

'Do you want to go for a drink?' I eventually asked. The screech of bus brakes drowned out my voice.

'What?' she shouted over the racket.

'Can I buy you a drink?' I shouted back.

The roar of bus engines died down like a drop in the wind, and all was suddenly hushed, as hushed as it had been within the college walls, as if the street itself waited on Antonia's answer. She appraised me with her arched eyebrow once more.

'Certainly,' she replied when she was good and ready. 'Certainly, you can buy me a drink, *Declan*.' She enunciated my name with pointed scepticism as if, no more than Glynn's title, she knew it to be a sham. There was something about her cynicism that endeared her to me then. She made herself easy to describe.

She led me to a cellar wine bar just past McGonagles, knowing full well that I could not afford such a place. I could see her smiling away to herself, enjoying my discomfort. She had style, Antonia. Style is everything, Glynn had told us, reeling off the names of the great prose stylists, urging us to devote our lives to them.

'I've never been here before,' I said after she'd ordered a bottle of Bordeaux. This information was of no interest to Antonia. She did not acknowledge it. They had seated us at a table in the corner. Her lipstick left a waxy cerise print on the rim of her wine glass. This pattern was repeated on the filter of her cigarette, a set of matching tableware. 'Sorry,' I said when I accidentally kicked her ankle. I glanced under the table when she registered no annoyance, and saw that it was only her handbag.

'I didn't realise Professor Glynn wore a hearing aid,' I mentioned. I couldn't think of anything else to say. It was that, or sit in silence.

'Not any more he doesn't, apparently. The man isn't prepared to listen to us any longer. He made that perfectly clear when he chucked the dirty little contraption into the bushes. A metaphorical act, I suppose you would call it.' Antonia gazed over my shoulder to see who else was in the room. No one took her fancy, and she returned her attention to me. 'What's all this fuss between you and Lady Guinevere? Break her heart, did we?'

'Oh,' I said. 'That.'

'Yes,' she said. '*That.*'

'What about you and Professor Glynn?'

Antonia shrugged and knocked back her glass of wine. He had called her Grendel behind her back a few weeks ago. 'Where's Grendel gotten too?' he'd asked in the pub, and we'd burst into laughter. Well, only I had burst into laughter – the girls had looked at the floor – but the point was, we all knew who he meant. Just one of our number fit that description. I'd felt sorry for Antonia then, and stopped laughing. I'm sure she'd have appreciated my pity.

'I suppose we have to make allowances for Professor Glynn,' I said. 'In his condition,' I added.

Antonia topped up my glass and refilled hers, emptied it, refilled it again. 'Jesus Christ, you make him sound like he's ancient.'

'Professor Glynn is ancient.'

'He's fifty-six.'

'Exactly.'

Too late I realised my colossal blunder. Age was a delicate matter amongst women who were past it. Antonia's mouth momentarily lost its footing, but it quickly regained its balance and she threw some more wine into it. 'So fifty-six is ancient now, is it, Declan?' She beamed that tight smile of hers across the table at me. *Ping.*

'I suppose it's not that old.' My father was dead at fifty-two. 'It's not that old at all, really, when you think about it.'

'How old do you think I am?'

'You told us how old you are.'

'Yes, but how *old* do you think I am? Do you think I am *old?*'

'No. Of course not.'

'Liar.'

She bent over to pick up her handbag, clipping the wine bottle with an elbow. It toppled over, and a broad ruby stain surged across the white linen towards me. I lurched to escape its path. This was an overreaction on my part. The tablecloth absorbed the spillage. I set the bottle upright. 'Sorry,' I said, though I wasn't the one who had knocked it. I threw a napkin down to conceal the stain, as if it were somehow shameful, which it somehow was. 'Shit, I'm really sorry.'

Antonia signalled to the waiter for a replacement bottle. 'Doesn't matter. It was nearly empty.'

The second bottle arrived. The waiter uncorked it and poured. 'I don't have the money to pay for this,' I said quietly when he was gone.

'I know. I will pay for it.' She stubbed out her cigarette. 'I will pay for it,' she repeated grimly. *There is always a price.*

The use of portent and double meaning featured prominently in Antonia's prose, as did the persistently bitter tone, imprinting itself on every word that flowed from her pen, as ingrained as her accent. I shifted uncomfortably in my chair and kicked her handbag a third time. 'Sorry,' I said again.

'For God's sake, stop apologising.' She excused herself to the bathroom, taking her handbag with her.

She was gone a long time. She was gone for so long, in fact, that I wondered whether she'd done a runner, leaving me with a bill she knew I couldn't pay. A master of plot twists and revenge tragedies. It was her sheer deviousness that gave her short stories their bite. I could all but hear her laughing down Grafton Street as she click-clacked away from the scene of the crime.

I was almost surprised when she returned to the table, her face freshly powdered, her mouth painted in, the lipstick so bright it drained the colour from her skin. 'What?' she said when she caught me taking it in.

'Nothing.'

'What?' she said again. 'Why are you looking at me like that?'

'Nothing. You look tired, that's all.'

Antonia shook her head in disbelief and finished off another glass of wine. 'Christ, you really know how to make a woman feel good about herself, don't you?'

'I'm sorry,' I said before I could help myself.

She slammed the empty glass down on the table. 'Stop fucking apologising. I am not a charity case.' She lit another cigarette. 'Why do you hate me?' she suddenly demanded. This, out of nowhere.

'Excuse me?'

'Even the way you look at me. You make this face. You're making it now.'

'I don't hate you, Antonia.' I was stunned that she cared what I thought of her. Stunned she was aware I even had an opinion.

'I'm not the only one to have noticed. The others agree with me.'

'You've been discussing this with the others?' Guinevere had lost her temper over it once. 'Stop talking about her,' she had snapped. 'You're always talking about her, Declan. Haven't you noticed that? You never

206

stop bitching about Antonia. Why can't you just leave her alone? You don't like her, she doesn't like you, so just forget about it.'

'She doesn't like me?' I had probed. 'Did she actually say that? Were those her exact words?' etc. Fuckhead, she had called me. Guinevere cursed and warned me to drop the subject.

Antonia allowed her head to loll forward into her hands. It was a display worthy of Aisling. I had never seen her this drunk before. She seemed to be laughing, but I couldn't say for certain. I was confronted with the neat white strip of scalp along her parting and was surprised to note that she appeared to be a natural blonde. I had expected grey. 'I used to be a looker in my day,' she said apropos of nothing, her voice muffled under her hair.

'I don't doubt it.'

I couldn't imagine Antonia young. I categorically couldn't see it. There was no ghost of lapsed girlhood in her, no inner child, the opposite of Glynn, who lacked an inner adult. She'd have been one of those prim little children he'd written about, no child at all but a miniature adult, silently making note of all that took place in the grown-up world, Mummy's little double agent.

'No really, Declan, I used to be considered something of a beauty. The boys were all after me. Shame I didn't have the good sense to see it at the time. And now look at me.'

Aw Jesus. She caved in on herself before my horrified eyes like a rotten roof, like a collapsed grave, like a – oh God, she reached across the table for my hand. The desperation with which she seized my wrist was dreadful. She was going to cry. She was crying. She deteriorated into a sack of shuddering bones. I don't know why women, with all their intuition, persist in believing that displays of vulnerability will stimulate the protective instinct in a man. All they provoke is the desire to run. Glynn has written illuminatingly on the subject more than once. *You stupid bitch,* he had called her. Antonia's weeping, intended to draw me instead repelled me, but she couldn't see my reaction through her tears.

'You're still a beauty,' I said, and clamped a hand to her shoulder, a dog giving the paw. 'You're still a . . . a looker.' That word. So dated. It only made things worse. I stared at my hand, fastened to her shoulder like a lump of meat, and wondered how to retract it without exacerbating the situation. Poor Grendel. She angrily shrugged my hand off, God bless her, and knocked back the red wine, what was left of it. A thin black line had formed on her lips, a ridge of high-tide seaweed.

She opened her purse and tossed a crumpled twenty onto the table with her usual level of disdain. 'Let's get out of here,' she said, and I was only too happy to oblige. I helped her into her coat and bundled her up the stairs before she got a chance to change her mind.

The cold fresh air of South Anne Street was a salve. A public phone in a row of phone boxes was ringing out. Antonia took my arm, and I escorted her, click-clack, to Dawson Street to put her in a taxi. When one pulled up, I opened the door and stood back gallantly, every inch the gentleman. 'Get in, get in, for God's sake,' she said, gesturing impatiently at the back seat, as if I was holding the whole street up. I hesitated for a second before doing what I was told. I could hardly refuse her. I could hardly refuse her in that state. That is what I tell myself.

25

Castle Rackrent

Her house had a name. I can no longer put my finger on it. Something genteel and Anglo. I would have expected no less of her. I can see the black font in my mind's eye to this day, but not the word itself, painted in duplicate in block capitals like a trespassing sign, warning me as I passed through her twin gateposts to turn back, turn back, but did I listen? She had me going by then.

In the back of the taxi she had linked my arm as before, and held it for the duration of the journey against the heft of her breast, easing herself towards me, a warm pliant mass, a long thigh pressed to mine, until I felt a longing for her that almost pained me. We travelled in silence. Antonia kept her eyes on the road ahead, but when I glanced at her face I saw the slight smile at the corner of her lips. She was pleased with her night's work.

She paid for the taxi, and it pulled away, leaving the two of us facing each other across a deserted street. A great, still moon was hanging in the sky, though it was not still at all but hurtling through the glittering wastes faster than I had the wit to understand. That the moon was serene was yet another delusion. Had I thought that, or read it in Glynn? 'Long way from home, eh soldier?' Antonia teased. The crunch of gravel on her driveway delineated the point at which the mark had been irrevocably overstepped. I found I couldn't turn back.

'Beware of the Dog' read the sign mounted above the brass letterbox on her lacquered door. Antonia laughed when she caught me looking at it. 'There is no dog, silly,' she said, shaking her head at my naivety in falling for that one. She swung the door open and pulled me inside.

I fucked her first on the stairs and then in her bedroom. I fucked her as many times as she wished to be fucked. Neither one of us was willing to admit defeat first, neither one prepared to lose face. She issued instructions and guided me into positions as if this tutoring role were the prerogative and duty of the older woman, as if she had something to teach me, and I had something to learn. If I was considerably rougher with her than I should have been, Antonia did not flinch, but took it on the chin, being the kind of woman who was pathologically unable to admit that you were hurting her, even if it killed her. Two could play at that game.

As the night wore on, I grew progressively more resentful. 'Fuck,' I remember crying up to the ceiling in sheer frustration and regret.

'That's it,' she gasped, throwing back her head, displaying her long white neck, which I instinctively placed my hand on, marvelling at its fragility, at how easy it would have been to throttle her. *You stupid bitch. Are you happy now?* I didn't really understand the grace of youth until Antonia drained it out of me, tainting it with knowledge of what it was to have lost youth, or to have never possessed it in the first place. It was a party she had watched all her life from the outside. And now the party was over.

Women only fall asleep in your arms in novels.

Antonia wanted to talk about her broken marriage, as if it were a subject I could cast light on. What did she think I could possibly say to her? I just kept nodding. She had married too young, she explained. Barely eighteen. Straight out of school. I nodded. She'd subsequently felt she'd missed out on so much. She had never slept with a boy my age when she was a girl my age. Edmund had been so much older than her, you see. I nodded.

'So that's why you fucked me. To see what you were missing.'

'I burgled your bank of youth,' she smiled. I didn't think it was funny. 'Oh don't be like that,' she cajoled, marching her fingers up the centre of my chest like a little man. I couldn't stand childish games in a grown woman and rolled onto my side to get away from her. There was a framed photograph of a blonde girl on her bedside table. I picked it up to change the subject.

'Is this you?'

'No,' she said, 'that's my daughter. She lives with Edmund now.'

I didn't know what to say. It had never occurred to me that Antonia could be a mother. She had never mentioned her child before. I put the photograph back on the table.

A terrible confession followed. It must have been four in the morning by then, no sign of it yet getting bright, no assurance of an end in sight. Antonia had just returned from the bathroom, and she climbed back into bed, shivering with the cold. Her eyes were enormous in the darkness. She rested her head in the crook of my arm. 'I've never slept with anyone other than my husband,' she said in a small voice. Then she started to cry.

I stroked her hair. Stroked it mechanically, back and

forth, a windscreen wiper. It seemed like the right thing to do, but it didn't feel like the right thing to do. Antonia was too grown up for me to stroke her hair. We would have to sit across from each other in class every Wednesday. 'We must never tell anyone about this,' she whispered, glancing up at me.

'No,' I agreed vehemently.

She was feeling emotional because she hadn't slept well last night. At least, I think that's what she was trying to tell me. She was feeling emotional, she said, she hadn't slept well last night, but she didn't use the conjunction 'because'. I don't know why she was feeling emotional. I didn't know what this term 'feeling emotional' meant, exactly, as it applied to her. I knew what it meant to me – it meant the desire to punch a wall – but it appeared to denote something altogether different to Antonia, something spongy and discoloured and spreading that would eventually get the better of her, a bruise on an apple. She also seemed to think that I would empathise, maybe even attempt to help. Where did she get such notions? Seeing as she was older than the rest of us, I had taken it for granted that she was better equipped to take care of herself, but it turned out her seniority made her even more vulnerable. The gradient increased as your resources diminished. And me assuming life got easier with every passing year. Me, in fact, counting on it.

'So you didn't shag Glynn then?'

'No, I didn't shag Glynn, as you so elegantly phrase it.'

'So why did he call you a stupid bitch?'

Antonia winced at the recollection. 'Letters,' she admitted eventually. 'I sent him some anonymous letters.

We had a relationship briefly, but he went back to his wife. I was terribly hurt at the time. He never knew who'd written them until I confessed in the pub that night. Shouldn't have opened my mouth.'

I stopped stroking her hair and sat up, dislodging her from the crook of my arm. 'You were the one sending those letters?'

'Jesus, Declan, doesn't anyone tell you anything?'

'No,' I said. 'They don't.'

Antonia looked unwell by the time the bleak dawn light came seeping through her bedroom curtains. It was obvious from the way she kept fiddling with her hair, pulling it forward over her face, that she was embarrassed to be seen in that state. I couldn't blame her. Her hands, when she sat on the edge of the bed to light a cigarette, were shaking. The sight reminded me of the prelude to one of my mother's rages. Wells of unhappiness so deep, so terminal, that they could never be appeased. The massive, obstructive fact of my mother's disappointment in life was distressing to the point that I had started to hate being near her. Which was little better in practice than hating the woman herself, after all that she had done for me.

I stopped responding to Antonia's words. I stopped nodding. Women want to talk when you least feel able. At first she kept offering sentences that trailed off, leaving gaps for me to jump in and assert the opposite. 'This has been a huge mistake, Declan . . .' she murmured, watching my face closely, inviting me to disagree, to extend some reassurance. I didn't open my mouth. 'No, really, it was all my fault . . .', 'I'm far too old for you . . .', 'I should have known better . . .' I didn't beg to differ.

Next thing she was telling me that her unhappiness

was my fault, that I was inconsiderate, heartless, cruel – that I had *used her*. All she wanted was not to feel reject- ed for once in her shitty life. Was that so much to ask? That's when I got up and left. I stood up and dressed quickly and walked out of her bedroom, feeling as guilty as a four-year-old boy, but there you have it. Knowing with every step that I was fucking up again, but without exactly understanding why, and without exactly caring.

'That's right!' she was shouting after me, standing at the top of the stairs in her nightdress, clinging to the banisters like a madwoman. How much smaller she was without her heels. Almost ordinary. Almost plain. 'Run away!' she screamed. 'You just run away!' My mother's words to the letter. Uncanny. Antonia had probably learned them from her mother, who had in turn learned them from her mother before her. Women were never happy. They didn't want to be happy. They deliberately pushed all your buttons, manipulated you into acting the bollocks, then derived a perverse satisfaction out of watching you crack and seeing their blackest suspicions confirmed. Fuckhead, she had called me.

Antonia's face up there on the landing was monstrous with disgust and triumph, as if she had finally tricked me into revealing my true colours, and those colours were even uglier than she could have hoped for, *You stupid bitch. Are you happy now?* I pulled on my shoes and grabbed my jacket from the floor. I could hardly bear to look at her.

She hurled a book down the stairs as I undid the latch. How symbolic. 'Tinker,' she hissed. 'Dirty little tinker.' I slammed her lacquered door behind me. Beware of the Dog. Was it then that my hatred for Antonia peaked? No, I was only getting started.

26

Good girl Sharon, that was A1

The street lights were still glowing orange. It was about half six in the morning, judging by the grubby light. I'd left my watch behind on Antonia's bedside table. No turning back. I crunched across the gravel driveway delineating the point at which the mark had been irrevocably overstepped and shut the wrought iron gate behind me. We had left it askew the night before in our haste.

I did not glance up at her bedroom window. It's the one thing a man's supposed to do – look over his shoulder to steal a last lingering glimpse of his beloved, displaying how he cannot get his fill of her. Antonia would be watching for the glance, or watching for its omission, rather, to add to her slate. She'd be standing by that window in her white nightdress like a ghost, her ashen face more ashen behind the pane of glass, eyes boring into the back of my skull until I disappeared from view. It was a long, straight street.

I pulled up my collar and tucked in my chin. A few flakes of snow drifted down, grey as the cloud that had issued them. My empty stomach sucked and squelched with every step, a drain being unblocked with a plunger. The last of the street lights petered out as it grew bright, if you could call it bright. I wouldn't. I reached for a stick of gum but the packet was empty. I crumpled it in my fist and jammed it into a hedge.

Antonia's road intersected with a thoroughfare. A general feeling of flintiness loured about the place, a prevailing lack of comfort. The pavement was as perishing as compacted ice. It was hard on the bones. The buses weren't up and running yet. I did not know that part of the city. I was as lost as I had ever been.

The second I rounded the corner out of Antonia's sight, I had the most unbelievable headache. I crouched over by a pebbledash wall and cradled the crown of my head in my hands, pleading for it to pass, practically praying, thinking at one point that something had burst, or was about to. *There is always a price.* Eventually, the headache lifted, and I floundered on as best I was able. The odd car was out on the road by then, windscreen frosted and exhaust pipe pluming. How people found the will to leave their beds at that godforsaken hour to climb into frozen metal machines, I did not know. It was beyond me.

Any self-respecting man would have retreated to an early house, but it was pity I was after, not oblivion. My thoughts alighted on Guinevere. She was their natural destination. I had loved her before I met her. She was in every book, every song, every poem. It was not too late for us, I felt certain in my desperation, and was buoyed up by the conviction. I would place my aching head on her lap and beg forgiveness. The prospect made me walk faster. A car screeched past with a broken fan belt. I would present myself at her door and make a full confession, then beseech her to absolve me. It was too much responsibility to place on a young girl's shoulders, but I didn't let that stop me.

The threat of snow had passed by the time I made it to her door. I had been walking for maybe two hours, half-starved and smelling of another woman. What a relief it was to turn the corner onto her familiar cul-de-sac, those sleepy redbrick cottages with their net curtains and pink geraniums. No crunch of irrevocable gravel, no twin block-capital trespassing signs. 'I love you,' I was chanting as I stumbled along the cracked uneven paving leading to her door. 'I love you, I love you, oh I love you, my love.' Guinevere's curtains were drawn.

The black cat from the house next door displayed itself archly behind the glass, as if it were the finest merchandise in the city's finest shop window. I rapped on Guinevere's door with the brass knocker. I gave it a good clatter. It took a few goes to rouse her. Her bedroom was at the back. I was finding it difficult to contain my excitement. When she finally answered the door, she looked dismayed to find me standing on her doorstep. It was not the reaction I'd been hoping for.

'Declan,' she said. Why was she whispering?

I rushed forward, but the door was not opened to me. Guinevere held it fast. 'What are you doing here?' she wanted to know, 'at this hour? God almighty, go home.' She was wearing her powder-blue dressing gown, and not much else besides.

I tried to get a hold of her waist to pull her to me but she back-stepped out of my grasp. 'Go home, Declan,' she warned me again, and tried to close the door. I jammed in the foot before she got it shut. 'Jesus,' she whispered in exasperation. Her eyes had a raw look. She had been crying. For a sickening moment I wondered whether Antonia had phoned her. *You stupid bitch. There is always a price.* But Guinevere didn't have a phone. I reached for her hand, but she wouldn't let go of the door.

'Oh my beautiful girl, I'm so sorry,' I blurted. 'I'm so sorry for everything. I've been a selfish bastard, and a stupid one, but I love you so much. I'll never hurt you again. Let's give it another go. Please don't shake your head at me like that.'

I attempted to kiss her through the chink in the door, but she averted her face. I groaned with the tender agony of it. There was a movement in the gloom behind her: I froze. She wasn't alone in there. I craned my neck to get a look over her shoulder. Emerging from her bedroom, and craning his neck to get a look at me, was Glynn.

'Oh sweet Jesus,' I said.

Guinevere glanced over her shoulder and saw Glynn standing there, the two of us squaring up to each other like dogs. She gasped and turned back to me. 'Declan, please,' she pleaded, but what was there to say? I looked at her, then at Glynn in the shadows, then back at her, as if doing some exercise for my focal length, though it was my brain that lacked flexibility, not my eyesight. They did not belong on the same visual plane. Ariel and Caliban. 'Oh sweet Jesus,' I said again.

Guinevere started talking rapidly, tears rolling down her cheeks in panic. Glynn skulked at the back of the cottage in his vest and kacks, letting the girl defend him, the craven bollocks. I didn't take my eyes off the prick for so much as one second. The prick didn't take his eyes off me. Everything had become abstract and disconnect-ed in my rage. Guinevere was saying his words, but in her voice. He was the ventriloquist, and she was his doll, propped up on his knee, doing his bidding. 'He needed me,' she was imploring me, *I wanted her, so I took her.*

'He was in crisis,' *I manipulated her into bed.* 'You didn't see the state he was in last night,' *I pulled every trick in the book, bud.* 'It's delicate, Declan.' *Now shag off home, son, can't you see we're busy?* Guinevere seemed to be trying to convince herself as much as anyone.

'Stop talking!' I shouted when I could bear it no longer. Guinevere saw what was going to happen next and slammed the door in my face before I could go in there and break the fucker's neck for him. It was the wall I drove my fist into. I smashed it into one of her red bricks and screamed as the shockwaves ripped through my frame. I sank down on my hunkers with the pain, clutching my wrist with my good hand, holding it to my chest like a wounded bird. I could hear them arguing inside. I like to think that Guinevere wanted to rush out to help me, but that Glynn wouldn't hear of it. That's what I like to think. I am entitled to my opinions. A rivulet of blood trickled down my forearm. I didn't know what to do with myself. So I started laughing. Mad, hysterical, unhinged laughing, echoing up and down the narrow cul-de-sac. It was a trick I had learned from Aisling.

Are you happy now? Guinevere had wanted to know. I pushed her letterbox open. 'Yes,' I screamed into the rectangular vault, 'yes I am Yes!'

27

De Profundis

Giz cleared his sinuses when he saw my smashed-up
fist. No 'Hate tha,' no 'State a ya,' no 'Fucken spa,' just
that plunging sound from the depths of his nasal cavities, a mixture of approval and recognition. 'Let me in,'
I said nervously, half-expecting to be turned away even
there.

He did not immediately respond but stood there
regarding his own knuckles, what was left of them,
gnarled and stunted as a pit bull's muzzle and pocked
with tattooed melanomas. I had a long way to go. There
was a long way down. Giz cleared his sinuses once more
before stepping back to admit me. His stack of television
sets was gone.

All day I had wandered around town on my own, all
day, all day, it went on for months, not knowing what
else to do with myself, not knowing where else to go, so
I went nowhere. Down the windy north quays, around
the courts, through the hilly cluster of streets riddling
Stoneybatter; nowhere. It seemed at one point that the
sun might break through – there was a concentration of
lemony light in the southern sky, then a sun shaft
beamed down, an escape hatch to a better world – I
stopped to watch, pinning my hopes on it, placing bets
with the Devil. But the clouds steamrolled in and sup-

pressed it, a crushed rebellion. The sunrays were hauled off and shot. The street became flat and oppressive once more as the sky darkened to silver, steel, and finally iron. I started on my rounds again.

When Glynn had emerged from Guinevere's bedroom, it had physically hurt. There'd been a sundering in my core, a tooth torn from its socket, leaving an unfamiliar hole behind, a hole which, though small, became the throbbing centre of my being. I couldn't stop exploring the aching cavity that had opened in her wake. It commanded every drop of my attention. 'Now you know how it feels,' she might have said to me, were she that type of girl.

I tried to stuff a shop-bought corned-beef sandwich down my throat as if posting a letter but ended up gagging on my tears. I ducked down a side lane to hide my contorted face. *Giz woz ere* was sprayed on the piss-stinking, slime-glossy wall. My friend, I thought wildly, and looked around for him, grinning like a maniac at this unexpected reprieve. I was clutching at straws.

Vast swathes of the city seemed darker than usual that night, as if there'd been a power cut, though the street lights burned. The air was draining the light out of things, I decided, just as Antonia had drained the light out of me and Glynn had drained the light out of Guinevere, the filthy rotten bastard. I was pleased with my pathetic fallacy, if nothing else. I hoped to find one of them waiting outside the flat on Mountjoy Square, wanting to talk. Either of them would have done me, even Antonia. Even Glynn, for the love of God. Anything but sit alone on my soldier's bed looking at my knees. The emptiness of the steps leading up to the front door was another blow. Giz's light shone through his nailed-up blanket, the moth holes twinkling like constellations.

His complexion was as ashen as Antonia's had been at dawn, except that Giz's face was faintly luminous, like the static afterglow of a television screen, and faintly marine, the milky-grey of a bottom feeder. His eyelids were inflamed, two blisters. Would you even call him a man, I speculated as I took my usual seat and waited for him to spread out his wares, which he kept in a rusty Jacob's Cream Crackers tin divided into cubbyholes. The tin was almost empty. His prices had been hiked.

He moved about the bedsit in an agitated state, barely five foot five. A man or a boy? Boy or a man? I had no idea how old Giz was. Anywhere between sixteen and thirty. He still bore the hallmarks of the local children – pallid, chilblained, puffy-eyed – but he increasingly resembled a pensioner. That stiff pigeon walk of his was getting stiffer. His joints were seizing up. A comfort, somehow, knowing that others were worse off than you. Pain was pounding through my mangled fist to the beat of my heart. I wished he'd hurry up.

'Wha?' he demanded, catching me staring.

'Nothing.'

'Wha?' he demanded again.

'Nothing,' I asserted again.

He flexed the tendons in his neck, then shook his head to indicate he'd let it go, this once. I watched him roll a joint and wondered when he'd last washed his hands. He had started to smell like that boy in school who nobody would sit beside, that mangy boy from the bad family who had no friends. It was the rank tang of ingrained dirt. There was a cold sore on his mouth, a big crusty scab. Giz handed me the joint and a tab. It was all that was left in the tin. I gave him all that was left in my pocket. He sat into his armchair and started tinkering about with a piece of tinfoil and a lighter, looking more boy than pensioner again, with that intent frown of concentration on his face.

'Whatcha making?' I asked, and then, 'Oh.' He was rolling up his sleeve.

There was something wrong with his forearm. It was swollen like a ham, but unevenly swollen, lumpy. I swung my head around and fixed my eyes on the empty space where his stack of television sets had been. I took my medicine and smoked steadily until it seemed the sofa was sliding towards the empty space, or the empty space was sliding towards the sofa. I shivered. My bowels had turned to ice. My stomach had sprouted teeth. I wanted to get up and leave but was scared my exit might antagonise Giz. You never knew what would trigger his rage, you never knew what would send him rampaging. So I sat there, quiet as a mouse, smiling probably, or trying to, demonstrating that I was good. I must have fallen asleep for a few seconds. I had been dreaming of ants.

'Bleedin perished,' Giz whispered.

'Plug in the heater,' I whispered back.

Where was the heater? It was missing, same as his television stack and collection of video nasties. All gone. His communion photo lay face down on the carpet beneath a chipped Toyota hubcap. Giz's skin was so clammy, so pale by then, that his freckles looked black in comparison, as if they'd been spattered onto him by the wheel of a passing car. He slumped forward in his armchair and held the flame of his lighter to the leg of the table.

'What the fuck are you doing?'

He sniffed. 'Bleedin perishing in here.' The varnish was flaring black.

'But Giz, that's–' Dangerous, I was going to say, but it seemed a bit late for that. He was shivering too hard to keep the flame applied to the table leg anyway. His body seemed not to be shaking itself but shaken by another agency, such was the force of it. The lighter flew out of his hand, and he gave a little cry of protest.

The detritus on the table juddered as if there were a poltergeist in the room. My ashtray slid off the armrest, landing upside down on the floor. Blood was trickling down Giz's chin. The scab on his cold sore had cracked. I sat there in confusion, taking it all in. Then – slowly, so as not to alarm him – I reached across the sofa to lay a steadying hand on his arm. My good hand closed around a rattling humerus, thin as the leg of the table he'd been trying to set alight. Giz recoiled violently from my touch.

'Get off of me,' he spat, though I hadn't been on him. 'Fucken puff,' he added, a quiver of disgust contorting his bleeding mouth.

'I'm not a puff.'

'I seen ya lookin at me. Don't try an deny it. I fucken *seen* ya.'

Oh Jesus, his forearm was rupturing. A septic fissure was splitting his skin. Something toxic was breaking through his flesh. It was red and yellow inside. I sat rooted to my seat. Giz had no sense of how wretched he had become. He did not grasp that if I were a bleedin puff, the last man I would touch was him.

His spasm abruptly subsided. He sank, head thrown back, limbs splayed, star-shaped on the armchair. Two crescents of white showed between his eyelids. I stared at him, my mouth as far agape as it would open. Was he dying? Was he dead? I couldn't take my eyes off him, terrified at the same time that his eyeballs would roll into place and he'd lash out at me for gawping.

'Giz?' I asked hesitantly, still whispering, as if some third party were present in the room, some prison warden, some dungeon keeper, behind whose back I might manage – were I stealthy enough – to make covert contact with my old friend. I was throwing pebbles up at his window, trying to wake him without rousing the house. 'You alright there, Giz?'

It seemed important to keep using his name, in case I had become as unfamiliar to him as he had become to me. 'Giz,' I whispered, louder now, 'Wake up, it's Declan. Deco. From upstairs.'

Repeating his name did nothing to summon him from the catatonic state. *Giz woz ere,* but not any more. Jesus, fucking *answer,* I wanted to scream before it was too late. Too late for what? I didn't know. I didn't know yet.

There was a whirring noise in the far corner, followed by a familiar mechanical clunk. The bedsit was plunged into darkness. The electricity meter had run out.

Giz did not react. I couldn't hear him breathe. I held my breath to listen for his. Nothing. Just the sound of a poor old dog howling away the night, the groan of a bus labouring up the square.

'Giz?' I whispered yet again.

Silent as the grave.

I was pleading with him by then, begging him to become Giz again, and not this awful lifeless changeling. I tried to make out his star shape in the darkness. I blinked and strained my eyes at his armchair, or at the spot I reckoned contained his armchair, because I was

225

entirely disorientated by then, had entirely lost my bearings, could barely tell up from down. The part of the room at which I stared remained the blackest. It was so black, in fact, that I got it into my head that it wasn't Giz at all. That thing which had split open his arm had been unleashed by the darkness and was taking form. It was right there in the room beside me. I could have reached out and touched it.

I tried to stand up but was unable to move, whether from fright or intoxication, I cannot say. My limbs pegged me to the sofa like a tent. I heard myself whimper, the sound loud and glandular in my ears. My head was issuing dogmatic instructions. Don't make any noise, it warned me. It'll hear you, and then it'll get you. It'll get you, and then it'll hear you. So don't make any noise.

'It's the tab,' I managed to say out loud, a eureka moment.

Hearing myself speak fulfilled some normalising function, and I propelled myself to my feet. From that elevation, a slit of white was visible under Giz's door, welcoming as a landing strip. Beyond it was the sagging corridor, the old carpet, electric light. If I could just make it to the door.

I lunged toward the light and collided with his coffee table. An almighty clatter as his wares crashed to the floor. 'Careful now,' warned my head, 'You'll wake it.'

I listened, my head cocked to one side like a bird. Not a whisper of breath out of him. I was hardly breathing myself. I had no notion of where Giz was presently located. He could have been hanging from the ceiling, for all I knew. I took another tentative step toward that three-foot-long chink of light, worried it would startle and take flight at any sudden movements. The thing to do was creep up without it noticing. That was the thing to do.

Something split in two underfoot with a loud brittle crack; I braced, ready for a hand to snatch my ankle. There were objects scattered about the floor that hadn't been there when the light was on. They scuttled around the room like rats. 'It's okay,' I assured myself, 'This isn't happening.' The one thing that I could be certain of was that Giz was seeing worse. If I was caught in the ninth level of Hell, he was trapped in the Inferno itself.

The floor lurched, and I lost my footing. The bar of light beneath the door started to ascend. Smoothly and evenly, it rose higher, as if we were descending in an old-fashioned elevator cage. 'Aw Jesus no,' I whispered. The bedsit was sinking into the basement.

A wild thrashing broke out behind me. I hurled myself at the bar of white and miraculously connected with the door. I did not expect it to open, but open it did, flooding a benediction of light over me. I was all but crying by then.

The arc of light from the corridor did not extend as far as Giz's armchair, just to his runners, which were no longer glaringly white as of old. He was flipping about like a landed fish. At least he wasn't dead. I pulled his door shut and, to my shame, held the lever of the handle in place with my good hand, just in case, God forbid, he tried to come after me.

When all fell quiet inside, as it quickly and ominously did, I crept upstairs to my room and got into the bed without undressing. A full day and a half without sleep, yet I was scared to close my eyes. I couldn't lie facing the wall because ghouls seeped out of the corner as soon as my back was turned, and I couldn't lie facing the corner because hands stretched out of the wall. I couldn't go downstairs because Giz, what was left of him, was waiting, and I couldn't stay in the bedroom because Giz, or whoever he was now, was on his way up to get me. I propped myself upright on pillows and sat facing the door.

At some point during the night, the sound of breaking glass roused me. I opened my eyes with a gasp. My light was still on. The room was empty. People were shouting, chanting. It was coming from outside. Not outside my door, but outside the building, down below on the street. It sounded like an angry mob. An angry mob, of all things, out in the dead of night baying for blood, like something from a different century. My imagination was getting carried away with itself. It was going to town. Jesus, you're worse than Aisling, I told myself, trying to make a joke out of the whole thing. When that didn't work, I put my hands to my ears and blocked the angry mob out with my palms.

Next time I opened my eyes it was daytime. Around about noon, judging by the light. I checked my watch. Gone. Sitting on Antonia's bedside table. *Fuckhead. Are you happy now?* My knuckles had puffed and dried to black scabs. I couldn't straighten my fingers.

I stood outside Giz's door and knocked with my good hand, but not very hard, if I'm honest. He didn't answer. It was the result I was hoping for. I headed down the stairs. My relief was short-lived. It occurred to me that Giz was dead.

I went back up to his door and knocked harder. 'Giz,'

I called. No response. I pressed my ear to the door. Silence. I tried the handle. Locked. I put my eye to the keyhole. His armchair was directly in my line of vision, and his armchair was empty.

Daylight was a strained compound of nerves after the lurid night that was in it. I had shed a protective layer. Everything in me blinked and blenched, a colony of insects when their rock is lifted. So when I stumbled out squinting onto the street and registered in my peripheral vision the funeral wreath hanging from the front door of the house on Mountjoy Square, my initial reaction was to assume that it wasn't actually there. It was another demon, the kind of thing Glynn saw in his cups, the kind of thing I saw in mine.

It was only when I slammed the door and heard something tinkle down the steps in my wake that I turned around to gape at the wreath. And then gaped at what had fallen out of the wreath. There by my feet, a hypodermic needle. I looked up. A star-shaped hole in Giz's window. Evil had come to our door as we'd slept. Evil had left a calling card. I ran up the steps and plucked the card from its holder. *PUSHERS OUT,* it read.

There was no dole queue trailing out the door of the labour exchange on Gardiner Street. That was the first bad sign. The roads were deserted, just the odd car here and there, as on Christmas Day. The local shops were shuttered. A grown man with a tricolour knotted around his neck planted himself in my path and vomited down his front. I stepped around him.

A cloud as faded and discoloured as an old military uniform was about to occlude the sun. I watched it loom over the Custom House with the stealth of a cut-throat.

The delirium of that last blast of sunlight before rain, the sun-shot world on the brink of condensing – Gardiner Street was fleetingly gilded with such beauty that I was overcome with sadness that it could not always be this way. The cloud dispatched its bright-yellow quarry briskly; there was no struggle. A tidal wave of shadow came racing along the pavement. My heart started to pound.

I gritted my teeth and kept going, kept going, kept staggering on regardless, with hardly a thought as to where I was off to, and in such a hurry too. The gulls were out in force, screaming their prophesies of doom as the first heavy raindrops spattered the pavement. The streets grew darker with every step I took, the city a coffin being lowered into a grave.

Very few cars on the quays either. I crossed Butt Bridge down the broken white line of the central traffic lane. The Liffey was an opaque limestone grey in the grainy light. Water that was not translucent was no longer just water, surely. That's what ran through my mind as I hurried along. There was more to that river than it was letting on. A thunderous rain was unleashed on us then.

On the side lane connecting the quays to Poolbeg Street, I encountered a woman sitting amongst dustbins. Her dress had ridden up to her hips, and she wore no underwear. The sight of her pubic hair was a shocking obscenity. Her thighs were dappled mauve, like Glynn's daughter. He'd have gotten a whole chapter out of the scene, but I averted my eyes. The woman tugged at the hem of her dress with fingers gone rubbery from booze or worse and shouted something after me that I didn't catch, something lascivious, judging by the tone. She was well pleased with the remark, such as it was, and threw back her head to laugh as best she could manage.

Crowd-control barriers had been erected along College Green. Teenaged boys had shinned up the lampposts. A lost child with a plastic flag was crying. A convoy of sodden floats and pipe bands trudged past in the rain, watched by people in anoraks. Jesus Christ, St Patrick's Day. Empty bottles and cans littered the streets. I kicked through them like autumn leaves. The gates to Trinity were shut. The walled city had raised the drawbridge. Ambulances and squad cars nudged the crowd along like cattle. There was news of a stabbing on Stephen's Green.

I crossed back over the Liffey to present my pounding hand to the Accident and Emergency in the Mater, thinking to get a head start on the crowd. I was too late. The crowd had a head start on me. The crowd had been there since time began. The casualties already outnumbered the staff a hundred to one. A fine big country nurse directed me to take a seat alongside the rest of the city's drunken, drenched carnage and wait for my name to be called. We had a painful night ahead, the lot of us, during which time we were more than welcome to take a look at ourselves, take a good long hard look at ourselves in the cold light of day, tufts of wilted shamrock pinned to our scruffs, worse than any dunce hat.

PART III

Trinity Term

April

28

Failing better

It was my turn to read. I shuffled my sheaf of papers and cleared my throat:

'The Professor's forehead positively bulged with metaphors and imagery. Full to the rafters, so it was, worse than a pub on Holy Thursday. He hadn't, of course, written a word in five years; not a publishable word, at least. Why let a minor detail like that impede you? Professor Flynn wasn't remotely ashamed of the ludicrous figure he cut, having long ago lost sight of the fact that he was a preposterous personage. At times, it was possible to pity him. Mainly, though, it was not.

'—Everybody hates me, he told the young girl.

'—I don't hate you, Professor Flynn, the young girl replied. She was beautiful beyond compare.

'—Don't you?

'—No.

'—You're the only one. Oh, what would I do without you? Come here and sit on my knee. That's it, good girl. Up a bit . . . *Ahhhhh.*

'There were huffing, slobbering noises as the priapic Professor's aged tongue explored the canal of the young girl's ear, then he murmured her name, possibly to remind himself of it, what with his creaky memory (not getting any younger), or else as a ploy to distract the innocent creature from the sly progress of his hand, which was creeping up her thigh, groping for the leg of her drawers.

'Genevieve panicked at the prospect of Flynn clapping eyes on her tatty grey pants, purchased by her mother many years previously in Dunnes Stores, Better value beats them all. Instead of slapping the old man's hand away, as any sensible girl might, she yanked off her knickers altogether and kicked them out of sight under his desk, so sweet and obliging was her nature.

'A happy sigh from Flynn, followed by a grunt and lurch as he parted the young girl's knees and took aim. There was some fumbling. Yes, an extended period of fumbling. The girl waited patiently, gazing over the Professor's shoulder at the array of trophies displayed on his bookcase. She didn't wish to rush him. He was a great man, after all.

'— Well now, said Professor Flynn, glancing down and clearing his throat. Would you ever look at that? *Romantic Ireland's dead and gone. It's with O'Leary in the grave.* He laughed hollowly as he tucked his lad back into his brown polyester trousers. The girl smiled weakly back. It was the most excruciating moment of her life. No wait, I am wrong. The most excruciating moment of the young girl's life wasn't to occur for another thirty seconds, when she had to crawl under Flynn's desk to retrieve her tattered knickers, then step back into them one leg at a time while the mighty scribbler hungrily watched.

'Professor Flynn burst into tears again. Fourth time already that night. It was a pre-emptive strike: the young girl was the one with cause for tears, but Glynn – I mean, Flynn – made sure to get the boot in first.

'—Boo hoo hoo, he said, then swivelled an eye at Genevieve to check that it was working. Good stuff, the job was oxo. Was there no end to his crusade for pity? Flynn inhabited a world which, through his own mismanagement, had spiralled out of control. His wife had left him, his only child despised him, and it was just a matter of time before the college fathers turfed him out on his ear. Flynn was in service to nothing but his own capricious gift, which had abandoned him. And who could blame it? His voice had been described as inimitable in the past, but to Flynn it had become uninimitable. He couldn't stop cogging himself. The descent into self-parody was complete.'

Of all my Chapter Ones – and there were more than a few – this was my favourite. It was the first thing I'd written that wasn't tainted by despair, the only few pages of the past hundred or so to have afforded me any pleasure at all. I had turned an important corner in my writing life.

Glynn raised his glasses to his artist's eye. 'Be the hokey,' says he, trading on that brand of Hiberno-English that had brought him so far, but only so far. Somewhere along the line, he had gotten it into his thick skull that the Irish were more charming than other nationalities, when the best that could be said of us was that we weren't the worst. 'Write that with your good hand, didya Dermot?'

'Begob, I did not. I bet it out with this one, sir!' says I, holding up my bad hand, wrapped like a parcel of meat. I'd as much a claim on that manic bog codology as he. We sat there grinning wildly at each other, the big Wicklow head on him, and the big Mayo head on me.

Odd as it sounds, I was delighted that we were all back together again, birds in a nest, snug as a gun, after the best part of a month's break. A beautiful afternoon in April, it was, so perfect it couldn't last.

My good cheer was inappropriate, which only served to reinforce it. My latest Chapter One hadn't gone down too well with the ladies.

'I find your abrupt adoption of the Continental style sheet pretentious,' was the only comment it elicited, from Antonia, who else? 'This business of prefacing lines of dialogue with em dashes – who on earth do you think you are? Joyce?' The rest of them just stared at me, the female gaze. Which was like the male gaze, only more observant.

'I like it, son,' Glynn concluded, his glasses still perched on his forehead. 'A terrible beauty is born. You've been falling the wrong side of earnest for too long.'

'I have, right enough, Professor Glynn,' I nodded. 'I am in firm agreement with you there. Wait till ye see Chapter Two! No more Mister Nice Guy, what?' I made a series of faces at him, the way we did as school children before we'd acquired vocabulary to equal our malice. My enmity towards glynn I mean Glynn outstripped my ability to express it.

He for his part grimaced back for all he was worth. 'Oh ho, no more Mister Nice Guy, indeed!' he winked, rolling up his sleeves. 'Every story needs a good villain, isn't that right, Dermot?'

I clenched my jaw and winked back. 'That's right, you fucking gee-bag.'

My notes on the workshop end at this juncture. What follows is drawn from memory and must accordingly be

238

treated as partisan, one-sided, hopelessly lovelorn, hammered thin by anguish and pain. Ignore it, ignore every word of it – it isn't worth the paper it's written on. I am only out for revenge, in so much as I can get it. A near-black trickle of blood shot out of Guinevere's left nostril, fast as a darting minnow. Glynn jumped to his feet. Faye delved for a tissue. Guinevere touched her top lip in surprise, and slumped when she saw her scarlet fingertips. My chair screeched as I lunged for her. I caught her in my arms and felt like a man.

'It's nothing, it's nothing,' Guinevere insisted when she opened her eyes again. 'Really, it's fine,' she kept telling us. Faye guided her to tilt back her head and pinch the bridge of her nose. Aisling wrapped her in her black coat. I sat rubbing her poor white hand. Antonia ran downstairs to brew strong tea. But Glynn, the bowsie, hadn't jumped out of his chair to rush to her aid, but to get as far away as he was able from the blood.

'Is she alright?' he asked from a safe distance. Nobody answered him. We, who had hung on his every word for so long, now ignored him. That was the moment he became extraneous. *There is always a price.* 'Is she alright?' he asked again. Third-person singular. *Go home, you're only impeding us.*

'Dunno,' I said to him. 'Depends on what you've done to her.' I was gleaming with animosity. My hurt polished me like a diamond; it changed the shape of my face. I was all sharp angles, hard edges, cutting remarks.

'Leave it, Declan,' Guinevere told me, but I didn't know how. I didn't know how to leave it.

Antonia returned from the kitchen empty-handed. 'The milk was off,' she said.

'The milk was off!' Glynn repeated with relish, as if it were a choice metaphor indeed. He felt an epiphany coming on. Maybe he'd beat a paragraph into his red notebook that very night, or lash out a limerick at least. Seemed more likely he'd traipse home after Guinevere, and mewl and pule at her door until she took pity and let him in again. The colour had returned to her face.

Glynn resumed his seat at the head of the table and threw my chapter back at me. He had underlined every use of the word 'seemed' and its synonyms. 'As if', 'like', 'appeared to', 'as though'. I shook my head at him in disbelief. People in glasshouses. Pots calling kettles black. I didn't lick it off the stones. If ever there was a writer who knew how to flog a simile to death, here he sat enthroned before us. The smell of death was on his breath that day, but perhaps this is memory speaking. The smell of death was on his breath every day, but until that day, it had smelt like books. It was Aisling's turn to read. Glynn dropped his glasses back into position like a welding visor, and waved her on.

She was five hundred pages into that Promethean novel of hers. Never did manage to understand a word of it. Couldn't make head nor tail out of a thing she wrote. All I ever deduced from Aisling's work was its innate superiority over anything I could have produced and her innate right to be in that workshop over me. Not an 'as if' or a 'like' in sight. Different class.

The extract Aisling read that afternoon further upset the balance in House Eight for reasons which are too elusive to quantify without the evidence once more in front of us. Unfortunately the evidence is gone. Why didn't I retain a copy? Why didn't I take more care? There was an alarming aura about the piece, not just in the content but also the form, its visual presence on the page, as if it were a composite of letters cut from magazines and pasted down, though it was typed, same as everyone else's. Perhaps the first letters of every line combined to spell out a message, a cry for help. That would not surprise me in the least. We cannot say we were not warned. But wait, I'm getting ahead of myself.

Faye chose that class to depart from her short, sweet elegiac meditations on human frailty to instead read a chapter from a novel about a battered wife. We sat there in horror listening to graphic descriptions of a drunken farmer kicking the living daylights out of his missus as she lay cowering on the bathroom floor. *You know her husband beats her, don't you?*

'She felt internal tissue tear,' Faye read, 'and muscle wall rupture as Kiernan's boot pounded repeatedly into her soft belly. She closed her eyes and prayed to Our Lady. He never had much stamina. It would be over soon.'

Antonia was staring across the table at me with a tight-lipped smile that was no smile at all. Looking around the room while somebody read was transgressive, like opening your eyes during the Sacrament in Mass. 'When he was finished, Kiernan turned away and wiped his mouth with the back of his hand,' Faye continued, 'thirsty from his labours. He would beg forgiveness in the morning, his wife knew, but morning was a long way off yet.'

Antonia's expression was turning violent. The whites of her eyes had begun to bulge. She was the wild woman screaming abuse from the top of the stairs again. I looked down at Faye's manuscript. One of us was trembling. 'His wife's blood had spoiled the new bathroom mat. In her confusion, she couldn't think where to hide it. Kiernan would go into another fury when he saw it.' The words were swimming. The words had come to life.

'Fucking hell,' whispered Aisling when Faye's reading was complete.

Antonia tossed her blonde hair. 'Here, Declan,' she said, reaching across. 'You left this behind on my bed-side table when you stayed the night.' She deposited my watch on the desk in front of me, where it glinted in the sunlight. That was when my hatred for Antonia peaked. *You stupid bitch. Are you happy now?*

'Oh ho!' said Glynn, rubbing his palms together in glee. 'Oh now! Bedside table, is it! Janey Mack. Look at little Pope Innocent here. Now that calls for a pint.'

He stood up and indicated with a swimming stroke, the over-arm crawl, that the lot of us were to follow. He threw the workshop door open, and Aisling gasped, but I had seen it too this time, the demon that had been hanging like a bat behind the door all along. A blink of an eye, and it was gone.

29

The Importance of Being Earnest

The other three went on ahead with him to the Buttery. Aisling and I hung back by the dismal patch of shrubbery into which he'd tossed his hearing aid. We sucked down a cigarette each without speaking, fast as we were able, as if it were a race. What was wrong with me? What was wrong with her? The seagulls had started to scream.

'I feel sick, Declan,' she muttered.

I nodded. Indeed she looked sick. 'We'd better go in, I suppose.'

'Oh Jesus!' she cried, and covered her mouth. I whipped around to see what had startled her this time. Sylvia. Their feral cat glared up at us reproachfully, a tiny, underweight slip of jet black and lollipop pink. It was unlike her to be out in broad daylight like this. It was unlike her to stand motionless.

At first I thought she was snarling at us. Her lip was curled back to reveal an expanse of livid pink, but when she turned to flee into the shrubbery – wait, it did not have the agility of flight, I cannot call it that – when she turned to saunter off, her gait uncharacteristically nonchalant, practically a swagger, I saw that the pink was not snarling lip but exposed flesh. The animal's muzzle had been partially torn off. Her teeth were set needle-thin into her gums. She was panting. No, she was dying.

Aisling dropped her cigarette and took off into the shrubbery on her hands and knees, her widow's weeds snagging on every twig and thorn, like there was a chance in hell of catching poor Sylvia, let alone saving her. 'There's nothing you can do for her,' I kept telling her bent form, but I may as well have been talking to the wall.

It was a good quarter of an hour before Aisling gave up the hunt. God knows what crack in the earth Sylvia had slipped into to die. I reassured Aisling that she'd done her best, but the girl would not be comforted. 'Did you see her?' she kept asking me, her gaze unable to settle. It flitted about the bushes like a butterfly. 'Declan, did you actually *see* her?'

'Of course I saw her.' I wasn't sure I understood the point of the question. The cat had been standing right there in front of us, after all, half-savaged, panting, dying. How could you not see her?

Aisling bit at her cuticles. 'We mustn't tell Faye,' she made me promise, then we smoked another cigarette each to seal the oath.

Glynn was well on by the time we joined them in the Buttery. It was barely five o'clock. He was shit-faced, rat-arsed, locked out of his tree. This is a stupid language. It was immediately evident that something wasn't right. More wrong than usual, I should say. The others were exchanging meaningful glances over his head – there'd obviously been an incident in our absence. 'Oh, here they are at last, Professor!' Faye announced with forced gaiety, trying to jolly the fucker along, as if he were already enrolled in the nursing home. Glynn's skin was the colour of an eyeball. His eyeball was the colour of skin. The glisten of dribble down his chin was new. In his paw was a pint which he clasped like a sceptre, the court of slobbering Glynn, king of porter. 'Where the fuck have you two been until now?' Antonia hissed under her breath.

'Look who it is,' Glynn murmured blackly as we took our seats. He reached across the table and plucked a leaf from Aisling's hair with a card-trick flourish, then turned to take me in, shaking his head. 'At it again, you dirty little bollocks. You're an awful man altogether, so you are.'

Aisling was wearing the manic grin she used to mask her profound self-consciousness, or to poorly mask it, rather. 'We were smoking, Professor,' she said, as if she had to explain herself to the likes of him.

'Can't a man have a drink?' Glynn bellowed in protest, as if one of us had tried to stop him. As if any of us would have dared embark on such a course of action. The thought hadn't entered our minds. It is possible that Glynn was dropping a hint – prompting us with one of his rhetorical devices to attempt to stop him drinking, seeing as he had long since gone beyond attempting to stop himself. Instead, Aisling went to the bar. What a disappointment we must have been to him.

Glynn watched Guinevere over the cream disc of the head of his pint, then caught me watching him over the cream disc of the head of my pint. He raised his sceptre in salute. 'Playboy of the Western World, isn't that right Dermot!' He elbowed Faye in the ribs. 'Get this one into bed and it's a royal flush!' His face twinkled, his gums sparkled, his eyes kindled, his brow darkened. I bridled and bristled, nettled and rankled, then drinkled and drankled some more.

Glynn coughed fleshily until it seemed his rotting

245

lungs would come shooting out of his chest and land wetly on the table, still gasping, unable to bear it in there a minute longer. 'Here, Professor,' Antonia said, and dealt the old fuck a good sound clap on the back, that bit too forceful to be benevolent. He hocked up a mighty phlegm and gobbed it into the waiting lap of his hanky. It burst out with the ripe pop of a wine bottle being uncorked.

'I'm going to vomit,' Aisling said, but didn't leave the table.

Glynn raised his glasses to his artist's eye to appraise the winnings, and judging by the look of rapture on his face, he was not disappointed. He was forever picking at himself, sniffing himself, tasting himself, sampling the compressed bits of self he found compacted beneath his fingernails, in a perpetual swoon of fascination with his own detritus. 'Glynn's great subject was the self,' wrote the *New York Review of Books*. Little did they know.

'Where's his pap?' Antonia asked. 'Give him his pap. The poor fellow: his glass is empty.' It was my turn to go the bar.

I set a rack of pints down on the table and headed for the jacks. Jesus, the fucker had snuck in ahead of me. He gave a nod as he tucked himself in, then proceeded to the exit without washing his hands. Icky sticky gicky Glynn, his urinal fingers contaminating Guinevere's skin. He paused in the doorway.

'She'll come back to you once her dreams turn to shite,' he told me. 'You just watch.'

I shook my head at him. For all his insight, he had no conception of who Guinevere was, or of what she was capable, and the tender years of her. He could not see her tremendous gift. Or maybe he could see it. Maybe that was the whole problem. Maybe he knew she'd out-strip him in the end. He cured me of my earnestness, I suppose, and I'll always owe him for that. Glynn cured us all of our earnestness.

I squeezed myself in beside Guinevere when I returned. 'So how are you?' I asked, perhaps a little aggressively. Been a few weeks since we'd spoken.

'I'm worried about Patrick,' she said. It wasn't the answer to the question I'd asked. She leaned in so he wouldn't overhear. 'Do his lips look a little blue to you?'

His lips? Why was she looking at his lips? How could I make her stop? 'So it's Patrick now, is it?' I sneered, 'Rat Prick now, is it?' I sneered. She lowered her head. I wished the others had overheard my fine piece of word-play. It was Aisling, most of all, I wished had been listen-ing. Aisling would have enjoyed it.

Glynn slammed down his emptied glass and expelled a flabby yawn.

'Dear oh dear,' Antonia chimed, 'the Professor needs another drink,' although another drink was patently the last thing the Professor needed. 'Here,' she said picking up her handbag, 'why don't I go to the bar this time? I'm sure it must be my round.'

Glynn blinked gratefully and eyed her handbag glut-tonously, as if he might like to wolf the contents down. It was Antonia who got him started on the spirits that night, avenging herself with the perfect crime. *There is always a price.*

'I think she's trying to kill him,' Guinevere said in wonderment when Antonia left the table. 'I think the woman is actually trying to kill him.'

'There's something going wrong with me,' Aisling blurted. 'It's like everything I'm thinking is written in block capitals. I can't switch off Caps Lock. My thoughts are all screaming. Do you know what I mean?'

'Do you know what I mean?' she asked a second time, clearly accustomed to being misunderstood, to having to go to great lengths to explain herself. She looked at our faces around the table. DO YOU KNOW WHAT I MEAN?

We nodded, I, we, they. Those assembled at the table nodded, all except for Glynn, whose mind had wandered. It did kind of bother me that I knew what Aisling meant. A few months ago, I'd have drawn a blank.

'Funny taste in my mouth,' Glynn complained, and belched graphically. Anything to be the centre of attention.

'Probably only a brain tumour,' said Antonia, placing a tumbler of whiskey on the beer mat in front of him. A double, we silently noted.

'Maybe you're having a stroke,' I offered.

'Oh now,' said Faye. 'Enough of that.'

Guinevere didn't open her mouth. She didn't denounce Glynn's whining, she, who had most to denounce. Why didn't she slap him? Why did she leave the job fall to others instead? Grizzling Glynn complained steadily for the guts of an hour, as if setting us an endurance test. He muttered and murmured and mumbled, maundered and malingered and moaned. Oh Christ, there was no end to it. On and on it went. He was teething, or required burping, or a nappy change. I looked at his old freckled hand in disgust, watched it perform gestures of self-regard. The urinal fingers, the breast-sized palm. It was not a writerly hand. It wasn't a lover's hand either. 'I'm finished as a novelist,' he concluded bitterly, and nobody contradicted him.

'Are we still here?' Aisling asked. She seemed surprised. If she had briefly fallen asleep, I can't say I'd noticed. She finished off her pint, knocking it back like water.

'Why are you still sending those hateful letters to me?' Glynn snarled at Antonia.

'Because I hate you.' She laughed. 'Because I hate you.' She laughed again.

'Stupid bitch,' he retaliated. We think that's what he said. His speech was slurred, his eyes had glazed. He was listing over the table in a limp, boneless manner, his hands dangling by his side as if he'd lost the use of them, which for an awful moment we thought he had, until he batted Faye away when she tried to prop him up.

Glynn pushed the table back from his belly for the final act. For this, he needed an audience, though whether he could distinguish our individual forms in the blizzard of his whiskey blindness is debatable.

His demons were everywhere by then. There was more to it than a bad pint. They had stolen up without us noticing and had him rightly surrounded. No matter which way he turned, a leering head popped up, provoking one wincing grimace after another from the writer. Great was his torment. Glynn had never witnessed such ugliness in his life. Hideous was the word he used. 'Hideous, hideous,' he declared, yet he couldn't tear his eyes from their disfigured faces either, couldn't get his fill, now that they had finally revealed their foul selves to him. They'd been hiding behind books and doors for years, lurking at the bottom of pint glasses and whiskey bottles, but now his demons were sitting right there at the table with us, bold as brass, defiant as you like. I am going to keep this short.

By the looks of it, we were outnumbered. There was one beside me, one next to Aisling, and a whole rack of them lined up in the wings. They even had names. Moloch, Ezekiel, Belial, Glynn called them, pointing from one to the other. He paused for a moment to reflect. His wife hated him. His only child wouldn't speak to him. He'd only gone and . . . he gestured in the direction of Guinevere and Antonia at this point. 'Oh Jesus, Mary and Joseph,' he cried in anguish.

The demons leapt up and down in delight at that, monkeys in a cage. Glynn cursed them mercilessly in his best demonish. No better man for the job. He had recourse to the language of Milton and Dante, works with which he had forged a deep connection for all the wrong reasons, regarding them not as the moral allegories they patently were but as early examples of kitchen-sink realism.

'Infernal Serpent,' he hissed. 'Arch-fiend, Chemos the Obscene, horrid king.' I put my arm around Guinevere. It quickly degenerated into vile street argot, which was evidently fresher in his mind. He must have picked it up the night the knackers spat in his face beneath the statue of Thomas Moore. Still possessed a keen ear for the demotic, Glynn.

'He's right,' Aisling exclaimed, looking urgently from one face to the next, nodding vigorously to canvass our support. 'Listen to him: he knows what he's talking about. He's *right*.'

'I'm fucking light-starved,' Antonia was saying, 'I'm fucking light-starved.' Everyone was repeating everything twice. Or maybe I was hearing everything twice. What follows is my version of events, unexpurgated, after the master.

Up Glynn reared onto his hind legs. We too jumped to our feet. Then what? Then nothing. The five of us just stood around the table staring at him in alarm, waiting for instructions. 'Do you mind?' he asked, and we shuffled out of his way, biddable as sheep.

'Go after him,' Faye said in panic, 'Go after him. We can't leave him alone in that state.'

Glynn ploughed through the mill of students to the exit. Difficult, keeping up with him. It was quiet as a church out on the quad after the clamour of the Buttery. A large moon was rising over Botany Bay, the colour of the head of a pint. It seemed to possess no third dimension but was instead wafer thin, a communion host.

We were barely a few steps into the darkness when Aisling collapsed. I turned around to see her in a whimpering heap on the ground, a small whorl of trembling black fabric. Two tyre tracks of mascara scored her face as if something had mown her down. She gulped convulsively, sheer terror in her eyes, and pointed at the corner. 'Look!' she cried. 'It's here!'

Faye and Guinevere tried to pick her up, but she wouldn't let them. 'Look at it!' she kept shrieking, thrusting her finger at the corner, but the corner was empty. There was nothing there. 'I don't know what's happening,' Antonia was chanting in the background, over and over like an unanswered phone. Glynn turned around and saw that he had lost his audience. We, like his gift, had abandoned him.

'You,' he said sharply.

I turned my head. 'What?'

He muttered something under his breath, deliberately inaudible to force me to approach. He lured me around the corner and out of sight. 'What?' I said again.

'That one. Your one.'

'Guinevere?'

'Yes, her.' He laughed. 'To think I thought she'd be one of those girls who look better with their clothes on than off.'

That did it. I took a run at him. He went down easy, not a bother. Nothing to it at all. I'd have straight out punched him only for my bad fist, so I shouldered him instead, and down the great writer went, face first, rigid, a statue toppling from its plinth, first slowly, then quickly, making a meaty, gristly sound upon impact with the cobbles.

He started laughing again once he got his wind back. I swung a good kick at his ribs. My foot connected not with bone but a dreary mass of fat. It was a disgusting sensation. I kicked him again to rid myself of it. He grunted. I didn't feel any better. And I didn't feel any worse. I hated the fucker, *hated* him. I hope he is reading these words.

'State of you,' I pronounced in lofty judgement over the writer's bent back and hawked a gullier just shy of his face.

He stopped laughing at that and raised his head to regard me, a smile of sorts smeared across his face. It was the hapless oafish grin of a simpleton – Glynn's front tooth had shattered on a cobble. A quivering string of snot-clotted blood dangled from his nostril, elongating and contracting with the rhythm of his breath. 'State of you,' I said again, but he didn't retaliate, just nodded in what for all the world looked to be agreement, then lowered his head onto the smooth cobbles again and closed his eyes to rest. I think that's all he wanted. Another good reason to wallow in self-pity. Or confirmation that he was a prick. I no longer cared. It was nothing to me. By the time we passed that way again, maybe half an hour later, helping Aisling who was doing her best to walk to her parents' car – still doing her best, in spite of everything, God be good to her – Glynn was already gone, having sought cover in some dark corner to lick his wounds, as any animal might.

30

Ní bheidh ár leithéid ann arís

You'll never see the like of us again

This is the order in which I said goodbye to them:

Aisling was the first.

She was gone before we knew it. Gone before she knew it either. St Pat's psychiatric hospital wasn't half as intimidating an institution as you might expect, and the VHI covered it, her mother told me, adding that I was so kind to visit, that all of us had been so kind. Aisling had been given a room of her own once they took her off the suicide ward, where she had been kept for just two nights. In the scale of things, this was very good news, apparently. Her wing was filled with tranquillised women in slippers and dressing gowns, some still carrying their handbags about. They bore the muted, slightly sheepish demeanour of drinkers in an early house. 'You should see the anorexics upstairs,' Aisling confided, enunciating her words with a slow deliberateness that was neither characteristic nor necessary. 'Mother of God.'

Antonia had spent a whole summer on that same ward two years previously, also being treated for clinical depression, which is where they got her started on exploring her creativity, painting at first, or 'daubing' as she called it, since she showed no aptitude. The writing suited her better. Though this information was offered with the best of intentions, I don't see how Aisling could possibly have taken heart from it. Antonia was far from cured. Nor could I fathom how two individuals enduring such diverse symptoms could both be diagnosed with the same condition. But then, I wasn't a doctor. Maybe Aisling wasn't telling us the full story regarding what had gone wrong with her. Maybe she hadn't been told the full story either.

It goes without saying that we barely knew her without the stark make-up, hardly recognised her in colour. We saw the few spots she'd been trying to conceal all year. They weren't so bad, after all that, nowhere near as bad as I'd imagined. You'd scarcely notice them at all, really, but there was no right way of telling her, so I didn't.

She was dressed in a pair of pink flannel pyjamas printed with teddy bears, a small cross-legged bundle on the bed, overcome with shyness. I felt like I'd come to babysit. Already she was changing, fading. She would not be herself much longer. The hospital would cure her of being Aisling. I missed her then, a crippling pang, though she was still right there beside me, sort of.

I gave her the Walkman bought from Giz in the end, and a Bowie compilation. The Ziggy years, not the Eno stuff, to be on the safe side. The girl had enough on her plate. She had told us once, in the early days before any of us really knew one another, that she didn't believe anything bad could happen to you while you were listening to David Bowie. I dismissed the statement as foolish at the time, but the bad things she'd been referring to took place in her head, so her theory made sense, when you thought about it.

Her face lit up. 'Guess what?'

'What?'

'Professor Glynn came in to see me today.' A diffident trace of pride in her voice.

'Really? That was decent of him.'

'Yeah,' she agreed. 'He showed up with a bunch of flowers and a black eye.' She nodded at her bedside locker. Amongst the *Get Well Soon* cards was a vase of white roses.

'A black eye?'

She nodded. 'And a broken tooth.'

I was surprised when she started to snigger. Surprised and relieved. A flash of her old self. Not gone yet, so. Not yet. Crippling, as I say.

He never saw his attackers. That's the story he put about. At least four of them had set upon him from behind and kicked the tooth right out of his head. He'd gotten the better of them in the end, overpowering them with a left hook followed up by a sharp right, but that's why he hadn't been there to help when she'd collapsed, he wanted Aisling to know. He'd since made a speedy recovery and was right as rain, he had assured her bravely.

I shook my head. 'Who could do such a thing to him?'

'I know. Desperate.'

'He told me that I was not to worry about all this,' she added, gesturing at her surroundings. 'He said it was just because I was young.' We let that hang in the air, both of us hoping Glynn was right. Aisling lowered her head. She didn't quite know what to do with her hands, now that she'd been stripped of her amulets. The pyjama sleeves were too long for her.

'It was too much for me,' she quietly admitted.

'I know,' I said, as gently as I could manage.

'It got too much for me, Declan,' she confessed again some minutes later, looking me anxiously in the eye as if I would think less of her for this admission.

'I understand,' I said, as softly as I was able.

Giz was next.

I'd seen him just the once since the Pushers Out vigilantes broke his window and nailed that funeral wreath to our door. He'd been evicted shortly afterwards. I was walking back into town after a visit to Aisling when there he was on the north quays ahead of me. The pneumatic white runners were gone, replaced by an old pair of builder's boots. They must have been weighted down with steel caps, the way he hauled them along the pavement, as if they were magnetised to it. No shoelaces, never mind socks. His left arm dangled limply by his side, and his left leg dragged, slightly twisted.

I trailed along behind him at a discreet distance. We made slow progress past the courts. He collided over and over with the railings. It was a beautiful, such a beautiful morning in late April, one of those gifts the world unexpectedly bestows on you, warmth and light flooding into your bones after the siege of an Irish winter, so long, so hard, so damp, that you'd forgotten how good the sun felt, the giddying glory of it on your bare skin. The railings turned a right angle, and Giz veered around the corner with them, involuntarily by the signs of it. His good arm reached for the other side of the street, flailing towards it like a swimmer caught in an undertow. I crossed briskly at the lights, pretending that I hadn't seen him, nor heard the moan of appeal that indicated that he had seen me.

I glanced back from the safety of the other side. The

broad splendour of the Liffey, glinting and sparkling in the late spring sun, the smoky blue of the distant mountains. Giz was still floundering by the railings, a stalled clockwork toy, needing to be turned around and set on his way again. He was making the noise, the junkie noise, a wheedling mixture of pleading and complaint, the terrible *wa-aa-aa* that was general all over Dublin during the heroin years, ringing out of every side street and back lane. *Wa-aa-aa;* how it carried.

During the numb, tentative weeks following Aisling's hospitalisation, small acts of localised kindness gained a new significance in the order of things. I finally left my bed in the dead of the night and went out to see if I could comfort the dog that had been howling away the year, lonely as a wolf. I wanted to feel like a better person.

I followed the howl down a lane separating two rows of back-to-back terraces. I hadn't considered what I would do if I found the dog. Talk to him, I suppose. Tell him he wasn't alone. The lane rounded a corner and opened onto a clearing where I encountered not a dog but a group of men, too far away to have noticed my intrusion. No, not too far away, but too intent on whatever was squirming at their feet. They were lit from above by a security lamp rigged up to a garage.

One of the men spoke, and the dog stepped up his howling. A dogfight, was my first reaction. Another of the men nudged the creature on the ground with the toe of his boot, and the creature raised its hands in defence. Not a pit-bull terrier, but a boy, no wait, a man, a thin scrawny man, head shaved. He was on his knees, wheedling ingratiatingly though they hadn't started on him yet. Merciful Jesus, it was Giz.

'Wa-aa-aa,' he was saying, palms upturned in supplication. The men started to laugh. They laughed for a good while at his distress, then Giz, the poor bastard, tried to join in. This brought abrupt silence. Even the dog stopped howling to listen.

One of the men said something, to which Giz shook his head in vigorous denial. The man kicked him. His foot caught Giz under the chin, snapping back his neck. That was the signal. The circle of men crumpled as if the ground had sucked them down on top of Giz. His screams were indescribable. I started to run, not to his rescue, but away from him, out of there, back to where I'd come from.

The first phone box had no dial tone. The cash lock had been jemmied open, 'Giz woz ere' scratched into the metal casing. The second phone box had no receiver at all. By the time I reached the third one, I knew there was no point in running any more. Whatever had been done to Giz was over with. I reported what I'd seen to the Guards.

I thought I'd never lay eyes on him again, and I wish I hadn't. I opened the front door the next day to find him huddled on the doorstep, his arm crooked protectively under his chin like a broken wing. There was a pouch of purple blood beneath his eye. His lip was torn, teeth were missing, matted black clots studded his scalp. I didn't look too closely. People on the street hurried past him. They'd been hurrying past him all morning.

I ran upstairs to phone an ambulance, then came back outside to sit with him on the doorstep until it arrived, afraid to touch so much as his finger in case it hurt him more. He had a horror of being touched anyway, a phobia, sparked by God knows what in his childhood. Giz did not regain consciousness during this period. It struck

259

me as inappropriate that I was the one stifling tears, not him. What had I to cry about, after all?

The tune of an ice-cream van lilted past, and, some time later, the ambulance appeared.

'Name?' a medic with a clipboard asked me before they took him away, as if he were a parcel to be signed for.

'Giz,' I said.

The medic sighed and redistributed his weight. It was all a great trial to him. He inserted his biro into his ear and scratched. 'Name?' he said again.

'Dunno.'

'Address?'

'None.'

They rooted through Giz's pockets for identification. A set of nickel holy medals attached by a nappy pin to the washing instructions of his ratty tracksuit top was all they found.

I said goodbye to Faye and Antonia on the same day, or, rather, they said goodbye to me.

Guinevere phoned one morning. Such a long time since we'd spoken. When I heard her voice on the other end of the line, it was Glynn who immediately sprang to mind. *Declan, he's gone,* I thought she was going to tell me. I closed my eyes and swallowed, surprised at the force of my reaction. I wasn't sure how much more I could take of all this. But all Guinevere wanted to know was whether I'd like to join the others in the workshop that afternoon. 'Just the four of us,' she said.

I hadn't been back to House Eight since the night that Aisling fell, presuming it would already be locked up for the year. No one was using it, not any more, not after all that had happened. But the door was open, and up the stairs I went, listening to the sound of female voices floating down. I had to stop halfway up, gripping the banister to compose myself: for a moment, it had been like the old days.

The three of them were sitting by the windows, sunshine streaming through their hair. I had never seen them in summer clothes before. Faye stood up when she saw me. 'Declan,' she said. 'I'm so glad to get a chance to say goodbye to you before I leave.'

'You're leaving?'

'Yes, I'm going home to Clonmel early. My train is at four.' I had noticed the large suitcase by the door downstairs. Faye put her hand on her abdomen. 'Declan, I'm going to have a baby!'

'A *baby?*' I repeated stupidly. I could barely fathom it. It seemed such a bizarre undertaking. This was no time to be thinking of other human beings.

Tears sprang to Faye's eyes, and she shook her head in wonderment as if she could barely fathom it either. 'A baby, yes!' She opened her arms and held me in her embrace, the joy radiating out of her.

'God, I'm so happy for you, Faye.'

She paused in the doorway of the workshop to take one last look at us. 'Write,' she said before she left. And then she was gone. Just like that. It was over so quickly. Her husband was waiting below on Front Square. We sat in silence listening to her descending footsteps, then the front door clicked shut behind her.

The three of us watched as her husband carried her suitcase in one hand and placed the other on her shoulder. *You know her husband beats her, don't you?* He was a big mucker type in a maroon jumper, a Tadhg or a

Mossy or a Micky Joe, and seemed a few years older than his gentle, pretty wife, though it might have been just that he was a proper grown-up. Someone had to keep the country running. I hardly knew her, I realised as Faye disappeared under the Arch. And now I never would.

'Well, that's that then,' said Antonia. 'Back to the real world, I suppose.'

Guinevere walked slowly around the workshop. 'Look at this place,' she said. 'It's like an empty theatre set.' She rested her hands on the back of Glynn's chair, then stooped to open his side drawer, her train of thought momentarily arrested – all our trains of thought momentarily arrested – by simple curiosity. What was in the drawer? How had it never occurred to us to look? All the months we'd sat there.

Inside was a map of Dublin. Guinevere flicked through it before replacing it and pushing the drawer shut again. She moved on, trailing her fingertip along our old desks. 'It's so sad to think we'll never sit in this room together again. I can barely believe it.'

'I'm leaving Dublin too,' I announced. Suddenly, everything seemed so final. It had been final for a long time, but it only hit me then.

Guinevere stopped walking and looked up. 'Oh?'

'Yes,' I said. 'There's nothing for us in this country. It's never going to change. It's never going to get better. *The sow that eats her farrow.* I'm off in two weeks. Will you come, Guinevere?'

'Listen to him!' said Antonia, as if I'd lost my wits.

Guinevere laughed. 'What, leave the country with you?'

'It's going to get worse here. Any fool can see that.

There'll never be any money, there'll never be any jobs, there'll never be any future. We have to get out fast if we want a chance at life. Come with me, Guinevere.'

'Where to?' she asked softly, 'Leeds?'

It wasn't an outright refusal. I crossed the room and clasped her hand. 'We'll go to Paris like Beckett and Joyce.'

Guinevere peeled my hands from hers to peer at the jagged purple scar where the metal pin had been inserted. 'Iron Nails Ran In,' she said.

'I'm being serious. Say yes.'

She lowered her head to avoid my eye. 'Declan, I have to go now. I only came to say goodbye to Faye.'

'Be there in two weeks. Meet me outside Front Arch this time two weeks.' I checked my watch. 'Three p.m., Wednesday a fortnight. Please.'

She picked up her bag and smiled apologetically before leaving. 'Goodbye, you two,' she said.

'You idiot,' Antonia scoffed as soon as Guinevere was gone. Fuckhead, she had called me. 'Don't you realise that if there ever was money in this country, no writer could afford to live here? Glynn would've starved before he even got started. Our literary tradition would perish. You better pray it doesn't change.'

'With all due respect, Antonia, I didn't invite you. I invited Guinevere.'

I instantly regretted the harshness of my tone. There was no call for it, not any more. Antonia dropped her chin onto her chest, where she kept it for some moments. 'You're right,' she said eventually. 'You're absolutely right. Don't let me spoil it for you. Don't let anybody spoil it for you.'

I frowned at what I assumed was more sarcasm.

Antonia reached up and cupped my head with her hands and tilted it down to kiss my forehead, allowing her lips to briefly rest there before angling my face to look into hers. She imparted something of great import and clearly meant every last word of it, the urgency with which her eyes searched mine. All I heard was seashell sounds. Her cool hands covered my ears. This I am sure was intentional. It permitted her the temporary freedom to say what she had to say. Antonia had no freedom in her life. She had never been carefree.

When she had finished speaking, she briskly and tightly embraced me, her brooch jabbing my chest. Then she released me and walked away, click-clack, down the wooden stairs in her high heels. She left the building, and I watched from the window until she disappeared through the passageway between the 1937 Reading Room and the Colonnades. She did not look back. I never saw Antonia again. I never saw Aisling again. I never saw Faye again. I sat down at the workshop desk in my old chair and remained in House Eight for the rest of the afternoon and much of the evening, thinking, thinking, furiously thinking, until it was almost dark.

There is so much that I have left out.

It was mid-May before I got around to saying goodbye to Glynn. I came upon him in a reflective mood.

It was one of those days that fills you with aching nostalgia for the summer that has not yet been. Such days in the past would have found me paralysed with regret. Regret for what, exactly, it is difficult to put into words. Regret for all the things that should have been happening in my life, but never would. I felt no regret that day as I walked through the broad leafy squares of Trinity.

The lawns were scattered with bare-armed girls lost in books. I was new to the sense of completion which engulfed me that afternoon, new to the awareness that a distinct period in my life had come to a close, an era so discrete that already I could see it as a finite entity, a car wreckage some yards back on the road behind me, from which I had escaped unscathed. This knowledge had been hard enough won all the same.

Glynn was in his office in the English Department. It smelled of books and sun-warmed carpet tiles.

'It's yourself,' he said when he opened the door. 'Come in, come in, sit down.' He lifted a stack of books from the spare seat to make way for me. The black eye Aisling mentioned had faded without trace, as if that whole hellish night had been a figment of our imagination.

Glynn made a point of shutting his red notebook and removing it from my reach. He stationed his fountain pen on top of it like a sentry, though I had not the slightest interest in trying to steal a glimpse at whatever was written there. Those days were over. He raised his glasses and peered at me across the desk. 'Your hand is out of the plaster, I see.'

I held it up and flexed my fingers. 'It is. Good as new.'

'The walls had better watch out!' The amusement Glynn derived from this witticism revealed the gap where his front tooth had once been. We contemplated each other's battle wounds for a moment.

'So anyway,' I said, 'I'm moving to Paris.'

'Go 'way. When?'

'Tonight.' My rucksack was propped against the wall outside his door.

Glynn raised his eyebrows at this information and nodded thoughtfully for a long old time. It was good to speak to him like that, finally. Like adults, with restraint and without rancour, as if we were talking about people we had once known. Which, I suppose, we were.

'Tell us: are you still writing about that Flynn fecker?'

'I am and I amn't.'

'Arra.' He tossed his head ruefully.

I forget most else of what passed between us as my head was suddenly crowded with fresh thoughts, thoughts which had nothing to do with Glynn but were instead a realisation of what it signified to inhabit the world as a man, to possess a past and a small degree of certainty. All new to me at the time, as I say, and a little previous as it turned out, but there it is, there you have it. One thing I clearly recall is Glynn's announcement of his decision to quit teaching. He issued this statement then coyly examined my face for a reaction. I did not react. What did he want? What did he expect me to say, after everything?

He averted his face. 'I've lost them,' he suddenly admitted.

'Who?'

'My fairies.'

'Your fairies?'

'The women. The four girls. I've lost them.'

I paused. 'Yes, I'm afraid you have lost them.' There was no point in lying to the man any more.

'They were so beautiful.'

'They were.'

'They are still in the world, I suppose.'

'I suppose they are.'

'Abroad in the world.' He liked that idea. His hand described a curlicue in the air, ever the maestro.

'Yes.'

'But no longer in my world.'

'At least you had them, Professor Glynn.'

'There is that.'

'And you'll see them from time to time, here and there, in unexpected places.'

'I dearly hope so.'

I didn't tell him that he had driven his fairies away, that he had nobody to blame for the early and terminal disbandment of the group but himself. I didn't need to tell him. Glynn knew. He was, after all, an artist of personal tragedy, not the noble, stoical kind but the self-inflicted variety. It was why the six of us understood each other so well.

I left him there, racked with remorse, shuddering in pain, already searching for the words to describe it, already groping for metaphors. He had lost the women and recovered his great subject – longing. They were his fairies, alright. Glynn was precisely where he wanted to be, in a paroxysm of torment approaching the condition of ecstasy. Suffering, whilst training a canny eye on that suffering, the artist's eye, the eye of the imagination.

'By the way,' he asked as I was leaving, 'what do you think of *Conversations with a Blackbird* as a title?'

Glynn took pleasure in teasing us this way, right to the bitter end. All year, he had led us on, flashing demure glimpses of his artistic self, a raised hem here, a lowered neckline there, taunting us with the notion that our opinions actually mattered to him.

'It's a beautiful title,' I averred as vehemently as I was able. 'It is absolutely stunning, Professor.'

I knew he would despise this response – the measure of a work of art's beauty as the criterion by which it was assessed – but that was the whole point. I wanted Glynn to despise my judgement. I wanted him to feel that he knew more than the likes of me and to thereby regain the authority, the courage, the audacity required to proceed. I indulged him to facilitate the engendering of a mood conducive to composition. Nobody wrote about September like Glynn.

Some writers preferred platitudes to no response at all. I had presumed before I knew him not to count Glynn among their number, which shows how little I understood about the chaos of the writing life, the dreadful tumult that descends upon a man. No instructions, no manuals, no progress reports. Just the wanderings of your own imagination. The chaos had to be calibrated every now and then. It had to be shattered by matters of no importance to remind the artist why he had devoted his life to it in the first place. Once Glynn got his dose of platitudes, he could reject their mundanity and feel confirmed in the choices he had made. All the man needed was to feel he had choices. It wasn't so much to ask. I hesitated before closing the door – the finality was momentarily unbearable – then I pulled it shut on him, gently, gently, so as not to in any way suggest it was a reproof.

He didn't go with the blackbird title in the end. *Electra Is Complex,* his novel charting the doomed affair between a middle-aged professor and his young student, was published two years later. His doomed affair and subsequent redemption. Glynn was a new man in his author's photograph. No longer meat-faced, liver-lipped, clown-haired, glowering. A big, unguarded smile for the female photographer, revealing a gaggle of mismatched teeth, at least one of which I knew to be fake.

*

Which left Guinevere. Guinevere Wren. The name became her. More so than Electra, but these are matters of taste and artistic difference. Would she be waiting for me at the gate?

The farewell to Glynn had taken less time than I'd allowed for, so I sat in the sun on the steps of the Reading Room to await the appointed hour, my rucksack at my feet. I put my head between my knees and contemplated Guinevere's absence in terms of imagery, how stark the black railings beyond Front Arch would look without her. If this were a Glynn novel, she wouldn't be there. I was under no illusions.

At one minute to three, the condemned rose and crossed the quad. It took my eyes a moment to adjust to the cool darkness beneath Front Arch after the brilliant May sunshine. A pigeon beat its wings in the vaulted ceiling with the violence of something trying to break. I did not falter. I would face whatever was there, or not there. I would go alone. I would leave Dublin without her. I had done it before.

The sunlight, when I emerged on the other side, was blinding. It bleached the world bare of detail. There was nothing. Nobody was waiting. Well then, I said to myself. Okay so. *Are you happy now?* I stood there in the middle of the entrance, blocking everyone, all the tourists, the undergrads, I didn't care. Then a hand touched my shoulder. I dropped my rucksack.

I stooped and gathered Guinevere up, lifted her off the ground and buried my face in her hair. *Thank you* she says I chanted into her neck, and I take her word for it, I take her word. Around and around we went, revolving slowly, her feet dangling in the air. 'Are you ready?' I asked when I was able.

She nodded. 'I'm ready.'

She accepted my hand and set her calm face to the street, as if joining me in a dance. Through the gates, onto Dame Street, uphill to Swift's cathedral. I will call this moment the beginning.

Acknowledgements

Thanks to those who read and commented on drafts: Mia Kilroy, Simon Trewin, Simon McInerney, John Boyne and Liz O'Donnell. A very special thanks to the Arts Council of Ireland, An Chomhairle Ealaíon, for its generous financial support, and to Angus Cargill of Faber and Faber, esteemed editor.

7